THE JOSHUA TRAIL

by Early Santee

THE JOSHUA TRAIL

VOLUME TWO
OF THE
JOSHUA TRAIL TRILOGY

by Early Santee

OZ
OSTEEN-ZALAR PUBLISHING
SACRAMENTO, CALIFORNIA

The Joshua Trail
Volume Two of the Joshua Trail Trilogy
By Early Santee

Copyright © 2002 by Early Santee

ISBN 0-9716437-1-7 (soft cover)

Library of Congress Control Number: 2002107001

This is a work of fiction. Names, characters and incidents either are the product of the author's imagination or are used fictitiously, and any resemblance to any actual persons, living or dead, events, or locales, is purely coincidental.

Cover art by Ty Johnson

This book was printed in the United States of America

To order copies of this book, contact:

OZ
Osteen-Zalar Publishing
P.O. Box 1349
Sacramento, CA 95812-1349
E-mail: *earlysantee@aol.com*
Telephone: (916) 383-6321

DEDICATION

To Richard Louis and Dorathy Sorensen Zalar, King Smith, Bill Walsh, Roz, BMW, Fazzi, Becky, the future Mr. J.L. Hampton, Richard Holler, and all members of The Wednesday Night Literary Guild. Carol Minard, my number one fan. Frank Adami, Sandra Williams and Jennifer Sparks, my editors. My lovely niece Trish. For Georgia Carol and my brother David Milton Osteen. (David! Read the book for goodness sake!)

CHAPTER ONE

Eli Llynne had been right all along. Jules Joshua was not dead; he was in Mexico.

Jules, as Eli had been, was befriended by the hard rock miners of Hornitos who thought they were rendering assistance to one of their own. Jules could talk mining lingo and they accepted him as a miner who had experienced a bad cave-in. Jules blamed the death of his brothers on "Mexican claim jumpers" and weaved a tall tale about how he had fought them off despite interference from Eli Llynne. Since Eli was unconscious, Jules' story went unchallenged — until he robbed and shot the doctor who was attending him.

Dr. Levi Immanuel was a legitimate doctor and an orthopedic specialist. He was the only specialist in California at the time and was a good friend of most of the miners. No one in the Gold Country could have saved Jules' right leg except Dr. Immanuel.

Jules did not see it that way. He saw that he.was left with a noticeable limp and a "toothache" in his leg. In his twisted mind, Jules figured Dr. Immanuel owed him. After all, the good doctor made a handsome living, had plenty of ready cash stashed about his home, and was a "Jew boy" no white man need feel the necessity to respect.

One moonless night, when Jules was fully recovered, he separated Dr. Immanuel from his money, his life, and his thoroughbred Arabian horse, Midnight. Midnight was a coal-black Arabian so fast that the miners who pursued Jules the next day had no hope of catching him. Jules had thought they would give up because of the distance he had put between them and their self-interest in their mining, but the miners had respected and, indeed, loved Dr. Immanuel. They pursued Jules for almost three weeks until he had made his way across the Mexican border. Jules had laughed as Midnight had plunged into a rushing river and swum it with ease, while their horses had balked and refused to enter the water.

Jules was very impressed by Dr. Immanuel's taste in horseflesh.

"That's one mighty fine horse you have there, doc!" Jules had told the doctor one afternoon when he was walking again.

"Thank you, Mr. Joshua. My one vice. I'm afraid I indulged myself, extravagantly, in this one instance. The shipping fees alone were … well, very substantial. He is handsome, isn't he?" Dr. Immanuel brushed his beloved stallion with gentle stokes.

"I hear tell he's a half-day faster than anything else in these parts?"

"No. That's exaggerated because we won the last mile race by several lengths."

"I heard it was more like a quarter mile?"

"Well, it really wasn't fair to race him against cow ponies." Dr. Immanuel smiled with pride for only a moment. "Mr. Joshua, I have done the best I can for that leg. But you have to take care of it. You have to keep that wound clean and use the medicines I've given you, religiously. You are a very lucky man … with, I must say, a very strong constitution."

"Yes, sir. I always did heal up good!"

"That may be so, but any serious neglect and you'll have trouble with that leg. Understand?"

Jules shrugged indifference.

"So tell me. Do you feel well enough to return to the mines? The foreman asked me about you yesterday. They are short-handed."

Jules feigned looking real sick. "I don't know, doc. If it's all the same to you I don't expect I'll ever be minin' in the earth no more!"

"Yes. Well, I can understand that …" Dr. Immanuel stopped as an impeccably dressed banker approached.

"Morning, doctor," Lew Zalar, the banker, said as he addressed Dr. Immanuel and ignored Jules.

"Lew, how are you?"

"Fine. Is this a bad time to resolve that matter?"

"No. No, come inside and we'll wrap it up now," he paused and looked at Jules. "Do you mind brushing Midnight … long gentle strokes, please, while I go inside with Lew?"

"No, sir. I'll be glad to do it."

"Thanks, Jules," Dr. Immanuel said as he and Lew moved inside the house. Jules took the brush and threw it down the moment the doctor left.

Jules slowly eased around to where he could get a peek through the curtains of a window into Dr. Immanuel's study. He watched without interest as he and the banker talked awhile. His eyes popped open when he saw Dr. Immanuel slide a panel of books and remove a strong box.

Jules salivated as Dr. Immanuel opened the strong box and removed the biggest stack of bills Jules had ever seen. He watched with envy as Dr. Immanuel counted out money to the banker.

He knew, immediately, he would find some way to quickly have the rest of the money in his possession.

Jules looked at Midnight and knew that such a fast horse would give him the edge he needed. He knew the doctor was well-liked by most of the miners and if he had trouble with the doctor he would have to get out of town fast.

Jules knew he had to strike in a few days. There were strong rumors that there was going to be a United States marshal appointed to this area soon. Jules did not like that idea. He liked it the way it was — where a man was a law to himself and need only shoot straight and have a good horse to survive.

The thought of organized law made him feel ill.

As it turned out he had trouble with Dr. Immanuel.

The night Jules decided to go for the strongbox, he thought Dr. Immanuel was sleeping. Jules had, he thought, made his way undetected into the study.

But the panel hiding the strongbox would not slide easily and Jules had made some noise getting it to, finally, move. Dr. Immanuel had approached so quietly that Jules, at first, had not seen him.

"Is this the way you repay me for all I've done for you?" Dr. Immanuel entered the room holding a kerosene lantern in one hand and a Colt in the other.

"Doctor ... no ... this isn't exactly what you think it is ..."

"You're trying to rob a man who saved your life and your limb. What kind of demented animal are you?"

"You got no call sayin' I'm an animal!"

"Well then, how would you describe such inhuman betrayal, such a malfeasance of trust? ... no, you are right. Midnight is an animal and to compare someone as despicable as you to an animal is not fair to the animals ..." He paused and cocked the Colt's hammer. "Now get the hell out of my house and I'd urge you to get far out of town before I advise the miners of your exploits!"

Jules, slowly, closed the panel. He smiled as he looked the doctor in the eye. "You ever killed a man before, Doc?"

"Of course not. I practice the saving of life."

"I thought so. You ain't supposed to be killin' nobody, no how!"

"My oath does not prohibit the extermination of vermin."

"Vermin? That's like rats, ain't it?"

"Precisely."

Jules put his hand on the handle of his revolver. Dr. Immanuel pointed his gun at Jules' head. "Don't even think about it. Just go, *NOW!*"

"You ain't gonna shoot me. You can't take back the life you done give a man!"

"I'll kill you real dead if you aren't gone in sixty seconds!"

Jules looked doubtful, then shrugged. "Okay. I'm goin'. Just point that thing away from my head. They go off accidentally sometimes, you know." Jules smiled.

Dr. Immanuel did not buy it, at first. But he, finally, uncocked the hammer and lowered the gun, slightly. In that instant, Jules pulled his gun and fired four rounds into the doctor's body.

"Hey, Jew boy! Who you calling vermin now?" Jules stood over Dr. Immanuel's dead body and waited for an answer that never came.

As Jules sat in the Mexican *cantina* drinking three fingers of raw *tequila*, he was glad to be alive and well. He was also glad to be in a place where no one asked too many questions as long as you could pay the bill.

Jules needed this time to plan what he wanted to do to settle the score with Eli once and for all.

Bitter, deep, burning rage built up in his heart as he thought of Eli Llynne. The miners had buried Jules' brothers in a decent, well-kept cemetery on the outskirts of Hornitos. Jules had heard rumors that Zack and James had been buried in unmarked graves in Sonora. Jules did not know when, but he knew he would return to Sonora and mark those graves, as well as the one he would put Eli Llynne in for eternity.

Stella read the paperwork with increasing fascination. "I, Isaiah Micah Hopkins, having no living heirs, do hereby bequeath all my worldly goods to Eli Llynne and/or his inheritors …" Stella looked at the San Francisco lawyer dressed in the fancy suit, and her eyes asked, "How much?"

"Pardon me, ma'am?"

"Do you have a hearing problem? How much money did he leave us?"

"Oh? Yes. I see. Well, his interest in the Silver Cloud was less than a quarter of a million dollars, but he held other property that puts his assets at ... well, in round numbers, they exceed two million dollars ... possibly three at the outside. You understand that is not liquid assets?"

"Two ... three million dollars?" Stella liked the sound of it.

"... Cash in various deposits amounts to only around seven hundred thousand. The real property, as you know, fluctuates in value ... especially the land and the house he owns in Boston. And of course you know about his shares in your local gold claim."

"A house in Boston? Well, we can certainly unload that as I don't expect to be going there anytime soon!"

"No! I'm afraid that is not possible."

"What? What is not possible?"

"He specifically provided that the house cannot be sold. It is an ancestral home."

"Captain Hopkins has an ancestral home?"

"Oh, yes. He was from a very old Boston shipping family. I'm afraid he was the last male heir."

"He told Eli ... us that he was a gang-pressed youth from a poor family?"

"Yes. Apparently, he loved to tell tales. I'm afraid his past was a romantic invention to compensate for a boring ... well-provided-for ... upbringing."

"I see. An old Boston family ... of good name, I suppose?" Stella appeared slightly interested.

The lawyer looked insulted. "Of course! Believe me, it is high praise that he leaves you this property."

"Well, I'm not living there!"

"I believe he intended for your husband to live there."

"Eli Llynne in a proper Boston house? Not likely."

"Be that as it may, it was the Captain's wish," he stopped and fiddled with his papers. "By the way, you said your husband was out of town and you don't know where or ... why?"

"That's the long and short of it."

"I did need to have this taken care of soonest. I really do have to get back to San Francisco."

"Soonest? I don't think so. For all I know he might decide not to come back. He's a little crazy, you know," Stella said coolly.

The lawyer did not know what to make of Stella but he had heard the exaggerated tales of Eli's fighting bears in public and killing scores of men. He believed only half of the tales were true, but that much was enough to make Eli an unusual man, indeed. "I see. Notwithstanding Mr. Llynne's alleged eccentricities, he is still the principal and only heir. There are no Hopkins kin left who can file a claim."

"I'm his wife. Why can't I sign the papers?"

"That just simply doesn't work, legally."

"Since when does anything work 'legally' in these parts?"

"We are trying to become a respected member of the United States, Mrs. Llynne. Even now marshals are moving in. Soon we will have a courthouse and be well on our way to being as civilized as the East."

"That's too bad." Stella mused aloud.

"Pardon me?"

"I said it's too bad that all the party poopers are coming. Laws and lawyers and fences and paperwork, and bluenoses who don't want anyone to have any fun."

"There are many who welcome it, madam."

"Well, I'm not one of them! So you need my husband to sign or else he doesn't get his inheritance? What if ... what if something ... if he had an accident or something?"

"I'm sorry?"

"If he died? What would happen if he was killed?"

"Oh, my goodness!"

"Don't give me that shocked look. Eli thinks he's a gunfighter. He's off now looking to get involved in one. I have to live with that reality!" Stella tried to look sympathetic.

The lawyer nodded reluctant agreement.

"Yes, I have heard this is true. Your position is not without merit."

"What does that mean in plain language?"

"It means, if ... if he should be, God forbid, killed. ... then you would be his inheritor. But I do hope he is returning ..."

"Maybe he is and maybe he isn't. If you must know, he rode off mad. When he's mad who knows what he might do? It has been difficult living with this uncertainty. I wish he were home. I wish I knew he would come home. ... but to not know, to never really know … I hope you understand?" Stella held a hankie to her nose and tried to force tears.

They did not come.

"Oh, yes. It must be very difficult. I wish there was some assistance I could render."

"I appreciate your concern, Counselor. There are many in this town who do not wish me well. If Eli were to die and I were to inherit money, they might accuse me of somehow being responsible."

"Oh, no! I can't imagine that."

"I don't know if I could even accept the money the Captain left under those circumstances."

"Well I would hope you could. You would certainly be deserving and legally entitled." He stopped and regained his professional demeanor. "Of course there would have to be proof of … of his demise."

"You mean his body?"

"… or a death certificate … this is all highly irregular. Perhaps we should not speak of these things?"

"That's me, 'Irregular Stella.' Thanks for coming, Counselor. I'll contact you as soon as I have news — one way or the other." Stella looked at him with flirty eyes. "You seem to be an upright and pleasant lawyer. I hope I will be dealing with you and only you?"

"Oh, my. I see. Yes, I will make sure this case stays as my personal project." He almost blushed. "Well, you know where … I can be found … where to reach me?" He put on his hat to leave.

Stella went to a flower vase and picked a bright red carnation. She pinned it on his lapel. "Of course I do. Good day, Counselor. Until we met again!" Stella smiled as she showed the lawyer to the door.

He took one last dubious look at her, tipped his hat, and scurried down the street.

Stella slammed the door hard.

She poured herself a tall glass of whiskey and grinned. She sat at the kitchen table and thought it over. "Two million dollars." She felt a little faint just saying the words. "Glory be! Two million dollars and where is he? He's … God knows where … and the devil be damned if I would even care! … except for the money." Stella tried to harden her heart. She knew, to do what she was planning to do, was going to take considerable hardening.

It was hard to hate Eli.

Eli was, basically, a good man. But he was also just as stubborn as she. Stella knew that in matters of money people changed. In matters of big money, they changed a lot.

For all she knew, he might decide to take all the inheritance for himself and leave her out in the cold. She decided she was not going to let that happen.

One of them would, eventually, lose.

She figured it had to be him.

She rattled around the big kitchen and kicked at the huge potato bin. It fell open and spilled several big potatoes. She picked one up and looked at it.

She did not know whether to laugh or cry.

The horrors of the potato famine of 1848 that had caused Stella's family to leave Ireland had permanently warped her soul.

Stella had seen friends and relatives die of starvation and had vowed it would never happen to her. Stella had endured the terrible Atlantic passage as a young woman. She had known what it was like to huddle in the cold, damp darkness below the decks of the stinking overcrowded ship. She had walked among human excrement and wallowed in vomit. She had endured the vituperative scorn of those who despised her people.

Stella had never known what is was like to be a child.

For one brief moment she had been allowed to taste childhood, but that was taken in a most brutal way.

She remembered the terrible pain of losing Lucy, her rag doll. Lucy, the only present she had ever been given. Lucy, taken from her because the rags were needed to fuel a fire. A fire that warmed no one for very long.

Stella had never been allowed to be a dreamer.

She had always had to plot to survive.

Stella did not look at things in black and white so much as in the color of money. In her mind, the highest morality was to provide for oneself and rely on no one else.

It took all her emotional strength to get it straight in her mind.

Eli had left of his own free will. Left her to survive on her own. He had not asked her — he had told her. In her rational mind she knew what Eli was doing, he did for her but Stella did not let herself entertain rational thoughts. Rational thoughts were not expeditious. Rational thoughts got in the way of going places fast.

Besides, it was lonely in the big old house and the loose tongues of Sonora were wagging. The bluenoses were saying Eli left her because of her past life. That now, being a respectable member of the community, he could no longer keep a wife who had been a whore.

"Whore!" How Stella hated that word. She wondered what they would do if they had not eaten for a week and were cold and outcast. She also knew that despite pretenses they loved money and power as much as she.

She knew if she had enough money she would have the power — and thanks to the good Captain, she would soon have the money. Stella was not poor. By most people's standards, she was, now, very comfortable. Scotty had made her a ring out of a part of a twelve-pound nugget he had found just the other day. If the claim continued to pay out at five to ten thousand a week, she would be very rich in her own right, soon.

But it was all Eli's doing. All his money. All power and respect to him. Eli Llynne, the only man she had ever known who dared to scorn her.

All the money in the world would not hide the fact that she could not hold him. That she did not have enough power over him to keep him close to home. That she, a woman most men begged to defer to, was shunned by the man she loved most in the world.

It didn't matter that Eli's motives might be honorable. Stella knew she could hire a man killed for a bottle of good whiskey. For a few thousand there were men who would hunt Jules and Eli both down and dismember them.

Eli did not have to go. He *WANTED* to go. She would never forgive him for that.

Stella really didn't care if Jules lived or died.

She *did* care to make Eli crawl on his knees back to her and beg forgiveness — or know that he was dead.

Eli sat in the shadows of a dusty saloon in Hornitos and watched people coming in and out of the door. His eyes were now adept at looking to identify someone without staring at them. He studied each man that came through the door and was ready with his gun if need be.

He waited, impatiently, for John Miller, the head of the Miners Brotherhood, to join him. John Miller, Eli hoped, would bring the information he sought. As he waited he sipped three fingers of rye whiskey. For a man who had disdained strong drink most of his life, Eli had developed a quiet fondness for the taste of good whiskey.

Eli could now afford the best and it was the one vice he allowed himself — stopping just when he felt it impaired his judgement or his aim.

"Mr. Llynne?" John Miller approached his table.

Eli stood up and shook his hand. Eli was glad John had a strong handshake. Eli trusted a man who gave firm handshakes. "Yes. John Miller?"

"Yes."

"Can I buy you a drink?"

"Don't mind if I do."

"Pull up a chair."

"Thank you," John said as he sat down and Eli called for the waiter.

After he had ordered a bottle of the finest whiskey in the house, Eli addressed John.

"You know why I wanted to speak with you, John?"

"Yes, sir."

"I'm sorry if I sound like a man in a hurry."

"Oh, no. I understand."

"As you know I'm seeking any information you might have on the whereabouts of Jules Joshua?"

"Yes."

"I was told you found the doctor dead?"

"I have no trouble telling you all I know. Dr. Immanuel was a friend of all the miners. We feel like it was partly our fault that the wolf got in the door."

"Don't blame yourself. This 'wolf' has a way of getting in doors where he isn't wanted." Eli paused.

"Do you mind tellin' me about the doctor?"

"He was a good and kind man. As good as there ever was. If a miner didn't have the wherewithal he would tend to them for free. He tended Mr. Joshua, and Mr. Joshua repaid him by putting a bullet in his head and stealing all that he had of any value."

"You headed the posse that chased him?"

"He took Midnight, the doctor's horse — it was the fastest animal ever in these parts. I'm afraid we just weren't fast enough. We turned back because we hope … and pray the Mexican Indians will not take kindly to his presence. Since we took California they don't welcome white men below that border."

"I wish I could believe in your prayers, but he'll find a way to survive. He's a *cucaracha* that you can stomp with your boot but the son-of-a-bitch will just get up and scurry away."

"He's ornery enough, but he's just a man."

"No. No, my friend, he's more like the devil himself. I expect to shoot him dead. Then, to be certain the deed is done proper, I will have to drive a stake through his heart," Eli said calmly.

John Miller looked dubious.

Eli smiled. "Now can you direct me to where he crossed the border?"

❖ ❖ ❖

Jules' foul breath was on her face and his gnarly hot hands were all over her body. She clawed at his eyes — hideous, red-glowing, satanic eyes. He only laughed as he took her again and again, as she lay in a coffin in a freshly dug grave. She fought him with all her strength until the bullet pierced her brain.

Stella woke up screaming. She was drenched in sweat, and she had chills and fever. She shivered and shook and cursed the dream.

Stella had felt the stirring in her womb for some time now. The timing was close but she knew the child was not Eli's — but that of the accursed Jules Joshua.

Her first thought was to have it cut from her body, but her strict Catholic upbringing would not allow her to entertain such thoughts for long. In her anger at Eli, she often thought of what his face would look like when she told him. The remnants of love she felt for him caused her to, quickly, dismiss that virulent thinking — and she vowed he would never know the child's true father.

She had never told Eli about the rape, and he had never asked. That terrible day before she lapsed into unconsciousness, she had barely managed to get into a clean dress and hide the torn one. Telling Eli would have served no purpose. Eli did not need any additional motivation to hunt down Jules Joshua.

But that was all yesterday's news.

This day it was time to think about the future and the new life she nurtured. It wasn't a difficult decision. There was no life in California for either of them. It was easy to decide go to Boston and see the great house Captain Hopkins had willed Eli. If she left soon there would be no danger to the unborn child if she made her way there by ship. Such was the power of Captain Hopkins' name, that she would be offered free passage aboard almost any ship sailing that way.

But she would not use Captain Hopkins' name to secure free passage. Stella was a wealthy woman who could afford to buy whatever she desired — except a good name.

Stella felt that even her parents would respect her if she could somehow manage to ease her way into Boston high society. She knew they wouldn't return money she sent them if she was a Boston *grande dame*.

She had been paying tutors and coaches for some time now to help her with the social graces. She had begun the process of having all her paperwork put in her dead first husband Dan Winslow's name.

The California courts being in legal limbo between a republic and statehood, it was easy to find a friendly judge. She smiled as she knew how easy the legal part had been. Her most arduous client in San Francisco was the best probate lawyer there. He had friends who, for a fee, would provide a legal death certificate with Jesus Christ's name on it. They had no trouble convincing Captain Hopkins' estate lawyer that Eli was "officially" dead. She had had to write him endearing letters and give him ten times the normal fee, but in the end he saw it her way.

Everyone always did — except Eli.

Well, Eli did not matter anymore.

When and if he ever returned, he would find that it didn't pay to leave her. Not that he would be poor. She left him the gold claim — only because Scotty would not have stood for her meddling in that. None of that mattered now. Now she was prepared to begin her dream journey to respectability. She was confident she could move about, easily, in polite society without interference from the past.

In her mind, Eli was lost to her. The pursuit of Jules Joshua was, to Stella, an ugly obsession that would either lead to Eli's death or Jules' or both. Stella had her reasons to wish Jules dead, but it was not a consuming passion in her life. Not like the passion to be somebody. To be somebody that was whispered about not as "… that San Francisco whore …" but talked about with respect and treated in an honorable manner by decent people.

Eli was lost to her, so she would have to make a life for herself and her unborn child.

As she packed her belongings, she put everything she thought she would need into large trunks.

She started to put in a picture of Eli but decided that she would not take anything with her that would remind her of the past.

Only one detail remained.

It had been a hard decision for Stella to sleep with, but one Stella knew she had to make.

To ensure there would be no future complications, she would have to make sure Eli was not only "officially" dead — but forever dead.

Her friends in San Francisco had recommended she hire three free-lance gunman they knew to be excellent in this area.

Stella had rationalized it so that she pretended in her mind they would only be "checking up" on Eli.

She would contract for them to, only, pursue Eli and report to her on his movements. To give her fair warning if he did manage to survive.

"You say he's headed up Hornitos way?" Lyle Jameson, a bear of a man with a scar on the left side of his face, had asked the day she hired them.

"That's right. He's riding a roan stallion with a Spanish saddle. He favors a black hat and a Navy Colt revolver."

"I see, ma'am. And our contract is to bring him back or just report his whereabouts? You mean for us to return him here? … is that alive, ma'am?"

Stella had paused before answering Lyle's question. She still cared enough for Eli not to speak of what must be done in plain terms.

"You just do your job however you have to do it. Understand?"

Lyle and his swarthy companions, Tom Manson, a tall quiet gunman, and "Smiling John" Beasily, looked doubtful.

"… are you sure, ma'am?"

"Just do it! There is five thousand dollars up front and five more when you report back. Isn't that enough, for God's sake?"

"Yes, ma'am," Lyle had replied before they tipped their hats and left.

Stella had wanted to call them back before they rode off, but the hurt in her heart had stopped her. Now, as she sat alone in her ornate parlor, she shivered from the fear that she had done something terribly wrong.

She dismissed that thought.

It would serve Eli right for having the audacity to leave her and miss out on Captain Hopkins' bonanza and the good life to come. She was not cold enough to cut him out of any inheritance. She would see to it that he was provided for if he ever returned — but she believed the odds were in her favor that he never would.

CHAPTER TWO

JULY 4, 1855

Jules liked Mexico. In California it was hard to tell, day to day, what the law was or who the lawmen were. In Mexico it was very clear. The man with the most *pesos* was the law, and thanks to the money he had liberated from the good doctor, Jules had plenty of *pesos*.

Jules heard the sound of the beating as if it was from a dream — the dream that haunted him almost every night of his life:

"You slothful slacker! Look at this pitiful fifty cents in script … not worth twenty cents you done brought home, boy!" Jules' father drove his huge fist full into Jules' young mouth. Jules was eleven years old and was supposed to be the breadwinner for the Joshua family of eight. The two daughters were frail, sickly asthmatics and could not tolerate the mines.

The other brothers were not quite old enough to be *trappers*.

"Damn you, boy! How in the hell do you expect us to keep body and soul together bringing home this pittance? Huh? Huh? Say something, boy!"

Jules let the blood spill though his fingers as he glared at his father with white-hot hatred in his soul. His father had broken both legs in a mining accident and they had not healed properly. As a result, he had limited mobility in his legs, but his arms and fists were as hard as the coal he had mined for twenty years.

Jules spit out two teeth and glared at his father. He looked at his mother, Miriam, for support.

Her eyes said she wanted to help but she backed into the shadows instead.

"This ain't gonna git us one day's rations at the company store. If it weren't past dark I'd have your lazy behind back down there doin' some real mining!"

Jules did not reply but looked into the frightened eyes of his younger brothers who cowered in the corner. Big John was only five, and big for his age.

But he was the most frightened of them all.

"Don't hit me no more, Pa!" Jules challenged.

"What?"

"I said don't hit me no more. I done been hit enough too many times …"

"You tellin' me what to do, boy?"

"No, Pa. But you know I done as good as anybody my age …"

"… except Eli Llynne! He's outdone you every time. He makes cash money. You know that?"

"Yes, Pa."

"Then you'd better listen up and start producing or I'll be hitting you a lot more than I am now! You hear?" Ephraim Joshua backhanded his son.

Jules fell backwards against a wall deep in the shadows of the small shack where Miriam cowered in a corner.

Miriam's hands trembled as she took her apron and dabbed the blood away from her son's mouth.

"Now don't go coddling the boy, Miriam. He's near to a sissy boy now anyways."

"You don't hit him anymore … please, Ephraim. Please?"

"Stay out of this, woman! I done told you not to interfere in my disciplinin'. So jes' hush up!"

Ephraim hobbled over to Jules and clenched his fists.

"I told you not to hit me anymore, Pa!"

Miriam stepped in between them. "Please, Ephraim … he's bleeding bad."

Ephraim grabbed Miriam by the hair and threw her to the floor. "Shut up, woman! Shut up!" Ephraim growled.

Jules looked at his mother prostrate on the floor and then looked at his father with unyielding hatred. Calmly, with measured detachment, Jules grabbed a pick axe and drove it into his father's chest.

His father looked at him in disbelief before he hobbled backwards and fell against the wall.

Jules followed him and pulled the pick axe from his chest. His father's blood spurted out of his chest and drenched Jules from head to toe.

Miriam got to her feet and moved toward Jules. "No, son! No! No!"

Jules raised the pick axe high. He glared at his mother. "Shut up, woman!" Jules said just before he drove the pick axe deep into his father's head — killing him with more joy than remorse.

The dream was broken by the screams of a young man being beaten in the alley outside the *cantina*. Jules downed his *tequila* and moved to investigate.

The young man was around sixteen years old and he was being beaten by two *federales* who took great delight in kicking him when he was down. Jules felt a strange kinship with the boy and wanted to interfere. But he had seen the inside of Mexican jails and he did not want to ever go there again.

He did remember that his sentence of three years for "having no papers" was miraculously abbreviated to three hours when he had paid a hundred-dollar fine.

"*¿Señores? ¿Por favor?*" Jules addressed the officers in his broken Spanish. "What has the boy done?"

"Go away, *gringo!* Go away or we will invite you to join him!" the heavy-set *federale* said.

"Go!" The thin one agreed.

The boy looked up at Jules with sad Spanish eyes. Blood dripped from his mouth and he was missing two teeth. Jules felt a cold chill of remembrance.

"If he's done broken some law ... if it's all the same to you, I could pay the fine?" Jules offered.

"Pay the fine? Ha! Ha! Ha! He is a *Juarista!*"

The heavy-set *federale* paused. "Are you a *Juarista, señor?*"

"No! No, I just thought ... maybe I had too much *tequila*. The *tequila* in the *cantina* is the best I've ever had ... it goes down so smooth, I think it's done made me *loco!*"

The *federales* thought it over a long moment.

"The fine is fifty dollars ... in gold pieces!" The heavy-set one announced. Jules thought it over a moment. He looked at the young man holding his bleeding mouth in his hands. He paid the fine.

Once the *federales* were gone into the *cantina*, Jules stood and watched the boy wipe his mouth on his sleeve, leaving a snail's wake of dark blood.

"*Gracias, señor*. But please ... I am not a sissy boy. I could not repay you in that way."

"Nobody said nothin' 'bout repayin'," Jules stopped. "... what's this here *Juarista*, anyways?"

"Benito Juárez, *señor*. He wants to make Mexico once again a proud place for Mexicans. He will drive the Spanish and their church from our land!"

"I see. Well, it sounds like politics and religion altogether. If you want some advise you stay plumb far away from both. Now git on home and git those teeth fixed as best you can."

"I am forever in your debt, *señor.*"

"I said git!" Jules insisted.

The young man paused only a moment before he vanished into the hot dusty afternoon.

BOSTON, MASSACHUSETTS — SEPTEMBER 1855

Stella remembered the disdain that New Yorkers held for the Irish and had heard it was even worse in Boston.

In order to give her unborn child the best chance at a good life in this town, she decided to use the name of her first husband, Winslow. Dan Winslow was of respected Anglo descent and he had never given her much. Perhaps, in this way, he would finally be useful.

She had secured passage on a fine windjammer that had made it around the Horn and on to Boston in near record time of three months, one week. As she waited for the driver to open the door of her carriage, she knew she had cut the timing close. The baby in her womb was pressing hard and seemed to press the hardest as she dismounted the carriage and stood before Captain Hopkins' majestic great house on the highest hill in the best section of Boston.

It was breathtaking. The great house was everything Stella had every dreamed of or wished for. It reeked of elegance, class, and instant social status.

"Mrs. Winslow, I have taken the liberty of seeing that you have a full staff of servants. I admit I'm partial to Irish for this vocation — but you need have no fear, if they steal anything I am good for it!" The snobbish real estate agent addressed her.

Stella did not recognize "Mrs. Winslow" at first. She was too busy fighting back her anger over his Irish prejudices.

"What did you say?" she challenged.

"Excuse me?"

"Irish servants?"

"Yes. If you don't like them … I understand. We can get English or French, maybe German, but they are more expensive and very uppity."

"Just show me inside, Mr. Tuttle. I'll take care of any servant problem."

"Yes, Mrs. Winslow."

Mr. Tuttle paused and looked at her ample girth. "Per your instructions, I have contacted Dr. James W. White. He is the best in this area. You are fortunate he agreed to take you on."

"I suppose a two-thousand-dollar retainer had something to do with that!" Stella stopped as she felt woozy. "… I think … I need to … to see him right away." Stella felt faint.

"Yes. He has you scheduled for first thing in the morning …"

"No! No, I mean right away! *NOW!*" Stella fell over into Mr. Tuttle's arms. He tried to hold her but she slipped to the pavement just as her water broke, soaking Mr. Tuttle's shoes with amnionic fluid.

"Oh, my God! Oh, my God!" Mr. Tuttle backed off. "Get her into the carriage, Michael!" he yelled at the driver. The driver hesitated.

"No! No! Go get the doctor! Go! My child … my child will be born here."

"Madam! Here on the street?"

Stella struggled to her feet.

She looked at the long climb up the steps to the great house. "No, you idiot. Up there! Up there in that great house!"

Stella doubled over in pain as she began to climb the steps.

Mr. Tuttle did not know what to do. The carriage driver drove off to get the doctor.

Stella was dizzy and near fainting as she crawled over the last step to the grand porch of the house. She smiled as she looked at the polished oak door and the shiny brass knobs. She forced herself to get to her feet and ring the bell. It seemed like an eternity before someone answered the door. Stella smiled as she saw a freckle-faced Irish girl open the door.

"Oh, my! Oh, my! I'm sorry, but you'll have to go to the servants' entrance. We are expecting the mistress of the house," the young girl fretted.

Stella pushed the young girl aside. She staggered into the parlor. She took one look around at the exquisite furnishings and smiled. She looked back at the young girl. "I *AM* the mistress of the house!" Stella said before she fell to the thick, imported carpeting of the parlor floor.

CHAPTER THREE

Eli Llynne eased into the north side of the dusty Mexican town. For a long moment he thought the town was deserted. There was no movement anywhere within his eyesight, and it was deadly quiet. Then, like iron filings attracted to a magnet, a hundred children came out of nowhere. They gathered around his horse with their hands held out and their mouths chattering away in Spanish.

"Go away, *muchachos!*" Eli spoke one of the half dozen words he knew in Spanish. "Git! Git out of the way!" Eli insisted. The *niños* ignored him and pressed closer.

Eli was irritated until he remembered the advice John Miller had given him just before he left for Mexico. "Smile and be generous ... money is social grease in Mexico." John had said.

Eli pulled his horse up reached in his pocket.

He withdrew a handful of coins. He threw them as far as he could. The *niños* scattered and Eli, quietly, thanked John for the advice.

"... and me, *señor*. I'm afraid coins will not satisfy me ..." A pleasant-looking young man in a huge *sombrero* and a brightly colored *serape* addressed him as he moved in front of Eli's horse.

"You seem to be old enough to take care of yourself. Now stand aside and let me pass."

"You are a stranger in this land. *¿Es verdad?*"

"I really don't have time to talk, *hombre.*"

"You will need help to survive down here, *gringo*. *¿Habla español?*"

"Are you going to let me pass, or am I going to have to get nasty?"

"*Por favor*. Please pass." He stood aside. "But when you call for help Pepito Baca will not answer ... and you *WILL* call for help. *Cuidado, amigo. ¡Cuidado!*" Pepito stepped aside.

Eli paused and studied the young man's face. It was a youthful, but solemn face that wore a forced smile. There was deep hurt in his eyes but he seemed to want you to believe he was a clown.

"It's a mighty hot day and I have had a long ride. You wouldn't know where I could get a shot of good whiskey? ... mind you ... not *tequila*, but good imported whiskey?" Eli posed.

Pepito shrugged then took Eli's horse by the reins. "I know anything you care to know and more than you want to know. But I will only tell you what you need to know ... and are willing to pay for. Agreed?"

Eli smiled as Pepito led his horse to a small *cantina*. Eli dismounted and slapped at the dust that coated his clothes.

"I will stable your horse and join you here. At that time you can ask me questions that will determine my worth." Pepito forced a smile before he took the horse to the stable.

Eli started to protest, but, instead, moved into the *cantina*.

Once inside, Eli moved to the makeshift bar and smiled at Mamacita, the large *señora* tending the bar.

"A bottle of your best whiskey, please."

Mamacita laughed. "Whiskey?"

"... I was told by ... I think it is Pepito? Pepito said ..."

"Where is your horse, *señor*?"

"Pepito, ... he ... took it to the stables."

"Stables? We don't got no stinking stables!" Mamacita almost fell down laughing.

Eli cursed himself for being so trusting as he turned to move for the door. He was almost through the door when he ran into Pepito.

Eli grabbed Pepito by the collar and lifted him off the floor. "My horse. Where is it, Pepito? Where the hell is it?"

Pepito looked hurt. "They told you I was a thief?"

"Never mind what they told me, where is my horse?"

"I am poor, but I am not a thief."

"Where the hell is my horse?" Eli paused as he heard a whinny outside.

He looked out to see his horse tied to a rail. He let Pepito go.

"I forgot, we do not have stables." Pepito looked sly.

"Just stay where I can see you until I've had a whiskey!" Eli sighed hard.

"They do not have whiskey here." Pepito looked at Mamacita. She looked at him with scorn.

"Do you tell the truth about anything?"

"What do you need to know?"

"Whatever it is I won't ask for it from the likes of you," Eli picked Pepito up and sat him down in a chair. "Just sit. Don't move. Don't even think about moving!" Eli insisted as he turned and moved back to the bar. *"Tequila* or nothing, is that it?"

"Or rum. You want rum?" Mamacita shrugged.

Eli smiled a moment as he remembered the good times he had with Scotty sharing "a pint o' rum."

"Rum. A pint of rum."

"¿Excúseme?"

"A bottle ... a bottle of rum, *por favor.*"

"A whole bottle for just one man? For a hundred *pesos*, I will share the bottle with you." Mamacita grinned a gap-toothed smile.

Eli did not want to insult her, but it was hard to keep a straight face. "No, thank you. I have some business with this scoundrel." Eli said as he moved to the table where Pepito sat.

"Oh, no! Our business is concluded." Pepito started to leave.

Eli grabbed Pepito's arm and pulled him back down in a chair. "Just shut up and drink!" Eli took a long pull from the bottle and passed it to Pepito.

"Señor, did I not tell you I would be useful? I think Mamacita has serious intentions!"

"Look! Stow it. I'm hot and tired and ..."

"You are looking for a man!"

"What?"

"¿Señor? No one comes this way on a good horse with money in his pockets unless he is *loco* or looking for someone. There is no gold in these parts ... and no good whiskey." Pepito looked serious.

It was hard for Eli to dislike Pepito. Pepito had an engaging personality and his eyes were compelling — yet sinister. "You lived here a long time, Pepito?"

"No, *señor.* I am here only a day longer than you."

"You're running from something?" Eli challenged.

Pepito looked impressed with Eli's insight. *"¿Quizás?* Perhaps ... and you are running after someone?"

"Tell me, how far did you get before you decided not to steal my horse?"

"¿Señor? Por favor ..."

"How far?"

Pepito smiled. He shrugged. "My brother Eduardo was one of the first to work a claim in Amador, before the *gringos* ... by the southern mines and the mother lode. When Santa Ana lost California, *Cabrone!*" Pepito paused. "Your people ... your people took his claim." Pepito paused again and waited for an apology from Eli.

Eli sipped from the bottle of rum without showing emotion.

"Eduardo returned to Mexico penniless and one night, when he had too much *tequila*, he blew his brains out ... right outside that door!"

"What has all this got to do with your stealing my horse?"

"Eduardo, he returned, penniless but with many stories. His favorite story was of a man, your size, who rode a horse with a Spanish saddle and favored a Navy Colt. This man had fought a bear to the death in Sonora." Pepito stared at Eli's Navy Colt.

Eli pulled down three swallows from the bottle and looked at Pepito with curiosity. "That's some story."

"I think so ..." Pepito stopped as he saw two *federales* walk through the door.

A look of terror filled his eyes and Eli turned to see what had frightened him so.

"*¿Pepito? Pepito, ¡mi amigo! ¿Qué pasó? ¿Dónde está mi dinero?*" The heavy-set *federale* almost spit into Pepito's face.

Pepito backed against a wall. The tall thin *federale* looked at Eli. "*Señor*, you are American?"

Eli nodded, "Yes."

"Go, my friend!" Pepito insisted.

"You are a friend of this man?" The heavy-set *federale* looked incredulous.

Eli did not reply.

"Maybe he is also a *Juarista*," the tall one growled.

"I have most of a bottle of rum here. Why don't I pour you boys a drink?"

The heavy-set *federale* back-handed Eli and sent him reeling to the floor. "*¡Cabrone!* You will keep your *gringo* nose out of this affair! *¿Comprende?*"

Eli looked at the huge Mexican and wiped a trickle of blood from his mouth. The two *federales* grabbed Pepito under the arms and dragged him screaming and kicking toward the door.

Eli pulled a Colt from his belt and fired a round that took a hunk of adobe out of the wall above their heads.

They released Pepito and started to go for their guns. Eli fired two more rounds that were near misses. They raised their hands in surrender.

"*Es verdad.* He is a *Juarista!*" the tall one said.

"I ain't no damn *Juarista!* But I don't take kindly to being busted in the mouth!"

"*Señor,* it is a serious offense to assault a federal officer."

Pepito eased to go out of the door. "Hold it, Pepito. You tell these lawmen, I'm just a visitor here. I'm not looking for any trouble. Tell 'em!"

Pepito started to object but Eli cocked the hammer of his gun.

"*¡Sí! Es verdad. Es un hombre muy malo.*"

"Not in Spanish, Pepito. In English!" Eli insisted.

"*Sí. Ese hombre es* ... this man is the man Eduardo spoke of. He is the one who killed the bear."

The *federales* looked shaken.

"Then can I see your paperwork, *señor?*" The heavy-set *federale* lowered his hands.

Eli uncocked his gun and slide it back into his belt. He kept his eyes on the *federales* as he thought it over.

He, slowly, reached into his pockets and withdrew five twenty-dollar gold pieces. "I'm sorry. This is the only paperwork I have."

The heavy-set *federale* smiled as he looked at the shiny coins. "Your paperwork is in order, *señor.* Welcome to Mexico. Have a nice visit."

CHAPTER FOUR

Benjamin David Winslow was twelve pounds seven ounces at birth. The nursing staff that had attended Stella called him "Big Ben" when they thought she was not listening.

But Stella always listened. Her ears were perked to hear any gossip that might indicate that, in any way, her past had followed her to this wonderful place.

Captain Hopkins' ancestral home was as beautiful as any she had ever seen in New York. It was three times as big as the house her mother and father worked in as servants. Her bedroom was bigger than the first "sporting palace" she had lived in California, and she had but to lift a finger and five maids attended her smallest wish.

She had never been here before, but she felt at home. She had always liked Captain Hopkins, and she said a quiet "Thank you" as she remembered him.

She held Benjamin in her arms and, reverently, pulled his sweet mouth to her engorged breast. She felt a wonderful, tingling sensation that flooded all her senses as he suckled her.

All the wealth in the world could not buy the feeling she felt as her son took his life from her breast.

For the longest moment, she regretted, to her soul, her past life and prayed for God to make her milk pure so as not to harm a hair on his thick blonde head.

"I love you so much, my son. I swear to you, no one will ever harm you, and I will see that you never have to do what I had to do. This is your great house. I will see that you have a great name! God help anyone who dares try to take anything away for us!" Stella sighed as Benjamin looked at her with innocent blue eyes.

"Madam, would you be carin' to receive any visitors?" Stella's thoughts were interrupted by Rosie, the upstairs maid, who was as Irish as freckles.

"Can't you see I'm nursing my son?"

"Yes, ma'am … but …"

"Just close the door and leave us alone."

"Yes, ma'am. But it is the good Reverend Dr. Talbot."

"Now why on earth would I want to be seeing a reverend?"

"Oh! Ah, … he's the vicar of the church where … where all the … the important people go."

Stella thought it over as she watched Benjamin fall into a deep sleep. She gave him a long kiss on the forehead and inhaled his sweetness before she replied.

"Is he a power in this community?" Stella asked.

"Yes, ma'am. The most respected."

"Then let me put on a proper dress … with a hint of cleavage and powder my nose."

"Madam! I have never!"

"Just tell him I'll be down in awhile … Rosie. Rosie, isn't it?"

"Yes, ma'am."

"I like you, Rosie. Let's get along. Don't try to flimflam me and I won't try to flimflam you. Okay?"

"Madam … I … "

"Just trust me, Rosie. I know I'm an outsider. I know how hard it is to accept someone like me. But it would be to your advantage to make the effort."

"Madam, I am here out of respect for the Captain. If he willed you this house then you are to be respected. I have no place to quarrel with that."

"There are those who don't like me here, Rosie?"

"Madam … please …"

"The Captain was my good friend, Rosie. Was he your friend?"

"Oh! Yes, ma'am. The best employer ever. It's so sad he died … out there … not at sea."

"I agree. But I think he loved the gold fields also. Tell me, Rosie. This Reverend Talbot, who is he?"

"The vicar, ma'am."

"No! No, WHO is he? Why is he here?"

"I see. Please forgive me. I forget you are new to Boston. He is here to … how shall I say it?"

"To pry?"

"Oh, madam!"

"He's snooping, isn't he?"

"Madam!"

"He wants to know how somebody no one knows is living in Captain Hopkins' house. He's curious but I'll bet he won't admit it. I've seen these mealy mouthed psalm singers before. They all want to get something for nothing … you know, take you for free then run you out of business." Stella studied the look of horror on Rosie's face. "You know, the collection box."

"Yes, madam. I'll tell him you'll be down directly." Rosie turned to leave.

Stella grabbed her by the arm and spun her around. "Don't you ever … and I mean ever, look at me with those condescending eyes! I've seen those eyes before and I don't like them one bit! You just attend me and do like you're told or you can get the hell out of here! Now which is it?"

Stella's Irish eyes met Rosie's Irish eyes and they reached a forced understanding.

"I will do as you say. Is thirty minutes adequate time to prepare, madam?"

"Is that a proper time to make him wait?"

Rosie thought it over for a long moment. "If it was me I wouldn't see him at all."

Stella smiled at Rosie with respect. "You're Irish Catholic?"

"Yes, ma'am. And he's right mean about being against the Pope and all."

"I see."

"It's mighty hard these days being Irish and Catholic. I don't hold anyone's religion against them, I just ask that they don't hold mine against me."

Stella looked sympathetic only a moment. "It is my wish that we do not discuss religion at all in this house. Now I want to ask you an important question. But first I want you to look at me as a friend looks at another friend," Stella insisted.

"Yes, ma'am."

"I am a stranger here with no friends. That is true enough. You might not like me or you might like me. But I ask you, please … please come look at my son. "

Stella took Rosie to the crib where Benjamin slept peacefully. "I would ask your help as a woman to see that he has the best possible chance to have a good life … here where he is also a stranger."

Rosie nodded agreement, slowly. "Yes, ma'am. He is a right beautiful lad."

"You, nor your family, nor your friends will regret it if you are a friend to him, and you will want for nothing in your life if you assist me in watching over him!" Stella insisted.

"Yes, ma'am. What shall I tell the Reverend?"

"Will it help Benjamin if I see him?"

"Yes, ma'am. The Reverend Talbot has much power in this town. He is also superintendent of the schools."

"Then help me with my most pious dress and we will go meet the bastard!"

"Madam! Oh, madam!" Rosie said just before she broke into laughter.

CHAPTER FIVE

Jules Joshua watched the gathering of Mexican Indians from a safe place on the hillside above them.

He had discovered that Mexico was in the early stages of a civil war with a young Mexican Indian named Benito Juárez stirring the *campesinos* to open revolt against their Spanish oppressors.

Santa Ana, who had failed miserably as a general, was elevated to power as governor of Mexico, where he was an even worse administrator than he had been a general. He represented the status quo which was okay for the elite but hell on the general populace.

The ferment in Mexico was racial, religious, economic, and ideological. A devil's brew of the things men will fight and die for. The "liberals" of Benito Juárez were mainly Mexican Indians and *mestizos*. Santa Ana's constituency was, mainly, Spanish, bankers and businessmen, and the church.

Benito Juárez, popular among his people, had made a major mistake of taking on the church. Not to destroy it but to make it pure. Benito was a puritan in the mode of Martin Luther. Benito wanted to purify the church and establish a kind of theocracy in Mexico. Called a bandit by some, a "murderer" and — the insult he hated most — an "atheist," Benito Juárez underneath it all was a pious man who only wanted Mexico to be ruled by men of God through "divine will."

Santa Ana had exiled Benito to New Orleans where he and Melchor Ocampo worked out the plan they would later use when they came to power. Meanwhile, the *Juaristas* struggled everyday to stay alive and keep his name in the people's minds.

Jules did not like it at all. Jules did not want any part of being involved in a conflict where ideas were being fought over. Jules knew you couldn't buy your way out of such disputes, so he figured it was time to leave Mexico.

In his mind, it was time to ease his way back to the United States and on to Sonora. He knew how short people's memories were in the Gold Country and how fast things changed.

It riled him to think that maybe Eli was now a rich man sitting in some fancy parlor fondling that gun with those damned notches in it.

Notches that signified each of his brother's lives.

Jules turned to move to his horse and walked into the cold end of a Walker revolver. On the other end was a mean-looking Mexican.

CHAPTER SIX

When Columbus sailed west he was looking for the Spice Islands where he could find black pepper. Instead, he sailed too far southwest and discovered red pepper.

The Spanish palate, indeed the palates of the world, have never been the same since.

Black pepper may season bland food and tickle the taste buds, but red pepper not only seasons food — it adds emotion.

Pepito smiled as he watched Eli try his first red *jalapeño* pepper. Beads of sweat broke out on Eli's head as he bit into the pepper. Pepito was impressed when he saw that Eli did not, immediately, call for a tall glass of water.

Pepito took two peppers from the plate and shoved them in his mouth. He swallowed them whole without flinching.

Eli looked at him for a long moment before he, also, took two peppers from the plate and swallowed them whole.

Pepito had never seen a *gringo* eat red peppers without flinching. "Maybe this really was the man who killed the bear?" Pepito thought to himself.

Eli saw it as a test of wills and he was determined not to lose any such test. His throat was on fire and he felt hot to the tips of his toes, but he would never let Pepito know that.

"*Señor* Eli! You are the most famous man for eating so many peppers. You have beat me by three and I am the grand champion. *¡Muy bien! ¡Muy bien!*" Pepito looked sincerely impressed.

Eli had, temporarily, lost his voice so he nodded agreement. He picked up a bottle of rum and took several long pulls.

They were both interrupted by the presence of a stunning Mexican woman who stood by the table and glared at Pepito.

"Where have you been? You were supposed to be home six hours ago. Where are the *tortillas?*" she demanded with Spanish eyes that lit up the dark *cantina*.

Pepito looked angry, but a little fearful.

Eli had loved Lydia and had great affection for Stella, but neither of them had leaped into his senses with such instant allure as this fiery woman.

"Maria, this is Eli. He is the man who fought the bear! Eli, this is my sister Maria Christina."

"The *tortillas*, Pepito? Mother and the children are hungry and you sit in a saloon with a *gringo!*"

"Nice to meet you, ma'am." Eli tipped his hat and she ignored him.

"I'm sorry, Maria. I will bring them in a little bit …"

"No, you will bring them now!" Maria grabbed Pepito by the ear.

"Ouch! Stop it! Okay! Okay!" Pepito broke her hold. Pepito looked at Eli and shrugged. "She thinks she is the boss now that father is dead. I think she needs a husband to beat her a little bit."

Pepito ducked as Maria took a swing at him.

She missed Pepito and hit Eli square in the jaw, knocking him off his chair.

Eli did not feel any pain as he looked up at her with admiration.

"I am sorry, *señor!* I am sorry. Are you okay?"

Maria looked genuinely concerned as Pepito looked worried, then laughed.

"Shut up, Pepito! It's all your fault," Maria insisted.

"I'm … I'm fine, miss … I hope it doesn't offend you to say you hit like a man?" Eli rubbed his jaw and got to his feet.

"Sometimes a woman has to be a man when the men act stupid like this one!" Maria pointed to Pepito. "Now we must go!"

Pepito, reluctantly, nodded agreement. "*Señor* Eli, would you like to come eat with us? Maria, he is the world champion pepper eater!"

"No! I'm sorry, *señor*, but you understand, these days one cannot have strangers in their houses."

"But he's not a stranger. I told you, he is the one Eduardo talked about."

"Eduardo is dead and you know why. So let's go now!" Maria's Spanish eyes flashed determination.

Pepito hung his head and started to leave. He looked back at Eli. "I will come see you after *la comida*. As soon as I have finished eating I will come back here. Okay?"

"No! You have spent too much time here. There is much for you to do at home!" Maria insisted.

Eli looked at her and did not like the anger he saw in her eyes. "Pardon me, ma'am. Have I done something to offend you?"

Maria looked hurt and turned to leave.

"*Señor* Eli. She holds all gringos responsible for Eduardo. He was her favorite. They were twins."

"Shut up, Pepito! That is family business. Now let's go!"

Pepito shrugged and moved to the door.

Maria waited until he was out of earshot, then turned and glared at Eli.

"I would ask that you leave my brother alone! He is stupid when it comes to *Americanos*. He has the romantic notions about them … but I do not! It is best for you that you return home as soon as possible. There is much trouble for everyone here these days. For *gringos*, it is even more dangerous," she warned.

"I see. Thanks, but I have business to attend to. When that is done … we'll see."

"You cannot deny you were warned."

"You know, you are a right handsome woman, but you are a mite too pushy. You don't seem to know much about people, do you?"

"I don't know what you're talking about."

"People don't like to be pushed. You push them in one direction and, like as not, they'll go the other just for spite!"

"I don't care which way you go. I told you what I thought. You do what you want. *¡Adios, señor!*" Maria said without smiling, then turned and left the saloon.

Eli watched her go. She was a charming spitfire and he admired her spunk. He also admired her beauty. He felt a little sad that he would never see her again. He sighed hard as he picked up a red pepper and ate it without feeling any pain.

Lyle Jameson, Tom Manson, and "Smiling John" Beasily rode, cautiously, into the far end of town. It had not been hard to follow Eli's trail. There were only a few roads traveled by *gringos* into the Mexican interior and there were only a few towns where they might not get their throats cut. A "big gringo" like Eli, who favored a Spanish saddle, was easy to track.

Lyle was not clear in his mind about what he would do when he found Eli. Lyle was a man of his word. He took pride in any job he was given. The money was important, but doing a good job was more important. Whatever he had undertaken in life he had excelled at. He took pride in being a craftsman — whether it was carving wooden figures or killing men. When he was sure about the work at hand, Lyle did it well.

He was not sure about this work, and it sat uneasy on his mind.

He pulled his horse up and motioned for the others to stop. He stared down the length of the dusty street and stared at the roan stallion with the Spanish saddle at the far end.

"Looks like his horse, Lyle," Tom offered.

Lyle nodded agreement.

"You got it figured ... how we're goin' about this, Lyle?" "Smiling John" wondered aloud.

"I reckon," Lyle sighed hard.

"Are we going in shooting, Lyle?" Tom asked.

"Is this like that time in Jackson? Are we going to give him fair warning?" "Smiling John" asked.

Lyle looked concerned a moment before he replied. "It's not like Jackson or nothing we never done before. He's done us no wrong but we made a contract. You know I don't take money unless I do the job right!"

"It's clear in my mind she wants the man dead," Tom said.

"I understand that, Tom! But we ain't no backshooters so we give him fair warning. Is that understood?"

"I heard he was a good shot, Lyle. He's mighty handy with a Colt." "Smiling John" hesitated.

"You want out, John? If you do you say so, now!"

"No. I just said what I said. That's all."

"You want out, Tom?" Lyle looked at Tom hard.

"No, Lyle. I just think we'd better go in slow. He does have five notches on that gun of his'n."

"Does that make you nervous, Tom?"

"Damn straight, it makes me nervous! But it don't make me scared." Tom looked offended.

"And you, John?"

"I just wish she had told us straight out to kill this man. That's all."

"She said enough and she paid enough. Ten thousand ain't tracking money — it's killin' money."

Tom and "Smiling John" nodded agreement.

"I understand what's on your minds. It's bothered me some too but we make our living on our word. We gave our word and we got ten thousand dollars coming. That's fair money for a good job. … and I intend to do a good job. Understood?"

Tom and "Smiling John" looked at Lyle with understanding in their eyes. They all turned and looked down the street at Eli's horse tied in front of the saloon.

They checked their guns and moved to go kill him dead.

CHAPTER SEVEN

The Boston of 1857 was trying hard to be America's greatest city, but it was still considered a second city to New York. Though rich Bostonians had a higher per capita wealth than New Yorkers, and had more proven "Yankee ingenuity," Boston could not command the respect that New York City did on the world and national scene.

It rankled descendants of the old "Massachusetts Colony" stock to take a back seat to New Yorkers. They knew it was Boston money that built American railroads and financed most of American heavy industry. It was Boston bankers that taught America about banking and finance, and it was Boston shipping that was the foundation of America's global greatness.

The West End and Beacon Hill where the Hopkins mansion sat, was, to Boston Brahmins, the center of Boston high society and, indeed, thought by many to be the center of world culture.

Stella was steadily trying to gain acceptance in that society as she penned her first letter home:

Dear Mother and Father,

I write to announce to you the birth of your grandson, Benjamin David Winslow. He is a fine strapping boy who favors his grandfather. I, regretfully, must tell you my marriage to Dan Winslow, a man of fine, respectable English stock has ended. He has died a most honorable death in the gold fields attempting to save a poor Irishman from drowning. Through the misfortune of his passing, I have inherited his home, and considerable holdings, in Boston.

Also, because of his respected name, your grandson, Benjamin David Winslow, is already accepted in the highest echelons of Boston society. I am enclosing a bank draft in the amount of five thousand dollars. I hope you will accept it in the spirit in which it is given and come, soonest, to see your grandson. I am attending Mass daily and have set Benjamin's

christeni\ng for Christmas Eve. Please plan to attend.
As always, Stella

Stella folded the letter and sealed it with wax. She stamped the Hopkins crest into the warm wax and sighed hard.

Stella had been raised a staunch Catholic, but she had put that aside to make friends with the Vicar Talbot. Her weekly teas with him were excruciatingly painful to her psyche, but for Ben she would put up with it and smile.

She dressed in her most pious dress and washed her face until it hurt, so there would be no trace of makeup. She picked up a King James Bible and walked gracefully downstairs to meet the Reverend.

Rosie, with Ben at her side, waited at the bottom of the stairs to greet them. Stella smiled at Rosie and gave Ben a hug. He gurgled something and wobbled away.

Ben was a little over a year old and already walking. He was big by any measurement, but he wasn't heavy. He was strong.

Reverend Talbot watched Ben stumble from one piece of furniture to another. "What a fine boy, Stella. You should be very proud."

Stella watched her son's bright eyes laugh at her as he slipped down to all fours.

"I am, to the extent that it is not sinful. I agree with the Biblical admonition that pride goeth before a fall."

"My, you have learned your scripture well."

"I've had the best teacher."

"Well, I don't know about that. I try."

"I do. You have been a godsend, Reverend. I was a stranger and you took me in. I understand the natural suspicions of people towards outsiders. I would still be an outcast in this town without your help," Stella smiled, sincerely.

Reverend Talbot looked somewhat embarrassed. He gulped down a swallow of tea. "I must say, I had my reservations also. But, this is a new Boston. We are no longer the isolated city of the past. The world encroaches more and more each day ..." he paused and looked at her with his cold, serious face. "Have you heard of the proposal to fill in the marshes and annex Roxbury?"

"No? No, I haven't."

The Reverend looked at her, suspiciously, then put his cup of tea down. "I have come to know you as a friend, Stella. Would you say we are friends?"

"Of course, Reverend."

"Please call me, James, or if you would like, Jimmy — but Jimmy only in private!"

"Jimmy? I like Jimmy."

"I, ordinarily, would not dare impose upon a friendship to do what I am about to ask you to do. But this is a special time and it must be dealt with in a special way."

"You sound serious?"

"It's business, Stella. I take business very seriously."

"I see."

"As I said, Boston can't stop the growth. There is nowhere to go but into the marshes. I believe that it is a good time to buy land on the peninsula and to invest in the gravel business. I would like to have you as a partner," he said with greed in his eyes.

"I see. They intend to annex Roxbury? The people over there don't have anything to do with Bostonians?"

"What they think is of no consequence. We have the power in the state legislature. Believe me. We can get the marsh land cheap. We can fill it in and in a few years make a fortune!"

"Oh? Please excuse my immodesty ... I already have a fortune."

Reverend Talbot looked displeased a moment, then he looked at Ben. "Perhaps it is something you should consider establishing for him. Whoever takes control of that new land will have the future of Boston in his hand!"

Stella looked at Ben then back at the Reverend. "How much money are we talking about?"

"An initial investment of only one hundred and fifty thousand. In any case, not to exceed half a million. An investment that will return a hundredfold."

"I see. We are to be partners? You have this kind of money, Reverend?"

Reverend Talbot looked embarrassed. "No! No, of course not. ... but I have the connections, Stella. I have the name and the respected reputation. A name is more to be chosen than wealth in these parts. Your money is no good ... without me."

"I don't understand."

"Stella, please don't force me to embarrass you. I want us to be friends.

"I detest equivocation. If you have something to say, say it!"

"Do you have some brandy?" Reverend Talbot asked.

Stella went to a table and poured him a glass from a decanter. He sipped it and looked at her with crafty eyes.

"Stella, I know you are of Irish descent. I know about your past. I have known it for some time. Others suspect it and I have eased their fears with lies ..."

"Jimmy! You bastard! You're trying to blackmail me!"

"No! No, I'm not! Please, I *AM* on your side."

"Get out of my house!"

"Stella, you don't want to do this! You need ..."

"Out now! Just get the hell out and don't darken my door again!"

"You Irish whore! I know all about you. Who do you think you're talking to? I can have you shunned and driven from this town in shame! You'll regret this!"

Stella picked up the brandy decanter and held it in a threatening manner. Reverend Talbot, slowly, backed out of the door. "Go now, before I get really mad!" She turned beet-red.

Reverend Talbot looked at her with contempt. He turned and moved out of the door, his words trailing behind him. "You'll be sorry. You'll be real sorry." He slammed the door behind him.

Stella put down the decanter and looked at Ben. The angry words had not shaken him.

He rarely cried.

He looked up at his mother with love in his eyes. Stella lifted him in her arms and hugged him, dearly.

She shivered with fear, wondering if she had destroyed his future.

Scotty was uncomfortable in the casual outfit he was wearing. Scotty had gotten used to tailored clothes of fine silk. He liked soft combed-cotton shirts with soft lace embroidery. The money had spoiled him rotten and he loved it. He had a happy life with his young bride and was a pillar of Sonora society. There was talk of his running for mayor and he was greeted with love and respect in every part of town. He was soon to be a father, and the claim was producing ever-richer ore.

It was no time for him to be riding off to find Eli and warn him.

As Scotty put on his old riding clothes he cursed Eli for his obsession with Jules Joshua. He cursed Stella for hiring gunmen to go after Eli.

For two weeks after he knew Lyle and his men were going after

Eli, Scotty had tried to ignore the import of that information.

Scotty's leg was still not completely useful And he hadn't sat a horse for months. He had never been a gunman and he had no exact idea of where Mexico was, much less how to find Eli.

He only knew he could not sleep nights wondering if Eli were alive or dead. For three thousand dollars, John Miller had agreed to accompany him at least as far as the border and secure him some men good with a gun.

As he sat in the saddle of his horse and looked across the Rio Grande at the vast forbidding territory on the other side, he sighed hard.

"This is where they crossed, Mr. Scott. I wish I could go on with you, but I've been away from business too long as it is. I hope you understand," John Miller apologized. "The men who will be riding with you are the best available. I know them to be trustworthy."

"Hell! Can they shoot straight, man?"

"Yes, sir. They can do that," John Miller insisted as he and Scotty looked back at the three men John had secured.

They looked a little seedy to Scotty but he was in no position to complain.

"Yes, of course. Thanks for your help, John," Scotty looked across the wide Rio Grande at the vast expanse of sagebrush and dust before them. "Good Lord, that's a whole heap of nothing!" Scotty sighed. "A man could get himself awful lost down here."

"Yes, sir. I respect what you're doing, but you're right. There's a lot of nothing out there. Mostly *pueblos* and sagebrush between here and Mexico City. I wish you luck my friend." John Miller shook Scotty's hand.

Scotty smiled as he watched John Miller turn and head back North.

Scotty almost turned to follow.

Jules looked into the mean eyes of the man holding the gun.

"You are in the wrong place, *gringo!* Give me your money and maybe you don't die right now!"

Jules backed away until he felt the barrel of another gun in his back. He turned to see he was surrounded by twenty men.

"Look, I don't want any trouble, but I don't have any money. I swear!"

"How sad to die with such a lie on your lips!"

The man cocked the hammer and was about ready to fire, when a young man stepped out of the shadows.

"No, *padre*. He is a good *gringo*. He is the one who saved me from the *federales.*"

The mean man looked doubtful before he relented and uncocked the gun. "You are a *Juarista, señor?*"

Jules had no idea what the man was talking about, but he nodded "Yes."

"Then you do not mind making a donation to the cause?"

Jules hesitated only a moment. He cursed under his breath and handed the man his money belt.

CHAPTER EIGHT

Eli sensed something was wrong. He, suddenly, felt the unsettling feeling he always had when the Joshua brothers were in close proximity — yet, this time it was different.

This time he wasn't nervous or angry or anxious. He was, perhaps, too calm. He was defiant and cocky and eager. He smiled, easily, as he thought about the possibility of a good gunfight.

The smell of trouble was in the air and he welcomed it.

His hands went to his Colts automatically. He hefted them to assure himself they were ready if need be. They were now a source of much comfort to him. They now belonged in his hands and he had total confidence in his ability to use them. Where a pick axe handle had once felt comfortable, the smooth walnut handle of the Navy Colts, now, seemed at home.

Mamacita sensed it also. She looked at Eli and looked nervous. "Three horses …" she almost whispered. "You are expecting *amigos?*"

Eli got up from the table and walked, slowly, to the door. He looked up the street and saw the three horsemen in the distance. He moved back into the shadows of the *cantina* and looked at Mamacita. "I have no friends in these parts."

"The horsemen, are they *gringos?*"

"It seems so."

"Then they are not from these parts!"

Eli eased deeper into the shadows and positioned himself so that he had a good view of the door.

Mamacita reached under the counter and withdrew a shotgun. She leveled it at Eli's head. "I will ask you to leave now, *señor!*"

Eli grimaced as he stared at the long barrel of the shotgun. "You have a point. If there is trouble coming down that street it isn't yours." Eli tipped his hat and started to leave. He was almost to the door when Pepito burst through it and they almost collided.

"Pepito! Pepito, what the hell?"

"*Mi madre.* She says you can come join us for dinner. I even made Maria agree! Please come?"

"Not now! Go home. Get out of here!" Eli snapped angrily.

Pepito studied Eli's eyes then backed up and looked at the horsemen dismounting their horses outside the *cantina*. He looked scared. *"Señor*, we can go out the back way. I know places no one else knows …"

"No! No back doors. Back doors are for cowards. We aren't cowards … are we, Pepito?"

Pepito looked doubtful.

"I don't care which door you use. Just go now!" Mamacita insisted waving the shotgun.

Eli watched as Lyle moved to within inches of the door, followed closely by "Smiling John," then Tom. "I don't think so …" Eli backed into the shadows and waited as Mamacita fumed.

Pepito was frozen in his tracks. Eli reached out, grabbed him by the arm and pulled him aside.

Mamacita eased her shotgun down as Lyle came through the door.

Tom followed, then "Smiling John."

Lyle recognized Eli right away. Lyle had seen him around Sonora in saloons and various places.

Eli had never paid Lyle much attention but his face was familiar. Eli knew he was from Sonora and that his being here was no accident.

"Mr. Llynne!" Lyle greeted him as he moved inside and toward the bar where Mamacita watched his every move.

Eli nodded as Tom and "Smiling John" moved to separate ends of the small bar.

"I know you don't know me, Mr. Llynne. But everybody in Sonora knows you."

"You came here to tell me that?" Eli asked coldly.

"I recognized your roan … with the Spanish saddle out front. Since we're … neighbors I thought I'd buy you a drink." Lyle paused. "I'm Lyle, this is John and Tom," Lyle offered.

Eli nodded acknowledgment.

"So what sort of whiskey can a man expect in a place like this?" Lyle looked at Mamacita.

"I have no whiskey. It is closing time, anyways. I am sorry, *señores*, but you must go somewhere else!"

"Now that ain't neighborly. From what I've seen there ain't nowhere else!" "Smiling John" wasn't smiling.

"Why don't you just set up a bottle of the best of whatever you got, *señora!*" Tom growled.

"It's *señorita!* And I told you I was closed."

"She's right, Lyle. It is closing time." Eli stepped toward the door, watching the three men all the way.

"We had a long ride, Eli. My men are thirsty." Lyle insisted. *"Señorita*, is it?" Lyle looked contemptuous. "Just stay open awhile longer. I'll make it worth your while."

"Three thousand miles is a long way to ride for a drink." Eli stepped up boldly. "Who sent you, Lyle? Jules?"

"I don't know anyone by that name. Do you boys?"

"Nope." Tom grinned. "Smiling John" shrugged.

"I see. Mamacita, give the boys a bottle on me and we'll take it outside and jawbone. Okay, Lyle?" Eli backed toward the door.

Tom's hand moved, ever so slightly, toward his Colt. "Smiling John" eased into a shadowy corner.

Lyle thought it over. He looked sinister then broke into a crocodile grin. "I told you, Eli. We came here for a neighborly drink. That's all. We don't know anything about … Jules? Did you say Jules? Jules Joshua? The one who killed Doc Immanuel?"

Eli nodded. "Yes." Pepito, standing behind him started to say something. Eli put his hand over Pepito's mouth.

"Why on earth would any man have anything to do with scum like that?" Lyle sighed hard.

"My mistake."

"Here's your bottle … gentlemen? Now leave, *por favor!*" Mamacita insisted.

Lyle hesitated. He looked at Eli then at his men. He looked back at Mamacita then at Eli, once more. "I say let's go outside, share this bottle and talk about old times in Sonora?" Lyle grinned.

Eli nodded agreement. They waited for him to make a move to the door. Eli was not stupid enough to outline his body in the light coming though the door. "After you, Lyle?"

Lyle did not like it. Neither did Tom or "Smiling John." They looked at each other, nervously.

"You know, Eli. It wasn't Jules who sent us down here … but someone did. Would you like to know who it was?" Lyle's voice was cold and his right hand began to move toward his gun.

"I don't expect it matters much."

"Well, I would want to know if my wife paid good cash money to have me killed!" Lyle's hand was almost to his gun as Eli considered the harsh truth of his words.

Stella was fully capable of doing such a thing. It stung a little to know she might hate him that much. Yet the fact was, these men were here, and they were here for no good purpose.

"I see. I expect it was a goodly amount."

"Well, considering you have one of the richest strikes in Sonora, I'd say it's a pittance. But she's a whore, so what do you expect?" Lyle almost reached for his gun.

Eli had killed five men and one Mexican, but he had never tried to outdraw a man and shoot him. Eli found the thought of doing that exhilarating, except for one thing — there were three of them. Eli was not afraid. He just did not like the odds. "Pepito, why don't you ease on home?" Eli insisted.

Pepito started to object until he looked in Eli's eyes. Pepito started to move toward the door. As he moved close to Tom Manson, Tom grabbed him around the neck and used him as a shield as he went for his gun.

Lyle and "Smiling John" went for their guns as Eli was distracted by Pepito's capture. Two rounds whizzed by Eli's ears before he could clear a Colt from his belt. The bullets smashed into the adobe inches from his head as Eli stepped back into the shadows and fired.

The muzzle flashes lit up the darkness and gun smoke filled the small *cantina*. The sound of the loud guns reverberated in deafening echoes.

Altogether, it was hard on a gunman to take good aim. Eli fired more by instinct than eyesight. He did not have time to consider Pepito's whereabouts or welfare.

Eli knew a bullet had struck well when he heard "Smiling John" yelp in pain then fall to the floor. A bullet burned into Eli's fleshy thigh with a painful, but glancing blow. He ignored it as he peered through the smoke at shadows of men and fired.

Tom Manson no longer needed Pepito as a shield so he put a bullet into his back. Pepito fell to the floor and doubled over in pain.

Lyle's muzzle flashes came from Eli's left. Eli returned the fire in that direction.

Eli did not see Tom Manson creep around to his right side. Tom snuck close to the floor until he had a clear shot at Eli's head.

Tom leveled his gun at Eli's right ear. He cocked the hammer and grinned.

He never heard the loud report of Mamacita's shotgun taking his head off at the shoulders.

Lyle watched Tom's body hit the floor. His gun clicked empty. He made a run for the door.

Eli had a clear shot at him but his gun clicked empty, also. Eli threw the gun down and started to run toward Lyle. He was almost to the door when he tripped over Pepito's body. Eli fell to the floor hard.

As he started to get up, his hands dripped with Pepito's blood. "Oh, God! No! Not the kid!" Eli struggled to his feet only to hear the thunder of Lyle's horse's hoof beats disappearing into the distance.

Eli moved to the door and thought about pursuit.

"Mr. Eli ... help me ... please .. help me ... please?" Pepito said weakly.

Eli watched Lyle ride hard toward the horizon and figured there would be another day.

Mamacita eased a pillow under Pepito's head and used an old towel to press against the bleeding wound.

"What sort of doc do you have around here?" Eli asked.

"*¡Médico!* Ha! I am the doctor, the nurse, and ... the undertaker!" Mamacita said, sadly.

"Damn! I'm sorry to bring my troubles to you. But thanks for the good shooting. I owe you, and I pay my debts!"

"I do not blame you. You tried to leave." Mamacita looked curious. "These men. They are sent ... they come because of your wife?"

"I don't know. God, I really don't ..." Eli paused. "Look, what can we do for Pepito?"

Mamacita thought about it a long moment. She examined him with care and tenderness. Pepito stirred, only slightly. "*¿Quizás?* Maybe if someone could ride fifty miles very fast. There is a doctor in the next *pueblo*. But he is a loyalist," she looked sad. "Pepito is very much a *Juarista.*"

"I don't think Pepito gives a damn about politics right now. Which way?" Eli got up and felt warm blood from his flesh wound trickle down his leg.

"Ride south. There is but one road. But you are wounded too, *señor.*"

Before Eli could reply Maria broke through the door and into the room followed by half the village.

"We heard shooting, Mamacita. Where is Pepito? Pepito!" She almost fainted. "The *gringos* have killed Pepito!" Maria looked at Eli with hate-filled eyes.

"No, Maria. It was not this man. The man who did this is dead over there!" Mamacita nodded towards Tom's body.

"But ... but they came here for you, *señor*. Did they not?" Maria glared at Eli.

Eli nodded, "Yes," as he moved toward the door.

"So, now you just leave us? You come into my village and do this and just leave us?"

Eli paused. He looked at her with a steady gaze. "It ain't exactly like THAT."

Maria had misty eyes on the verge of tears. She, obviously, loved her brother Pepito dearly.

"What? I hate you and I hate all *gringos* sons-of-bitches!" Maria shook her fist at Eli.

Eli looked hurt only a moment before he moved to his horse. He said nothing as he mounted his horse and rode south at full gallop.

"Damn! Damn him!" Maria started to run after him shaking her fist.

Mamacita restrained her. "He goes to bring the doctor. This is not his doing!"

Maria looked doubtful as she pushed by Mamacita and knelt beside her brother. She kissed him gently on the forehead, then withdrew a rosary and began to pray.

CHAPTER NINE

Jules Joshua was, suddenly, a poor man in a country where money was only slightly less venerated than the Saints of Holy Mother Church.

General Nogales, a nasty-looking bear of a man, had relieved Jules of his money belt. He now made Jules sit still at gun point while he counted the money out on a table in front of him. Had General Nogales known the depths of hatred he generated in a man that always evened the score, he might have counted the money in secret.

"You have made a most generous contribution to the revolution, *señor. ¡Muchas gracias!*"

"Go to hell!" Jules spit back.

"No, *señor!* Hell is where I think you will go if I do not like what comes from your mouth. You are nobody here. This is my country and my people. I am a general and deserve respect!" He got up from the table and loomed over Jules.

Jules was not easily intimidated but General Nogales was a frightening figure of a man. Jules shrugged and looked away.

"Because you have saved my son's life you are still alive. I have a short memory about such things. Do not test me, *señor!*"

"It ain't right just to up and take all a man's money!" Jules looked at his money on the table.

General Nogales looked angry then grinned. "*Sí,* perhaps you are right. What would be a fair amount for you to contribute to the revolution? You tell me?"

Jules thought it over a moment. "I don't take no interest in other people's politics."

"Oh? So what is it you are doing in my country with all this money at this time?"

"I was just riding through."

"No! I think you are an agent of the *Directorio Conservador* and in the service of Governor General Felix Zuloaga. I should have you shot as a spy!" he threatened.

"I don't know nothin' about none of those guys! I told you I don't take no interest in any politics. If you'll give me my money I'll head north to Sonora and you won't see me in these parts again."

General Nogales laughed a hollow, macabre laugh. He looked at Jules with a certain degree of admiration. "You are one stupid or smart *gringo*! I think maybe more stupid. You do not seem to know the position you are in … you do not tell anyone here what to do about anything! This is not Mexico City where the French and Spanish and other foreigners tell that weakling Zuloaga what to do. This is Puebla. I am the law here, and I grow weary of you." General Nogales was no longer amused. "Sonora?" He paused and motioned to one of his men. "Bring in the other *gringo!*"

Moments later Lyle Jameson, bleeding about the face from a beating, was shoved into the room.

General Nogales looked at Jules then at Lyle. "This man is from your city. Does he ride with you?"

Lyle glared at Jules. "The men what was riding with me is dead. I don't know this man."

"… and you?" General Nogales looked at Jules.

"I ain't never seen him before!"

General Nogales studied their eyes. They did not flinch, but he did not believe them. "I think you are mercenaries in the hire of Zuloaga and the conservatives. I think the money this Joshua man brings is to buy guns for them. Is this true?"

Jules spit on the floor in reply.

"I think, maybe I will have to execute you in the name of the people," he said calmly — coldly.

"Joshua? Are you Jules Joshua?" Lyle wondered.

"I ain't talking to you, mister!" Jules snarled.

"If he's Jules Joshua he's a murderer and deserves execution. I'm a deputy sheriff … a duly appointed lawman. We came to take him back to Sonora for hanging for the murder of a good doctor." Lyle lied smoothly.

General Nogales studied Lyle's eyes.

Lyle forced himself to keep his gaze steady. He could not stop the sweat from pouring off his brow.

"I believe this. I believe this man is a murderer and he has said his name is Jules Joshua. But it is not necessary to go so far. We will hang him here. Is that good with you?" General Nogales seemed sincere.

"Yes. Of course. Either way … I suppose. My only concern is to see justice is done."

Lyle did not get the words out of his mouth before Jules was on top of him. Jules pounded his fists into Lyle's face. "You ain't no deputy sheriff! And ain't nobody hanging me! You hear? You hear!"

Jules started to swing again but a rifle butt cracked into the back of his head and he blacked out.

Lyle, slowly, got to his feet and wobbled until he leaned against a wall.

"Yes, he is a murderer. I believe this … you, I do not know yet." General Nogales looked at Lyle. "You stay with us tonight and watch the hanging in the morning. I will know then what to do with you." General Nogales motioned for his men to take them both away. A soldier reached for Lyle's arm. He shook him off.

"Did I mention the reward of ten thousand dollars for Jules?" Lyle exaggerated the amount.

General Nogales eyes were full of interest. "Ten thousand, American?"

"Yes, dead or alive. If you'll allow me to take the body back … you can send an escort with me, I will see that you get the full amount," Lyle hoped.

"Such a large reward. He killed a doctor? Maybe this is true. Maybe it is not. But for such money I should not act too fast. You agree?"

"All it'll cost you is a few weeks time."

"These *gringos* in Sonora? They will gladly give this humble Mexican so much money?" he scoffed.

Lyle knew where he was going and knew his life was on the line with his answer. "No! No, they won't! … but they will give it to me!"

General Nogales picked up a cigar and lit it, filling the room with acrid smoke. "And how do I know you will see that it is given to me?" The General paused and looked angry. "You know, *señor*. I had a claim in the Amador City long before the *gringos* come. I am panning out much good gold. Then the *gringo* comes and he digs in the earth … in the hard rock. He takes my claim and he runs me out of town. My friends tell me where my claim was is now the *grande* mine … the Keystone. Many, many *mucho* gold comes from this mine!"

"I'm sorry, General."

"No! They will not give me the money, and they will not give it to you if they think you will give it to a Mexican!" His face shivered with rage. "If I cannot have this money, no one will have it. You understand this?"

"You are not a man to be lied too. I can only tell you that I will do what I say I will do." Lyle gave the General his best steady gaze.

The General puffed on his cigar a long moment. "It would be good to believe this, but I cannot."

"I have a wife and five children. If I do not do right by you, I would expect you to send someone to exact your revenge upon my family." Lyle said as coolly as his nerves would allow — since he was not married and had no children he knew of.

General Nogales was impressed. "This is something men who do not trust each other might agree on. I salute you. I will allow this," He paused and looked sinister. "If this be a lie, I will find a way to hurt you that will bring much pain. You understand this?"

"I understand. It is no more or less than I would do."

"Simpático. Have some wine with me. You are simpático. Yes, we will do this. Tomorrow we will hang this one and you will be free to go," he stopped and looked around the room. "Of course some of my men, they ride with you." General Nogales congratulated himself.

Lyle sighed hard in relief.

Jules started to get to his feet.

General Nogales smiled at Lyle.

Lyle kicked Jules back into oblivion.

CHAPTER TEN

Stella regretted throwing the Reverend out moments after she had done it. She knew he had the power to make it hard, if not impossible, to progress in Boston society, but she was a stubborn Irishwoman and she would not sit still for blackmail.

She looked at Big Ben's cherubic face and his innocent blue eyes. If what Reverend Talbot had said was true, if Boston was going to expand into the marshes, Ben's future did lie there.

Stella had a good head for business and she understood that whoever bought the land now would reap great rewards once it was developed. She did not, inherently, trust the Brahmins who ruled Boston. However she figured she knew enough high-powered lawyers to have any agreement drawn up, be drawn in her favor.

"Are you alright, madam?" Rosie entered the room and looked concerned.

"Yes, Rosie. You heard?"

"Madam, when you give 'em what for, I think they hear it in heaven and hell."

"I doubt they listen to me in heaven but in the lower world I'm sure I have friends."

"Would you like some hot tea?" Rosie asked as Big Ben wobbled up and grabbed at her skirt. Rosie reached down and picked him up. He put his oversized baby's arms around her neck.

Stella was a little jealous of how Big Ben took to Rosie. Rosie had such a way with all children. They naturally gravitated to her and she often could stop Big Ben from crying when Stella was unsuccessful.

"I think I made a big mistake. He's not the kind of man you want as an enemy." Stella mused aloud.

"I think he likes prowling around in people's lives. But I have heard he is not so clean."

"Oh? Tell me what you know."

"Nothing you can prove. But there were some banking failures where he ended up with money and everyone else lost all they had. I would not trust him, madam."

"I understand. But there are times when you have to do business with the devil to get what you want."

Stella reached out for Big Ben.

Big Ben ignored her.

Stella's heart sank a little but she did not reveal any emotion. Rosie, finally, pulled Big Ben's arms from around her neck and handed him to Stella.

He came to her, but did not put his arms around her neck.

"I best be getting back to my chores." Rosie seemed a little embarrassed.

"Yes. Fine …"

Rosie turned to leave.

"Rosie?" Stella stopped her.

Rosie turned and nodded. "Yes?"

"What are Benjamin's chances of having a decent life here if I don't apologize to the Reverend?"

Rosie looked sad before she answered. "I think he would take great delight in having you shunned by polite society. If you are shunned then Ben would not be able to attend any decent school. There would be no invitations to any respectable social occasions."

"In other words, I have to make amends no matter how much it sticks in my craw?"

Rosie looked very sad.

"If you wish to stay in Boston and make a good life for Ben. Yes, ma'am."

"Thank you, Rosie. Please take Benjamin up for his nap. I have a letter to write." Stella handed Ben back to Rosie.

Ben, immediately, put his arms around Rosie's neck, lay his head on her shoulder and nodded off.

"Yes, ma'am." Rosie turned and moved upstairs.

After they were gone, Stella took pen in hand:

Dear Reverend Talbot,

I write this in order to apologize for my unseemly display of temper during your recent visit. I have been feeling melancholy lately as the anniversary of my husband's death approaches. I hope you understand I was not quite myself.

If the business proposal you offered is still open to my partici-

pation, perhaps you would like to discuss it over tea Wednesday, next.

As always, Mrs. Daniel James Winslow

Stella was interrupted by a knock on the door. She started to call for Rosie but decided to answer it herself. She pulled the heavy door open to see a fine-looking young man with a twinkle in his eyes.

"Good day. May I speak with the lady of the house?" he asked with a heavy Irish brogue.

Stella started to shut the door. He had a lost-puppy countenance and she could not. "I am the mistress of the house."

"Oh! Pardon me, madam. Madam Winslow, is it?"

Stella nodded "Yes."

"Allow me to introduce myself; I'm Shannon O'Bannion. May I come in?"

"I'm sorry I don't know you …"

"I am an acquaintance of the Reverend Talbot."

"I see. He sent you?"

"Not exactly …"

"… then why are you here?"

"Excuse me, but would you give me just a minute to discuss a matter of importance in private. Please, madam?"

"I don't think so …"

Stella stopped as a distinguished looking gray-haired priest appeared on the porch. Stella could never close the door on a priest.

"Glory be! Climbing those steps every day would be the death of me!" Father Brennan huffed and puffed.

"He's with me. Father Brennan, let me introduce Madam Winslow," Shannon said.

"Lord, son! Let me get my breath first," Father Brennan sighed then reached out his hand for Stella's.

"Father," Stella smiled. "Please come in."

"Thank you," Father Brennan replied as Shannon entered ahead of him.

Stella looked at Shannon with disdain as she led Father Brennan into the sitting room.

"Would you have a spot of brandy to warm an old man's bones?" Father Brennan looked thirsty.

So did Shannon.

"Of course. Please have a seat and I'll pour you a glass," she replied, talking to Father Brennan and ignoring Shannon. Shannon watched, hungrily, as Stella poured Father Brennan a glass of brandy and handed it to him.

Shannon stared at the brandy bottle and asked for a drink with his eyes. Stella shrugged.

"I'm glad you came, Father. I was going to look for a church. I meant to get to Mass but I've been so busy settling in …"

"I understand, my child but I do not say public Mass anymore. I'm retired," he sipped the brandy.

Shannon, boldly, poured himself a glass and smiled at Stella. She did not smile back.

"I see. … then how can I help you?"

Father Brennan put down the glass and sighed hard. He looked at Stella with sad eyes. "Please excuse me, Madam, but I have information from a reliable source that you might be inclined to help with Irish relief?"

"Oh? And who might that be?" Stella asked coldly.

Father Brennan looked embarrassed. "I have begun this badly. Forgive me for forsaking the truth for expediency. Permit me to begin again. The rumor is that you are of Irish ancestry. If this is merely a rumor than we are here on a fool's quest. If it be true, then glory be, one of ours has made it," he said as he looked at her with kind eyes.

"My name is Winslow, Father."

"This is your maiden name?"

"It is the name I choose."

"I understand. It was wrong of us to be so rude as to suggest you are one of us. It's plain to see that this is no Irishman's house. Have you seen the hovels they live in on Samuel Maverick's island? Sometimes I'm ashamed to call myself an Irishman," he stopped and looked over the elegant decor. "There'll be none of our kind in the Boston Assemblies or in fancy pants on Commonwealth Street come Sunday, where you belong. … and I do believe we are intruding here. Thank you, Madam … Winslow." Father Brennan moved to leave.

Shannon gulped down his glass of brandy and moved to leave also.

Stella looked at Shannon's handsome features and admired his strong frame. She thought to herself he was worth a second look. "Wait a minute, Father. Just because I'm not Irish doesn't mean I can't listen to what you have to say. Please, tell me why you're here and I'll see what I can do for you. Please have another glass of brandy and sit by the fire."

Shannon smiled as he went immediately to the liquor table and poured himself a full glass.

Stella wanted to laugh but Father Brennan looked too sad.

"You are new here and, perhaps, are not familiar with the plight of the Irish. The potato famine of '48 devastated an already poor country. We came here because we thought of America as the pot of gold at the end of the rainbow. I'm afraid it was not very golden. It has been a struggle against disease and prejudice and illiteracy."

"So, I've heard," Stella tried not to appear over-interested.

"It is said that the Negro slaves are better treated because they are, at least, worth something in the market place."

"I see. You are with a charity?" Stella moved to her bureau to find a bank draft.

"The Emerald Society is that and more!" Shannon chimed in.

"It's not entirely Irish relief I'm here for ... not directly," Father Brennan continued.

"I see. Tell me, would a thousand dollars be of help?" Stella poised her pen.

Father Brennan looked at Shannon.

"The truth is, we're here because I want to run for political office. The only way for Irish to make it here is through politics. I am going to be the 'Mahatma' of the Eighth Ward and maybe the mayor of Boston one day!" Shannon announced proudly.

Father Brennan looked at Shannon with censure. Shannon shrugged and drank his brandy

"I'm afraid my friend Shannon is much ahead of himself. We are only twenty or thirty thousand in a city of five times that many ... and we are Catholic in Mr. Winthrop's Protestant stronghold," he paused.

"But Shannon is right. Politics is our only hope. We came to you in hopes of finding a major benefactor. It seems my information is as faulty as my circulation these days." Father Brennan stopped as Rosie walked into the room holding Big Ben.

"I'm sorry, madam, but he awoke and said 'Mama!' I thought you would want to hear ..."

"Yes. Yes!"

Stella ran and took Big Ben from Rosie's arms. "Mama! Mama!"

Stella cajoled Ben to speak. She did not notice Rosie and Shannon make familiar eye contact. "Oh, please dumpling! Please say it for Mama!" Stella begged.

"I suppose we had better be going. Thank you for your time ... Mrs. Winslow," Father Brennan moved to leave.

"Wait. Let me at least give you a check for a thousand to be used for, only for charity." Stella paused and looked at her son. "You understand that I cannot become involved in politics for his sake," Stella insisted.

"He's a fine lad!" Shannon offered. "Can I hold him? I've always fancied having a boy child."

Stella did not like the idea but Big Ben did not pull away from Shannon's outstretched arms. She reluctantly let Shannon take him.

As Shannon held him, Big Ben burped, then said "Mama!"

Stella and Shannon laughed together as Stella took Big Ben back in her arms.

"I don't think so, dumpling. My goodness, I'm going to have to teach the boy some things about the birds and bees right away!" Stella was a little hurt Big Ben would not say "Mama!" for her.

"He's a fine boy, Madam. A fine boy!"

"If you please. I will accept the money for charity and I assure you ... Mrs. Winslow, that we will not make mention of our presence here to anyone who is anyone," Father Brennan said, reassuringly.

Stella handed Big Ben to Rosie. She wrote the check and gave it to Father Brennan.

He smiled in acknowledgment.

"Thank you for your time. Maybe we'll meet some Sunday on the common?" Shannon looked hopeful.

Stella did not reply. Instead she walked Father Brennan to the door. When they reached the door, Father Brennan turned and looked deep into their eyes.

"I do not say public Mass, but I will be happy to hear your confession and attend to your religious needs. Rosie knows ..." he stopped. "I am easy to find. Good day, Madam Winslow." Father Brennan apologized to Rosie with his eyes then turned and left.

Stella looked hard at Rosie as she put it all together in her mind.

Shannon paused in the doorway. He sighed hard. "This was not her idea, Madam Winslow," Shannon nodded toward Rosie.

"I am her brother. It was all my idea."

"I see. Good day, Mr. O'Bannion," Stella said coldly.

Shannon started to say something else but thought better of it. He turned and walked briskly out of the door behind Father Brennan.

Stella slammed the door. She turned and glared at Rosie. "What is going on, Rosie? Is the whole damn town going to know I'm Irish? Maybe I should put a bill on every fence post announcing it? You're fired!"

Stella jerked Big Ben from Rosie's arms.

Big Ben started crying immediately.

Rosie started sobbing also. "I did not tell him anything. He is a ward healer and knows everything that goes on in this city. He is my brother but I left him on the island three years ago and have not seen him since. I swear, madam!"

Stella tried to soothe Big Ben without effect.

She finally handed him back to Rosie. Rosie was able to hush him quickly. Stella shook her head in disgust and amazement.

"If you wish, you may stay on. But you had better let your loyalties be known to me, to this house and this house only! Is that understood?"

Rosie looked through her tears at Stella and nodded agreement.

Chapter Eleven

Scotty hated horses. He had not ridden one in over a year and his backside was sore. Scotty had spoiled himself rotten with his new-found wealth. He had purchased the latest in steel-sprung carriages to sport himself and his bride around town. A carriage cushion was no way to prepare for the hard leather of a saddle and the rude meeting of flesh of a long ride.

Shorty delighted in watching Scotty's discomfort. Sam Johnson and John "Chief" Thomas smiled also as they watched Scotty dismount his horse and rub his butt.

"I don't know, laddies. This was a good idea in Sonora, but it don't seem like near as good an idea now," Scotty sighed.

"Mr. Scott, if you like we can change animals. This mare is a mite easier on the backside than that stallion of yours," Sam offered.

"Thanks, Sam but I'll be alright. Where the hell are we anyway?" Scotty looked at Chief.

Chief, who was half Cherokee and half Sioux, was looked to as the pathfinder even though he knew no more about tracking than anyone else. The fact he had some Indian blood and Indians were said to be good at tracking meant he had to be good at it also. He was never asked if he knew anything about it. It was simply assumed that he did. He went along with that belief because the money was good. He survived as a tracker by trusting to luck and asking a lot of questions to find his way. He had paid for the information that led them to Puebla. For ten dollars in gold he had learned of a "shootout among *gringos*" in Puebla "with the man that fights the bears." Chief hoped that man was Eli.

"This is Puebla. It's a popular watering hole for *gringos*. A good place to look," Chief offered, acting as if he were sniffing the wind for tracking clues.

Scotty looked at the dusty streets and the stark adobe buildings. He looked at Chief and shrugged. "So let's go have a drink, laddies." Scotty rubbed his backside. "No, let's go have a lot of drinks. Chief, lead me to the nearest saloon!" Scotty, reluctantly, remounted his horse.

"Right down the street on the right, Mr. Scott," Chief said.

"Very good, Chief. The sign does say *cantina!*" Shorty needled.

"The man has a nose," Sam joined in.

They laughed as they rode to the hitching rail and tied their horses down.

Mamacita watched them with interest as they strode inside her *cantina*. She had just finished cleaning up the mess from the gunfight and was not particularly happy to see more *gringos*. But she knew they had cash money and she greeted them with a smile. "*¡Buenos dias, señores!* You would like a drink, *¿no?*"

"A drink, yes, lassie. A bottle of your best whiskey."

"Whiskey! Whiskey! Whiskey! All you Americans want whiskey, but this is not Kentucky. You can have *tequila* or rum. So tell me, which is it?" Mamacita shook her head in mock disdain.

"Rum? Haven't drunk much of it since my sailing days. Rum it is, lassie," Scotty said as the others looked doubtful.

Mamacita gave them a bottle of rum and four glasses. Scotty poured his glass full and drank a good portion of it as the others watched.

Shorty took a pull from the bottle and spit it out.

"If you don't mind, make mine *tequila,*" Shorty said.

Sam and Chief agreed.

Mamacita gave them a bottle of *tequila*. They all poured a glass and sipped their drinks quietly.

Chief looked around the room at the bullet holes in the wall. He figured he had gotten his ten dollars worth. There had been one helluva gunfight here, and maybe Eli had been in it.

Shorty watched Chief's eyes, he looked at the bullet holes and knew what Chief was thinking. Shorty was the real tracker in the group. He had spent ten years in the Army, in and around Fort Laramie. He had even done a little map-making before he quit the Army due to their bias against promoting "short people." He was the world's oldest living private when he left the Army and never looked back.

Shorty accepted Chief's role as the tracker because he never wanted to interfere with a man's livelihood. Shorty was only five foot one and one half inches tall in his boots, but he was nobody's whipping boy. You could call him "Shorty" but not "half-pint," or "short-stuff", and never, "dwarf" or "midget." Shorty would fight the biggest man over what he considered an insult. Shorty had lost many fights to bigger men but had won their respect for his courage in taking them on.

Sam Johnson also saw the bullet holes. Sam had been in his share of gunfights. He had been a deputy sheriff in countless gold rush towns from Copperoppolis to Mount Zion. Towns that had sprung up and disappeared as fast as the money he was to be paid. Sam liked "sheriffing" but there was no money in it. The thousand dollars John Miller had paid him to come along was more than he had made as a deputy in the last two years.

Scotty saw the bullet holes, also.

"The *banditos* they come in here and they drink too much and they shoot too much. I have stopped putting plaster in the holes," Mamacita sighed.

"Seems they were in here not too long ago?" Chief mused aloud.

"*¡Sí!* But you can relax. I do not expect them today," she smiled.

Scotty looked at her and reached into his pocket. He withdrew a twenty-dollar gold piece. He lay it before her. "A big *gringo*. He wears a black hat. Steel blue eyes. He favors a Navy Colt and a Spanish saddle for his horse. Was he one of the *banditos?*"

Mamacita played with the coin. "You are looking for this man?"

"Yes."

"Does he want you to find him?"

"He's a friend of mine. I have reason to believe he is in great danger."

Mamacita looked into Scotty's eyes. She studied his honest face. She picked up the coin and bit it.

Eli had almost ridden his horse into the ground, but he had returned with a doctor for Pepito. Pepito lived now because of Eli. Even now, Eli rested in her back room. Mamacita could not betray him.

"*¡Sí!* Yes, such a man was here. He rode south two days ago. ... he was also looking for a man. Is every *gringo* in the world looking for someone else?" Mamacita laughed.

Scotty studied her eyes. She seemed to be telling the truth — or the partial truth. "South? Did he say exactly where?"

"No, *señor*. He did not."

"This shootout with the ... *banditos*, was he involved?" Chief stepped in.

Mamacita started to lie until she saw the steady look in Chief's compelling chestnut eyes.

"*Sí.* Yes, he put many bullet holes in the walls and many bullet holes in the *banditos!*"

"These *banditos*, they were *gringos?*"

Mamacita hesitated. She wondered at Scotty's motives but thought these men did not look like the kind of men Eli had killed. "It was said these men came to kill him."

Scotty sighed with relief and broke into a smile. "Hot damn! Eli, you old son of a gun! He got 'em! Hey, boys he got 'em!" Scotty almost danced a jig.

Chief looked disappointed. "... this means we don't get the bonus?"

Shorty and Sam looked disappointed also.

"Hell no! I'll be glad to pay up and maybe double them! This just means I don't have to ride that damn horse another thousand miles. It means my friend ... wherever he is, is safe," Scotty paused and looked at Mamacita. "... he did get them all, there were three men after him?"

Mamacita looked sad for a moment. "No, *señor.* There is one that ran away."

"Damn! I knew it was too good to be true!" Scotty rubbed his backside. "Which one?"

Mamacita shrugged. "They all looked alike to me but I think he was the leader."

"Lyle Jameson. Damn! I guess we have to saddle up again, laddies!"

"So! No double bonus?" Chief asked sadly.

Scotty did not reply. He pulled down the rest of his glass of rum. He looked at Mamacita. "For one hundred dollars in gold can I ask you for the truth? Which way did they ride?"

Mamacita almost trusted Scotty. Scotty had an honest face, but she had been betrayed by honest faces before.

Scotty counted out five twenty-dollar gold pieces. Mamacita stared at them for a long moment. "This man, your friend. What is his name?"

"Eli. Eli Llynne."

"How do you know this man?"

"We go back a long way. I was best man at his wedding. I am not out to kill him … I am out to stop him from being killed," Scotty said sincerely.

Mamacita thought it over a long moment. "I told you, *señor*, he rode south. The man who came for him … I do not know which way he rides."

"Well, I sure do! Drink up and let's go, laddies. Thank you, *señora*." Scotty pushed the coins toward her.

"*Señorita*. And for such little informations I don't take thees much money," she gave him back twenty dollars. "… only thees much!"

Scotty laughed and pushed the twenty back at her. "Keep it and if you see my friend again you tell him, Scotty came to help. Will you remember that?"

"Scotty?"

"Yes."

"I will remember, *señor*. I will remember but I do not think I see Mr. Eli again. *¡Vaya con Dios!*"

Scotty grimaced and turned to leave. He was almost to the door when Maria Christina stormed in and almost knocked him down.

"*¡Excúseme, señor!*" Maria said quickly as she brushed by Scotty. "Where is *Señor* Eli, Mamacita? I need to talk to him!" Maria stopped as she saw the look on Mamacita's face.

Scotty froze in his tracks.

The others followed his eyes as he looked back at Mamacita.

"Yes, where is *Señor* Eli, Mamacita. I too want to talk with him." Scotty fought to keep his temper.

Mamacita sighed hard and pushed the gold coins away.

CHAPTER TWELVE

Jules chafed in the iron restraints that held him to the wall. He hated being held or restrained and he hated small rooms. In the years since he had left hard-rock mining, his claustrophobia had increased to where he broke into a hard sweat every time he was closed in.

Jules prided himself on his ability to escape from any bad situation and even come out a winner. He had always managed to, somehow, weasel his way out of every tight situation.

He had a bad feeling he wasn't going to weasel his way out of this one.

The small adobe hut where they held him was isolated from the main buildings in General Nogales' compound. They had him guarded by only one man and that man seemed bored with the job. Jules figured if he could get free of the restraints, he had a good chance of getting away. He hit the heavy shackles on the hard floor and pounded them against the wall.

He did not even dent them.

Jules had hardened his heart until he rarely felt fear. He despised people who were easily spooked. He thought of them as cowards. He had always enjoyed striking terror into the hearts of the timid. He took delight in watching their eyes get big and their hands tremble.

Until this night, he had never felt his hands tremble. General Nogales meant to hang him in the morning and he saw no immediate way out. He swallowed hard as he thought about the rough feel of the rope about his neck. He remembered the slow choking death he had seen when the hangman's knot was done poorly. He shuddered as he thought about how men had messed themselves and their eyes had bulged as they jerked at the end of a rope for what seemed like an eternity.

Jules figured he would have an instant before he was hanged to grab a gun and either shoot his way out or go down with a bullet in his head. A bullet in the head seemed a whole lot more inviting than a rope.

He decided that if he got free he would hunt down Lyle before he finished his business with Eli.

He relished the thought of hanging Lyle with a bad knot in a thin rope. He wanted to make Lyle dance in the air a long time before he died.

That seemed a good way to dispatch Eli, as well.

Jules pulled hard at the chains and rattled around his small room. He stopped when he saw the key turn in the door.

He backed into a corner and waited.

The door opened slowly, as Jules watched intently. For a long moment, Jules could not see who entered. Finally, Carlos moved out of the shadows and smiled.

"*¡Buenos noches, señor!*" Carlos said.

Jules watched him a moment before he replied. "It ain't mornin' yet. I ain't ready. I ain't said all my prayers."

Carlos looked at him with a mixture of fear and understanding. "It is three hours until morning. That is the head start I give you," Carlos said as he took a key and undid Jules' shackles.

Jules couldn't believe it. He sighed in relief. He looked at Carlos, suspiciously. "They waitin' outside to shoot me down?"

"*Señor*, you saved my life. I give you a chance to save yours. This means we ... we are even?"

Jules thought it over a moment.

The boy was setting him up. Or was he? "A chance? No! I need a gun and I need money and a good horse. My horse, Midnight."

Carlos looked sad. "I'm sorry, *señor*, but my father he likes your horse very much."

"That son-of-a-bitch! I'll kill him!"

"No, *señor!* No killing. You just go. I have a good horse for you and I give you all the money I have ... it is not much but ..."

"... and a gun. I need a gun!" Jules took the three twenty-dollar gold pieces from Carlos. "The guard? Where is the guard?"

"He is with my friend Carmelita. I am sorry I do not have a gun. You must go, now!" Carlos insisted as he looked around, nervously.

"And where do I go?"

"North, *señor!* You must go home as soon as you can. The best way is to ride the ridges of the hills. The soldiers, they do not like the mountains."

"The soldiers? How many?"

"*¿Excúseme?*"

"How many troops does your father have?"

Carlos looked worried. "How many?"

"That's right. You can count, can't you?"

"*¿Señor?* Why do you want to know this?"

"I like to play army. How many?"

Carlos did not want to answer. He now regretted he had helped this man. "No one knows. Sometimes he has many. Sometimes the men go back home and he does not have so many."

"Now! How many does he have now?"

"*No sé.* This I do not know."

"You know alright. But that's okay. There'll be time to count them out later. A gun. Just get me a gun and I'll be goin'."

Carlos shrugged. "I do not … I do not know how to do this. I am sorry."

"Yeah, I'll just bet you are."

Jules did not like going anywhere without a gun but he knew he had to go. He stuffed the money in his pocket and shoved Carlos aside.

Jules moved outside and looked at the moth-eaten horse Carlos had provided. He looked disgusted. He mounted the horse and looked down at Carlos. "One more thing. Lyle? Where is he sleeping?"

"*¡Señor!* You must not think of such things. You must ride!"

Jules grabbed Carlos by the collar and jerked him off his feet. "Where?"

Jules heard the click of the hammer of a Colt from behind his back. He lowered Carlos and turned to see Lyle.

"I couldn't sleep so I thought I would take a walk and see what crawled out of the woodwork."

Jules started to jump Lyle.

Lyle leveled the gun at Jules' head. "Don't even think about it."

Jules backed off. "Then shoot! If you intend to shoot, do it!" Jules spit at him as Carlos backed into the shadows.

"Maybe … maybe not," Lyle lowered the gun, slightly.

Jules looked puzzled.

"I'm looking for a man. A man that killed two of my best friends just like he killed your brothers," Lyle said calmly.

Jules did not know what Lyle was up to, but he saw an opening. He smiled thinly. "Eli? He killed your friends? That's too bad. I'm ... I'm mighty sorry to hear that."

"No, you aren't. But that doesn't matter. I need a good gun hand to go after him. You need a gun and some help gettin' out of here." Lyle put his gun away.

Jules licked his chops.

"So ... so ... so you got a gun for me?"

"Not for awhile. I don't trust you and you don't trust me. General Nogales doesn't trust either of us. I figure he has a rope for me right beside yours. I have a commission to kill Eli. If you want to help there's a thousand dollars in it for you."

"A thousand? No! If you been paid then it's for a helluva lot more than that. Who sent you? Scotty? Scotty wants him dead. That's it. Scotty wants the claim to hisself!" Jules admired his logic.

Lyle shrugged.

"Well Scotty is worth a whole lot more than that. I'd say ten thousand is more like it. I'll take five of that," Jules insisted.

Lyle thought it over for a long moment. "You're a lot smarter than I figured, Jules. Five thousand it is. Now we'd better get going."

Jules nodded agreement. "A gun. First a gun."

Lyle hesitated.

"I ain't goin' nowhere's without a gun!"

Lyle sighed hard. He reached in his belt and withdrew his extra Colt. He handed it to Jules.

Jules eyes took on their devilish countenance. He looked at the gun with a reverence that bordered on worship. Suddenly, he raised the gun and fired.

Lyle jumped ten feet as the bullet whizzed by his ear. He drew his gun to return fire. He was about to pull the trigger and blow Jules away when a soldier dropped to the ground dead behind them.

"He had a dead bead on your head," Jules grinned.

"Whoa! I would say a proper thank you but I expect we had better be riding." Lyle sighed hard.

Jules grinned an evil agreement.

CHAPTER THIRTEEN

Eli thought he was dreaming. Scotty's smiling face looked down upon him, as did Maria's. He shot up in bed and rubbed his eyes as he saw that he wasn't dreaming.

"Scotty? Scotty, is that you?"

"Eli, you old son-of-a-gun. How the hell are you?"

"Fine, Scotty ... fine. It is you. What the dickens are you doin' in these parts?"

"Just payin' my neighbor a friendly visit. We don't see enough of each other these days." Scotty laughed.

"Well, I don't know what's goin on here. I've got to wake up some ... but I have to say it's mighty nice to see you!"

Eli looked past Scotty to Maria's face and looked puzzled.

"I believe this young lady has something to tell you. Me and the boys will wait in the *cantina*. You come see us in awhile, okay laddie?"

"Boys?"

"You'll be meetin' up with 'em later. We'll share a cup of rum just like the old days. Okay, laddie?"

"Yeah ... sure," Eli replied as he watched Scotty walk out of the room.

Maria waited until they were gone before she addressed Eli. "Please excuse me for bothering you, *Señor* Eli. I have made a mistake and I must make amends."

"I don't understand ..."

"... I misjudged you. Pepito is going to be alright. I just wanted to thank you for riding for the doctor. I have been accused of being too quick to judge. In this case it is true," Maria said with flawless English.

Eli was still woozy with sleep, but not too woozy to admire her stunning beauty. Maria had the classic beauty of the Castilian Spanish women mixed with the mystery of the Aztec blood that flowed in her veins. She had the beauty that made strong men as weak as schoolboys and she had the power to make Eli forget his serious purposes.

"You speak better American than me," Eli wondered.

"My Jesuit teachers insisted upon it."

"I see. Jesuits?"

"Scholarly priests."

"Oh?"

"I did not mean to disturb your rest. As I said, I just wanted to thank you ... for Pepito's sake." Maria turned to leave.

Eli got up and put his hand, softly, on her shoulder. She turned and looked up at him. Their eyes did not turn away from each other in shyness; but held a steady gaze that only comes with time or when ancient souls meet.

"Thank you for coming, Maria. I like Pepito. I'm glad he'll be alright."

"Yes. ... and you will be leaving us soon?"

"I ... I suppose," he paused. "Is there some problem?"

Maria turned slightly away. "I believe that if you are here the man who ran away will return. Please, *señor!* We are a small village. Maybe this time Pepito does not survive."

Eli understood but he did not like her eagerness to get rid of him. Eli liked her — more than he cared to admit. He was sad as he thought about leaving. "In the morning. Tomorrow? *¿Mañana?* Is that okay?"

Maria detected the hurt in Eli's voice. She turned and smiled. "You understand I say this because it is the best thing for the village?"

"And you? You want me gone, maybe tonight?"

"I did not say that, *señor.*"

"Eli. Just Eli, please?"

"Yes. Well I have to go now. I thank you again for me and Pepito."

Eli smiled acknowledgment as Maria moved to the door. "Maria?" he called after her.

She paused and turned. "Yes?"

"Look ... is it okay ... I mean I would like to come by and see Pepito before I take off?"

Maria thought it over a long moment. "He is still not too well."

"I just want a couple of minutes. My God, that can't bother you that much? If it does, forget it. Just forget it, okay?"

"Okay. If that is your wish, *Señor* ... Eli." Maria toyed with him.

"No! No, it isn't my wish and besides Pepito has something to say about it. Let me say it another way ... a way even you can understand it." Eli paused and moved closer to her. "I will be by tonight to see Pepito. If you don't want to be there that's fine. Understand?"

Maria seemed to enjoy the wordplay. Her eyes danced with mischievous light. "I do not tell you what to do. You do what you wish. ... and I? I will do what I wish. *Buenas tardes*, Eli." Maria left, almost laughing.

Eli fumed inside long after she was gone. He hated the way she stirred his blood. This was absolutely the wrong time to be involved with a woman, any woman. But more importantly, this woman. This woman was dangerous.

Perhaps deadly.

He moved to the wash basin and splashed cold water on his face. It didn't help. Her smell, her aura, her being stayed in his mind. He knew he wasn't going to her house to see Pepito.

Eli knew if he went it would be for one reason — to be close to her.

He thought to drown those thoughts with rum as he moved to meet Scotty.

Scotty sat at a table in a far corner of the *cantina* and took long swallows of rum straight from the bottle. Chief, Sam, and Shorty had a bottle of their own and were matching Scotty drink for drink.

Eli joined them and Scotty handed him the bottle. Eli took a pull from the bottle. He stopped, then took another longer pull. He then sat down and smiled at his friend.

"So, you came all this way just to say hello?" Eli kidded.

"Not likely. Mamacita tells me you eliminated the reason for my trip. Had I of known that, I would have saved my backside a lot of hurt. Damned horses! God never meant man to ride a horse," Scotty moaned as he shifted his sore behind in the chair.

"It's that soft life you've been leading in Sonora." Eli paused. "So, how are things in Sonora?"

Scotty hesitated a moment before he replied.

"Fine and dandy. The claim is producing high grade ore. The town is growing up mighty fine. There's all sorts of Eastern finery coming in and Pa Jensen built hisself a brick outhouse!"

Eli looked unsatisfied.

"I don't know about Stella, Eli. God knows what got into that woman. She didn't talk to us much and one day just up and took off for Boston."

"Boston?"

"The rumors have it that Captain Hopkins had a great house back there. He left you his share, Eli, but I think she's doing some sneaky legal stuff. I know why you came here, Eli, and what you want to do, but maybe it's time to get home and take care of business."

"There's still some business to take care of here, Scotty."

"Eli, pardon me for saying so, but he ain't worth it. This is a big country and he could be anywhere. I'm not sayin' Stella is a bad person but she's up to something and it ain't something that's for your good." Scotty paused. "Don't take offense. I'm your friend, Eli. I don't want to see you lose it all."

"I understand, Scotty. I appreciate it. But it ain't exactly like that. Stella is gonna do what she takes a mind to. I have to do what I came to do. Then I'll see about Sonora. I want to thank you for coming … and your boys here," Eli reached out his hand.

"I'm Johnny Samples, but they call me Shorty." Shorty shook Eli's hand.

"Nice to meet you, Shorty."

"John Thomas, I'm called Chief." Chief shook Eli's hand next.

"Chief."

"Sam Johnson, Mr. Llynne. I heard a lot about you. It's good to shake your hand."

"Sam. I hope what you heard wasn't too damning," Eli chuckled.

"No, sir. You have a might hefty reputation seein' as how you killed three bears single-handedly,"

Sam laughed.

"Oh? It's up to three now? By the time they lay me away I expect it'll be a hundred." Eli shook his head.

They all laughed.

Scotty stopped laughing and looked at Eli soberly. "I do wish you'd ride back to Sonora with us. But if you intend on stayin' we'll be stayin' to help. Is that alright, boys?"

They all nodded agreement.

"No, Scotty. You know me. You know I don't expect anyone

else doin' my business for me. You got a new bride and I expect a lot of business to attend to."

"Damn you! You stubborn Welshman. I'm your friend, and I'm not coming here begging. There ain't nobody I know who's so big they don't need a helping hand. I know Lyle Jameson by reputation and he ain't likely to forget you killing two of his boys. Even you can't look both ways all the time. Somebody has to look out for your backside!" Scotty looked angry.

Eli looked serious then broke into a smile. "There ain't no Scotch whisky down here, Scotty."

"Well, that makes it unpleasant but it can be got used to."

"You're a growed man, Scotty. If you want to stay then that's your doin'." Eli smiled at his friend. "I can't say you won't be welcome."

"Well that ain't exactly a fancy invitation but it'll do. You got it straight in your mind what you'll be doing next?"

"Not exactly. Just riding and asking and looking."

Scotty looked at his men. "You boys didn't really sign on for this. Your job's done, and you deserve the bonus I promised." Scotty reached into his money belt and started to count out their pay. "If you want to ride on back home, I'll understand."

They looked at each other and made a silent agreement.

"I expect as long as Lyle is on the loose we ain't exactly done what we came to do," Chief offered.

The others nodded agreement.

"Then it's settled. We ride with Eli!" Scotty announced.

Eli thought it over and welcomed them with another handshake.

CHAPTER FOURTEEN

Charles Dickens' writing about Boston in *American Notes* published in 1842 said "the tone of Boston society is one of perfect politeness, courtesy, and good breeding." Stella had read those words and laughed. In her mind Mr. Dickens had only seen the face Boston society showed to the world outside. He must not have seen the face of the cutthroat businessmen and members of the Know-Nothing political party that tried to keep the Irishmen "in their place," which meant down. Stella rankled at the way her people were treated. Watching the Irish immigrants fight each other over low-paying heavy labor jobs made her more determined than ever that Benjamin would never be thought of as Irish. Stella watched the light snowfall out of her living room bay window. In the distance, she could see the white tower of Faneuil Hall where she imagined, even now, Know-Nothing party members were railing against the Irish.

Rose and her assistant maids were cleaning the attic and Ben was asleep. Stella was bored and even though it was still morning decided to have a glass of brandy.

She started to pour it when she heard the loud knock of the iron knocker on the solid oak door.

She started to ignore it but finally went to answer.

She was not completely surprised to see Shannon standing there holding two pairs of ice-skates in his hand.

"And good morning to you, Mrs. Winslow."

"Mr. O'Bannion? I thought we had settled our business."

"Yes, ma'am. But this is not business. This is sporting fun. Boston Harbor is frozen thick with ice. It's a fine winter's day, and I thought you might enjoy a bit of ice-skating."

Stella had not ice-skated since she was a little girl. But she remembered she had enjoyed it, and the idea was appealing. As to Shannon, Stella was not quite sure how appealing he was. Stella had known the cunning charm of Irish men all her life.

They were delightful little leprechauns until they got what they wanted, then they, sometimes, turned into disgusting trolls.

They were the only men she feared.

She did not fear Shannon, though he was an exceptionally handsome man and his smile lit up the gray winter's morning.

"I don't think so. Rosie and the others are busy so I'd better stay with Ben."

"I see. I can understand that. A mother's love is the purest expression of love that there be. It warms my heart to think of it."

"Shannon, don't give me that Irish blarney! Save it for the little seamstress with the dimples and the empty head."

"Ah, God bless you, Mrs. Winslow, but you are one smart lady. And I must say that today you are one handsome lady. It would be my pleasure to parade your beauty before all those Brahmins who think they're the only pretty things God has made." Shannon's Irish eyes danced into Stella's resolve. She knew he was full of blarney but she didn't really care.

He had already relieved the boredom of the day and getting out was a pleasant thought. But he was Irish and loudly Irish. Anyone who saw them together would place her as Irish. For Ben's sake she did not want to risk that.

"I don't think so. And I have to ask you to, please, not come around. I am not receiving gentlemen. Do you understand?"

Shannon looked hurt. He knew what was going on. He had had doors slammed in his face before. He looked deep into Stella's eyes and let the hurt show.

"What you mean is that you are not receiving any "Irish" gentlemen. That's it, isn't it?"

"What if it is?"

"You can turn your back on me, Mrs. ... Winslow. That is one thing that can be understood. But I think it is wrong to turn your back on your people ... your mother and father because of what some pious bluebloods might say."

"Just leave, Mr. O'Bannion. Or I'll have the constable summoned."

"That's not necessary. I'll be going!"

Shannon shivered as a cold wind blew ice and snow. His puppy-dog eyes were not convincing but they did evoke a certain sympathy. Stella started to close the door. She looked at Shannon's sad eyes and thought it over. "Come inside a moment and get warm before you depart."

Shannon was surprised but he obeyed and stepped into the foyer. Stella closed the door.

"Wait here and I'll bring you a glass of brandy. But you drink that and warm yourself a moment then you'll be going for sure. Understand?"

"That's kind of you, Mrs. Winslow."

Shannon brushed the snow off his coat.

Stella poured a glass of brandy for Shannon and one for herself. She took a quick drink then brought a glass it to Shannon.

Shannon took it and toasted her quietly before he took a sip.

"The saints be praised for your hospitality, madam."

"Don't mistake kindness for weakness, Mr. O'Bannion. I would do the same for a stray animal."

"Aye! A lost little puppy dog. That's me alright."

"More like a lost wolfhound." Stella could not avoid laughing.

"Pardon me, Mrs. Winslow but you do have the prettiest smile."

"I told you no more blarney! Now drink up!"

"It's not blarney to tell you something you know inside is true. A beautiful woman knows of her beauty. You know of yours."

Stella did not want to like this man, but she was bored and he was, at least, entertaining. She had confidence that she could enjoy being entertained but disallow him to sneak his way into her good graces. "Tell me, Shannon. Does everyone in Boston go down to the harbor to skate?"

Shannon thought about it a long moment. "Yes. But I know places where no one goes. I respect your need for privacy. I know places no one else knows …"

"… but getting there would be a problem," Stella wondered aloud.

"I have a covered carriage and a discreet driver waiting."

"Oh? You presumed?"

"No! No, I hoped. I would never presume anything about a fine woman of your elegant bearing."

"Ah, Mr. Shannon, I have seen so many of your kind. On the Barbary Coast the saloons were full of them. Shallow men who believe they can get their way with their smooth talk. Oh, I know it works on some of the dimwitted girls. I have seen it and felt shame for my gender. You show no respect for me by this approach."

Shannon looked at her with a steady gaze and his eyes lit up with admiration. He finished his drink and put the glass down on the table. He turned to leave.

"It wasn't easy for me to come here. I have my pride also. If you want the brutal truth, I'm bored by most women. I have no time for most women." He paused. "But you? You fascinate me and that is not blarney! Good day, Mrs. Winslow. I am sorry I bothered you." Shannon started to leave.

Stella grabbed him by the arm and spun him around.

"Hold on, big fella! Since we both know where we stand, let's make the most of it."

Shannon looked flustered.

"You have been fortunate enough to catch me on a dismal day and an outing is appealing. With discretion uppermost in our minds, it is damn appealing!" Stella hesitated. "You understand that this is merely an outing. You are not to think of yourself as a suitor. You are not to get familiar. You are not to speak of this to anyone. Agreed?"

"My, that's a heap of rules. I hope I can remember them all."

"Don't worry, I'll see that you do," Stella said as she studied his strong face.

Shannon had the chiseled face and strong jaw line of the very masculine North Country Irish — and the ancient Kelts. He was built as sturdy as Eli but he had much more charisma. He exuded strength but with a quiet softness.

"So tell me, Shannon. You have a pair of lady's skates for me?"

"Right here."

"And which colleen might they belong to?"

"None but my sister Rosie, who says your feet are her size."

"You don't miss a trick, do you?"

"I try to be of service."

"I don't suppose you would want another glass of brandy while I change and talk to Rosie?"

"Oh, glory be! You are truly a dear lady, Mrs. Winslow."

"Stella! Just Stella. The way you say 'Mrs. Winslow' makes me feel old."

"And you certainly aren't old."

"Just go have a brandy and I'll be down in awhile." Stella paused. "Try not to drink the whole bottle, please."

Shannon laughed as Stella turned and walked upstairs.

He watched her go with eyes that shone with a glimmer of sincerity — a strange sentiment for his lying soul.

He poured himself a healthy glass of brandy and was very pleased with himself as he waited for her to return. Shannon had not always been a con artist. He had been a farmer along with his father and two brothers in County Wexford, Ireland.

Shannon had watched as his father died of heartbreak when the "bumpers" or "horse potato" crop failed two years running. He had seen friends and neighbors, already poor, become destitute and many die of starvation. In the spring of 1850 he had taken what meager possessions he could gather together and, through the most humble begging, had come up with the twenty dollars needed for passage to America. His brother had also managed to scrap together the twenty dollars and they all departed the seaport of New Ross with hope in their hearts. They had no idea how dangerous passage on the British "coffin ships" was to be. In the year they sailed, almost fifty thousand Irishmen died either en route or shortly after reaching Canada as a result of the depredations of the voyage.

The voyage took six to eight weeks and the overcrowded ships were breeding grounds for diseases. With rank water and overflowing privies, anyone with a weaken immune system was apt to catch a fever and die.

Both of Shannon's brothers "caught a fever" and died only a few miles from the shores they had wanted so much to see.

Had they reached land they would have found it little better than the strife they had left. Because of the British Penal Codes that denied an Irishman the right to school, Shannon's brothers were illiterate. But Shannon had been the benefactor of a kindly priest who had taught him to read and write in secret. Shannon had read everything he could get his hands on and he felt he was the intellectual equal of most men.

Shannon was not as cocky as he portrayed himself to be, but was rather coldly cunning. He had felt the pain of hunger and cold and he was determined to never feel it again. As he sipped the quality brandy in this elegant house, he swore, quietly, that he would own it someday.

Upstairs Stella dressed in her most expensive furs and put on her most provocative makeup. She was going to have some fun with this man.

Stella liked wrapping self-confident men around her finger. It was great sport to cut them down one ego level at a time and do it so deftly they never knew what hit them.

Stella's only problem was picking out the right hat. She knew the symbol of status in Boston was headwear, particularly on a lady. Stella had paid exorbitant amounts to get the latest hat fashion direct from Paris. But they all seemed too elegant and nonfunctional for ice-skating. She finally decided on a purple and gray broad-brimmed hat with a mixture of colored ostrich feathers. When she thought she had made Shannon wait long enough, she moved to meet him.

Shannon's eyes lit up as Stella descended the staircase. She was a beautiful woman and he knew if he wasn't careful she could turn his head. Shannon did not plan on any woman turning his head. He was going to have political power, then wealth in Boston someday, and to do that he had to keep his wits about him.

He knew a woman like Stella could make him into a babbling idiot if he didn't proceed with the utmost caution.

"Am I dressed warm enough? California weather spoils you, you know?"

Stella modeled her furs for Shannon.

"It's mighty brisk out there. That's a lovely hat, but maybe it's …"

"It's fine. Let's go!" Stella led the way out of the house and down to the waiting carriage. Shannon had been as good as his word and the carriage had drawn black curtains. The driver opened the door without comment. Stella looked around for prying eyes and saw none. She relaxed and felt safe.

They did not speak much, and Shannon was a perfect gentleman as they arrived at a wooded cove in a remote corner of Boston Harbor. Stella was excited about the outing as she saw the ice and remembered the fun she had as a girl on skates. The wind was brisk but she felt she had her hat pinned down firm enough. They dismounted the carriage and walked to the side of the frozen water. Shannon took some dry wood, a bottle of brandy, and blankets from the carriage. He dismissed the driver and joined her. Shannon handed her the skates. Stella looked doubtful. She moved to a big log, brushed the snow aside and sat down. Shannon took a while to get a fire going. When it was crackling he looked for Stella. He did not believe what he saw.

"You put them on," she insisted as she hiked her skirt up way above her stocking-wrapped ankle.

Shannon was both shocked and pleased to gaze upon Stella's lithe ankle and lower leg. Shannon had seen his share of naked women but in the privacy of a boudoir — and they were not ladies.

To see a real ladies' ankle, clothed in a thick stocking or no, in public was risqué and exciting.

"Don't get any ideas, just put the skate on!" Stella picked up the glint in Shannon's eyes.

"Yes, ma'am." Shannon grinned as he strapped the skates on Stella's shoes. He, quickly, strapped his on as he watched her wobble out on the ice.

Stella could not find her bearings at first.

It had been many years since she has skated and she started to fall. At the last moment, Shannon was there to catch her in his strong arms.

Stella let him hold her for only a moment before she broke free. "Let me be. I have it now. See!" Stella laughed as she remembered and began to skate well.

Shannon nodded agreement and joined her on the ice.

Shannon was an accomplished skater and could not resist showing off. He cut tight figure-eights in the ice and did barrel jumps over imaginary barrels.

Stella pretended to ignore him but he was quite a show not easily ignored. Shannon was a big man but he had a grace worth watching.

"Stay well in toward shore. The ice thins out real quick if you get too far out," Shannon warned as Stella started to speed-skate.

"I know! I know!" Stella insisted as she delighted in the steady improvement in her style and speed.

Stella was happily skating along when she stumbled and fell hard on to the ice. Shannon was there in an instant to give her a helping hand. He pulled her to her feet and she looked embarrassed.

"I didn't see the rough spot … that's all."

"I know."

"I'm as good a skater as anyone!"

"I know."

"Oh, you! You don't believe me. Watch this!" Stella took off with long strides, going faster than she wanted to.

The wind picked up and helped blow her along. Suddenly, she

was going a lot faster than she wanted. The wind blew ever harder and Stella's cockiness turned to fear. She had no control and she was headed straight for thin ice. She wanted to stop but knew she would fall hard if she stopped too quickly.

A harsh gust of wind blew her hat off and it tumbled along in front of her. She found courage as she watched it go. Instead of caution, she now felt anger as she dug her skates in to speed toward her hat.

"Stella! Stella! Good God, don't go out there!" Shannon sped after her.

Stella ignored him as she saw her hat come to a stop. She sighed in relief as she started to slow to pick it up. The faint, but unmistakable, sound of thin ice cracking brought her to her senses. She looked down to see a small linear crack begin right by her right skate. The small crack paused then broke into three larger cracks.

Stella was no coward but she was scared to death as the loud cracking sound preceded a huge breakup of the thin ice.

"Oh, my God!" Stella cried as she felt herself falling, She saw the dark cold water just below the ice and remembered childhood prayers she had not used for many years.

The icy water was numbing. Stella had never felt such cold. She had never felt so heavy. Her layers of clothes were instantly soaked and she felt them pulling her down.

Stella sucked the freezing water into her mouth and she felt a thousand knifes stabbing her all over. She thought she would be dead in a moment. She reached toward the surface of the water with both her arms. She struggled with all her might to reach the surface.

She despaired at her weight.

It was pulling her down to her death. Stella saw only darkness before her eyes. She had finally found a foe she could not defeat.

Chunks of ice swirled around her as she started to slip into an almost welcome feeling of paralysis. She thought to sleep and maybe wake up in a warm place.

She was about to give in when she felt Shannon's strong hands grab hers and yank her from the water.

Shannon was lying flat on the ice only inches from the gaping hole. His strength was such he pulled her to safety with ease — just before the ice beneath them began to give away also.

When he was safely on thick ice, Shannon lifted Stella in his arms and carried her to the fire. She was soaking wet and shivering violently.

Shannon did not hesitate as he began to pile all the dry wood he could find on the fire until it roared high and hot. When the fire burned to his satisfaction, he turned to see that she still shivered uncontrollably.

She was still semiconscious and frostbite was a real possibility.

Out of respect for her need for privacy, Shannon had found the most isolated place on Boston Harbor. He had paid the carriage driver to stay away for five hours. He knew he could yell as loud as he could and no one would hear him. No one would be along to rescue them any time soon.

Shannon looked at the freezing Stella with deep affection.

He decided there was only one thing to do — take off her wet clothes and wrap her in warm blankets. For all his faults, Shannon was a gentleman. Stella was a lady, and he would treat her like a lady.

It was a great temptation to stare at Stella's nakedness, but he undressed her in a businesslike fashion — only pausing a moment to admire her most beguiling parts.

Stella coughed ice chunks and water for a long moment after Shannon had her wrapped in warm blankets and her clothes hung by the fire.

He moved her as close to the fire as he felt safe and watched her with deep concern.

She was more beautiful than he had let himself realize. In the glow from the fire she looked angelic, and he had to fight hard not to pull the blankets aside and take his pleasure with her.

Slowly, Stella came back to consciousness. When she saw her clothes hanging from tree limbs she almost fainted. "Shannon? Shannon? Am I? I am alive ... oh, I am!"

"Are you alright?"

"Alright? I'm naked under these blankets! What did you do to me?"

"I saved your life! Although, now I can't imagine why."

"What else did you do?"

"Nothing! Jesus, Joseph, and Mary! You are something else!"

"I'm ... I'm naked!"

"I should have just left you in the damn water! I should have left you to freeze in your wet clothes!"

"Maybe you should have!" Stella coughed water and looked out at the broken ice in the distance. She saw the gaping hole she had fallen into. She shuddered.

Shannon turned his back on her and sat on a log by the fire.

"God, what I'd give for a glass of brandy," she sighed.

Shannon looked at the bottle of brandy by his boot. He picked it up and took a drink. He did not offer it to her. "You're a hard woman, Stella. But there's a place for being hard." Shannon took another pull from the bottle.

"Look, I said I'm sorry. But I don't wake up naked with strange men very often, you know!"

"Well, it was me or the boys down at the morgue. Maybe I made the wrong choice ..."

"Oh, shut up and give me a drink!"

"Is that your way of saying 'thank you'?"

"Thank you, Shannon. Now give me a drink!" Stella stopped and sighed hard. "Please?"

"You're welcome, Mrs. Winslow. Please join me in a drink," Shannon took her the bottle. Stella reached for it. As she reached her arm from beneath the blanket she exposed her right breast.

Shannon did not try to look away.

Stella took the bottle and covered herself without comment.

"Since you've seen everything I have no mysteries to keep from you," Stella said.

"I did what I had to do. I did not mean to be familiar. Your clothes are almost dry. The carriage will be back soon. I'll leave and let you dress in privacy." Shannon seemed a little embarrassed.

Stella smiled as she thought Shannon was truly ashamed of what he had done. She looked back out at the gaping hole in the ice. It was ugly and frightening.

She took a long drink from the bottle. She had never enjoyed good brandy so much. She had never enjoyed the act of drinking anything so much.

She had a new turn at life and everything felt good.

The cold ice-wind coming off the harbor stung her face, but the sting was pleasant.

The fire was hot, and the heat was welcome. The woolen blankets scratched her naked skin, and the scratches were delicious.

She took several swallows of the brandy and laughed. Shannon took exception with his eyes, thinking she was laughing at him — when she was laughing at the pure joy of being alive. She shivered beneath the blankets and enjoyed the goose-bumps on her skin. She wondered how close to death she had come.

She looked at the handsome man who had saved her life. She took one last long drink of brandy from the bottle. "How long before the carriage returns?" Stella asked.

"Within the hour," Shannon replied.

Stella sighed hard as she lay on the blankets and looked up at the dark gray winter sky. "Then we do not have much time," she insisted as she opened the blankets and invited Shannon in.

CHAPTER FIFTEEN

Lyle did not like riding with Jules. It was difficult to keep one eye on the road ahead and one eye on Jules gun hand. Lyle tolerated the situation only because he wanted Eli dead and he needed Jules' help. It occurred to Lyle that, if he were lucky, he would be able to get Eli and Jules at the same time. The thought made him smile and Jules eyed him suspiciously.

"You done found somethin' funny in this godforsaken place?" Jules grunted.

"Nope. Just smilin' to stretch my face out a little. You're right. Ain't much to smile about in this dust and dirt." Lyle stopped as he heard the distant sound of gunfire.

Jules heard it also and his hand went automatically to his gun.

Lyle looked at Jules hard and Jules reholstered his gun. "It's coming over from beyond that hill. Sounds like all hell is bustin' loose."

Jules nodded agreement as Lyle started to turn his horse in the other direction. Jules held up his hand for Lyle to stop. "It sounds like there's people killin' other people over yonder." Jules paused.

"That's why we'd better ride the other way."

"Nope! If they kill each other off maybe there'll be some good pickin's for us."

"Are you crazy? Yes! … yes, you are. I heard tales about you, but … tell you what … go on if you have a mind too, but I'm riding the other way!"

Jules spit into the wind as he eyed Lyle hard. "You do that. But you gonna be needing an extra gun when you come up against Eli Llynne. Ain't no way you gonna take him by yourself!" Jules turned his horses head toward the sound of the gunfire.

"That's at least a dozen guns doing that shooting. You are going take on a dozen guns?" Lyle smirked.

Jules shook his head in contempt. "No, stupid. I'm gonna find a good lookout and just wait and see what I can see. Them Mexicans took my money back there and I aim to make it up anyway I can!" Jules paused to sneer. "You understand?"

Lyle watched as Jules turned and moved off at a slow gallop toward the sound of the gunfire. "You are crazy. Like everyone said … and I must be crazy to ride along with you." Lyle started to head in the opposite direction.

Jules did not look back as he rode into a group of rocks poised just above the arroyo where he heard the sound of gunfire. He dismounted and crept his way to a position where he could see down into the arroyo without giving himself away.

Lyle had been right. There were more than a dozen guns. Just below Jules there was a running gunfight between almost fifty men. Twenty men already lay dead and the blistering gunfire dropped one more man with each blink of the eye.

Jules saw, immediately, what the gunfight was over. There was a wagon loaded with gun cases between the two groups of men. Jules' mouth watered as he imagined what the guns might be worth. Jules watched as the numbers of men continued to diminish until there were now less than twenty. He could tell that one side, the side with uniformed men, was in trouble.

The soldiers were about to be flanked by the *banditos*.

Jules could only hope the soldiers took out most of them before they were killed. He almost leaped out of his skin as a shadow fell over him. He turned and withdrew his pistol with one motion. He almost fired until he saw Lyle standing above him. "Damn you, Lyle. Don't you know better than to sneak up on a man like that? I should shoot you dead just on general principles!"

"Looks to me like you're going to need all the help you can get to commandeer that load of guns," Lyle said coolly.

Jules, reluctantly, admired Lyle's perception. He slowly reholstered his gun. Well, they's all Mexicans so that's on our side. But there's about …" Jules grinned and looked the situation over. "… there's about … let's see? A dozen left. It's almost fair odds."

Lyle soberly looked the situation over. "Those are General Nogales' men. See that ensign. That means those guns are for him. I don't want any part of it."

"You're a big yellow coward, Lyle Jameson. General Nogales is fifty miles in the other direction. He was about to kill us dead. Anything we take from him is our just desserts."

"Oh? Now you're a gun runner? We just take the guns and walk into town and sell them like that?"

"You sure don't know much about Mexico. That ain't how you do it!"

"Oh? Suppose you tell me how to do it. Please, mister smarty-pants?"

"No, sir! I'll just say I know how and that's that. If you want a share then you stick around. If you don't then ride out the way you come."

Lyle watched the gunfight below. There were now less than ten men — four soldiers and five *banditos*. He moved to his horse and withdrew a long rifle from its saddle holster. He moved back beside Jules.

"If you can work your way around to those rocks down there we can get them in a crossfire. The *banditos* have only pistols so I can outgun them with my rifle. You concentrate on the soldiers … if there are any left," Lyle said calmly.

Jules grinned sardonically. He quietly got up and moved to flank the *banditos*.

Lyle settled into a comfortable nook where he had a clear shot at the soldiers. He was just out of pistol range and he felt confident his rifle would even the odds. He took careful aim at the apparent leader of the *banditos*. He took a deep breath and blew it out hard and squeezed off a round. The rifle barked as it sent a thirty caliber round whistling down the arroyo.

The chief *bandito* heard the report of the rifle and turned to see where the sound came from. In that instant, the bullet entered his mouth and took off the back of his head.

The soldiers and *banditos* stopped firing at each other and looked in Lyle's direction. Lyle dropped another *bandito* before they could scurry for cover. They all turned their guns on Lyle as Jules moved into position.

Jules was above and to the right of the soldiers' position. They had their backs turned to him, a fact that would have concerned a decent men. Jules saw it as a wonderful opportunity. Coldly and methodically, Jules fired into the backs of the soldiers. Two were dead before the other two knew where the gunshots were coming from. They turned only to be shot in the face. Jules was more than proud. He had dropped all four with only four rounds.

Lyle had stopped firing to watch. In that time the three remaining *banditos* made it to their horses and began to ride out of the arroyo.

Lyle did not want any living witnesses.

Lyle pulled down on the lead horsemen and dropped him with one shot. Jules thought the same as Lyle. He ran from cover to fire at the other two *banditos* .His next shot missed.

Jules' did not. He put a bullet in the second *bandito*'s chest.

The *bandito* spilled from his horse and Jules put another round into him for good measure as the last *bandito* bore down on him. Jules raised his gun to fire. It clicked empty.

The *bandito* grinned from ear to ear as he leveled his gun at Jules.

Jules ducked for cover as bullets hit the dust all around him. As he did, he tripped and fell into the dust. He tried to struggle to his feet spitting dust, and he turned to see the muzzle of the *bandito*'s gun in his face.

The *bandito* cocked the hammer of the gun and was about to pull the trigger when a bullet from Lyle's rifle broke his backbone. The *bandito* tumbled from his horse, dead.

Jules sighed hard in relief.

Lyle looked down at Jules and waited for some sign of "thank you" for having saved Jules' life. Instead Jules began searching the dead men for valuables.

Lyle watched in disbelief and cursed himself for what he had done.

CHAPTER SIXTEEN

Maize, the first Mexican gold. Eli could smell the mouth-watering scent of corn *tortillas* being cooked in the open hearth oven. He watched as a world-weary *señora* poured dry maize into a crock full of wood ashes and water, as her Indian ancestors had done many centuries ago. Another *señora* was grinding the wet meal into *masa* with a *mano*, a stone rolling pen, smashing the glob into a *tortilla* on her three-legged stool, *metate*. Stone, water, wood, and fire were the only ways to make good *tortillas*. Any modern contraption would take away from the flavor and, more importantly, the soul of the meal.

There are those scholars who date the beginning of civilization to the day Mexican Indians found the "grass with the sweet seeds" and began making it into "bread."

Even the lordly Brahmins of the Massachusetts Colony owed much to this humble grass.

Eli had on a clean shirt for the first time since he could remember. He had even splashed his face with toilet water and shaved without cutting himself over three times. He felt he was, at least, presentable as he knocked on the house where Maria Christina lived.

He knew it was a partial lie to say he had come to visit Pepito. Eli liked Pepito well enough, but the truth was he had come to see Maria Christina.

Eli considered himself to be a no-nonsense man of purpose. Whatever his hand found to do, he did it with all his mind and soul. He did not tolerate interference in his pursuits — except that interference that females often supplied.

Females were a continuing mystery to Eli. He could put them completely out of his mind for months at a time. Then he would meet one that eased her way into his being so softly he never saw her coming.

He did not like it, but every time he closed his eyes he saw the face of Maria Christina. She haunted him and he had come to try to purge her from his system.

He knew better than that. He knew he liked her more than he wanted to.

He knew she had rekindled long-forgotten desires. He knew he liked the way he felt whenever she was around.

Eli was a proud man. A proud man who did what he wanted when he wanted — except when he was around her.

Eli was a hard man when he had to be, and he had had to be of late. But Eli was also a lonely man, and he never knew how lonely he was until he met up with a woman like Maria Christina.

As Eli waited for someone to answer the door, he wondered at his feelings for the women he had known.

Eli had no real feeling for the word "love." He had seen the word misused so many times he thought it had little real meaning. As to true love, Eli figured that was something people hoped for but rarely obtained. He thought it was like the love he had once felt for the willowy Lydia.

In the beginning, Lydia was Eli's true love and the base from which to measure all other love. Eli had loved her more than his life, and he had endured a terrible hurt when she was killed.

Stella had come to him when he needed her.

Stella had been a comfortable woman. Stella had been handy. Stella had been desired by many men and in that was a compliment to Eli. Stella had been treacherous, and for her treachery Eli could find no forgiveness.

There would be a day of reckoning for her.

Even so, he was a little surprised at how easily she was dismissed from his thoughts. Eli wondered if he loved her why had it been so easy to leave her, and now that she had turned on him there was a certain bitterness in his heart. He knew he would never return to her. These thoughts eased his mind for he truly believed before God they were no longer man and wife.

"*Señor* Llynne. *Por favor*. Please come in." Maria answered the door.

Eli tried to mask the admiration he had for her but she saw it before he could hide it. "Maria … here I brought these …" Eli handed her some flowers.

"For me!" Pepito shouted as he hobbled up behind her.

"Pepito? Pepito, how are you? You look fit." Eli gave Maria the flowers and greeted Pepito.

"¡Muy bien! ¿Y tu? How are you?" Pepito beamed.

"Fine. I also brought these." Eli handed Pepito a bag. Pepito opened the bag and laughed. The bag was full of red peppers.

"So we have another contest?"

"No. Not today. But a *cerveza* sounds good."

"Maria, you heard our guest. *¡Dos cervezas!*"

"You both seem able-bodied to me. Get them yourself." She paused. "Thanks for the flowers, Mr. Llynne. The pigs they love such a treat." Maria smiled and left them.

Eli watched her go and shook his head in wonder. "I don't know why she doesn't like me."

"Oh, but she does. Do you not know about how to understand women?"

"Look, kid! I'm a lot older and I don't need any lessons about women from someone not dry behind the ears. Okay?"

Pepito looked sad. "Okay .. but I'm not a kid!"

"I'm sorry. I come to visit a sick friend and I act like bad company," Eli reached for the bag of peppers and withdrew one. He gulped it down.

"That'll serve my mouth right. Where's that *cerveza?*"

"This way. It is this way." Pepito laughed as he led Eli into the small kitchen.

The adobe house was small but neat and clean. All about it were the fine touches a woman gives to a house. Eli liked the way Maria had decorated it with small, inexpensive but colorful things.

Eli took the beer and pulled down two quick swallows.

"You want another pepper?" Pepito kidded.

"Not today. Today my throat has to rest." Eli paused as his eyes searched for Maria Christina.

"She is always angry when she speaks of you," Pepito offered. "… and she speaks of you often. I have not seen her so upset since the last time she was in love," Pepito continued.

"If that's love I think I can do without it. Thanks just the same."

"I do not think so, *señor* You are not a man who gives up so easy."

"You think I came to see her?"

"Yes, *señor*. I have had a pretty sister for some years. It is an old thing for me." Pepito grinned.

Eli laughed. "But, really, it was to see you also." Eli paused.

"You have been out of circulation for some time. You have heard nothing of the man I told you about?"

Pepito shrugged. *"¿Quizás?"*

"Oh? Forgive me. I forgot the memory pills." Eli counted out twenty dollars in gold.

Pepito took the coins and smiled.

"Good news! General Nogales has arrested two *gringos* and they are said to be the men you are looking for!"

"When? When did you hear this?"

"Only … five … six days ago. A gun caravan passed through here only last week. It is only three days ride to his camp." Pepito beamed with pride. "I would have told you sooner but there is no hurry."

"No hurry! Pepito, they could be gone to hell and back by now!"

"I do not think so."

"Oh? And why pray tell do you not think so?"

"Because by now, General Nogales has already hung them." Pepito sighed.

Eli gritted his teeth then took a long swallow of beer. He looked out of the window at Maria by the pig sty throwing one flower at a time at the pigs.

"You do not think to go there, *Señor* Llynne?"

"What?"

"To go see the dead men?"

"Of course."

"¡No, no! You must not think of this!"

"Why?"

"General Nogales, he does not like *Juaristas* or *federales*, but he does not like *gringos* more. He would kill you dead for sure!"

"Whose side is he on?"

"The side with the most money and land at the time."

"So you know this General?"

"Yes. He comes from the village not far from here. He was a peasant before the war. Then he said he was a General. He shoots anyone who says he is not. Maybe some day he will say he is *presidente?*"

Pepito laughed at his little joke.

Eli did not reply, but stared at Maria out of the window.

Maria looked back at Eli and smiled as she threw another flower to the pigs. The pigs squealed in delight at their treat.

"Well, there sure ain't nothing to keep me here, is there?" Eli pulled the beer down hard and started to leave. He was almost to the door when a big *señora* entered with a plate full of fresh-baked *tortillas*. She put them on a table.

Eli's anger dissipated into hunger.

He took one more look out of the window at Maria as she threw the last flower to the pigs.

She looked at Eli and laughed.

He hated her. He loved her.

Pepito moved up behind him and looked also.

"She must really love you to do such a thing, *señor*." Pepito said sincerely.

Eli turned and looked at Pepito in disbelief. "Good Lord. What does she do to men she hates?" Eli wondered aloud.

"They are never seen again," Pepito kidded. "Let's enjoy *mi madre's tortillas*. Dinner is served." Pepito led Eli to the small table.

Eli took several *tortillas* and a big helping of beans and *guacamole* mixture. He liked the heartiness of this kind of Mexican food but he missed beefsteak. He wondered if he was dreaming when he smelled the aroma of beef cooking on an open fire. He dismissed that thought and reached for another helping of beans.

He stopped when Maria put a plate in front of him that held a large steak.

Eli looked at her in disbelief.

"This will make us even for the help you gave my brother," Maria said as if it were the final word.

Eli looked at the beefsteak with love. He looked at Maria with confusion. "I don't figure you. Tell me, do you hate or not?"

"This has nothing to do with you. I am a honorable person. I pay my debts ... and those of my brother."

"I see."

"I hope so, *señor*. Enjoy." Maria turned to leave.

Eli got up and grabbed her by the arm. He spun her around and looked hard into her eyes. "I don't know what kind of saddle burr is scratching your behind, but I don't take kindly to being treated un-neighborly. You just spit it out and we'll be done with it!"

"Unneighborly? You have the only beefsteak in the whole of this region."

"That may be so, but it is served to me like I was bein' hanged in the morning. So why don't you take it and feed it to the damn pigs?"

Maria looked angry then smiled. Then she broke into laugh-

ter. "Feed a beefsteak to the pigs? Is that not funny, Pepito?" Maria
rocked with laughter. Pepito joined her and Eli let himself smile.

"But, *señor*, they like the flowers more." Maria laughed even
harder.

Her laughter was infectious and Eli joined in.

As he laughed he marveled at how she lit up a room. He had
never met anyone who made him feel so bad and then so good —
that made him feel so alive.

They laughed until Pancho entered the room and slumped over
the kitchen table.

Blood from a gunshot wound leaked onto the tabletop and
spilled over onto the floor.

Maria immediately ran to his aide. *"¿Pancho? ¿Pancho? ¿Qué
pasó?"*

Pancho reached up and pulled Maria's head down to his lips.
He whispered something in her ear, shuddered, and died.

Maria kissed him on the forehead and, gently, closed his eyes.
She looked at Eli, once again with hate in her eyes.

Eli gave her a steady gaze.

"¡Gringos! Damn you! *¡Gringos!"* Maria leaped at Eli and tried
to scratch out his eyes.

Eli grabbed her arms and stopped her assault. He shoved her
into a chair. "What the hell are you talking about? You think I
killed this man?"

"No, *señor*, but your people did!"

"My people?"

"Just go! Leave this house, now!"

Maria wiped a smudge of blood off her face.

"No! Not until I know what I am accused of."

"Death and destruction. That is what you are and what follows
you. You have brought nothing but pain to our village. Please go,
now!"

Eli looked at Pepito.

Pepito shrugged. "What is it, Maria? What did Pancho say?"
Pepito wondered.

Maria's eyes misted but she did not cry. She looked at Pancho
than at Pepito. She pointed her index finger at Eli. "The friends
of this man … they killed all the men we sent for the guns. They
left Pancho for dead but he lived to come here and tell us this."

"What friends? I have no friends down here … Scotty? No!

Scotty would not do this."

"No! The one who came for you. The one who rode away and his partner. Pancho said it was the man who came for you and a man with *uno ojo!*" Maria paused.

"Uno ojo? What does that mean, Pepito? What is she saying?"

Pepito swallowed hard. He looked sad. "Do you not search for a man with one eye?"

"Jules?" Eli wondered aloud as he nodded "Yes" to Maria's question.

"Jules and Lyle? I don't understand. I thought you said the general had them?"

"We are to believe you innocent?" Maria snarled cynically.

"I don't give a damn what you believe. You just tell me where this happened and I'll take care of the men who did this," Eli said coldly.

Maria studied the serious look in Eli's eyes. She thought it over. "You will do this all by yourself?"

"Just tell me where it happened. Please."

Maria looked at Pepito.

Pepito shrugged. "He is not a government spy, Maria. I believe he wants to help us."

"Sí, he has been so much help already?" Maria did not agree.

"Look! Whatever you think of me, as you said, I came here for the one-eyed man and I want Lyle. Do you want the men who killed Pancho or not?" Eli growled.

Maria sighed hard. "There is more here than your revenge or my revenge. It is *por la revolution!* Pancho was one of our Generals. Not like Nogales. He was a man beloved of the people. He was my brother."

"I'm sorry. I'm very sorry," Eli said as he watched some men reverently carry Pancho's body away.

"He was to bring us guns. Guns that Nogales will use against his own people. Now your friends have these guns."

"They ain't my friends!"

"Maria, we need his help. Please?" Pepito said.

"No, Pepito. He rides for his own reasons. He does not ride for us. Thank you, *señor,* but we will take care of this matter ourselves."

Eli shook his head in dismay. He looked at Pepito for help.

"No, Maria! I trust him and we need his help."

"Stay out of this brother!"

"No! We can do nothing without those guns. You are wrong, my sister." Pepito paused and looked at Eli. "Pancho was to ambush the soldiers at the arroyo that passes between the hills in Guadalupe. I will take you there myself!" Pepito stood tall.

"Pepito! You are wrong to do this."

"No, sister. You will see that I am right."

"*Gringos* do not care about our problems. He will betray us. You will see." Maria turned away, angry.

"Thank you, Pepito. I'll take you up on your offer. Why don't you draw it out for me. You are in no shape to be riding."

"I am well enough. I must go to show you places that cannot be drawn on maps." Pepito paused and took on a very serious look. "Now that Pancho is dead, I am the new General!"

Eli thought it over and nodded agreement.

Maria started to storm from the room. She stopped as she looked at the determination in Pepito's eyes. "*Es verdad.* This is true. This is sad that we fight a war with children as generals."

"I'm sixteen, Sister. Do not call me a child any more!"

Maria looked impressed.

"Maybe so, but if you insist on doing this, I will go also."

"I don't think so …" Eli started to object.

"This is not your decision, *señor.* It is the General's," Maria snapped.

Pepito liked the sound of Maria's words. "And the General gives Maria permission."

Eli shook his head in dismay. He didn't like it but he had little choice.

"Would you be ready to ride out tomorrow morning early, Mr. Eli?" Pepito asked.

"Yes. Tonight if you want."

"No, tonight we must have a ceremony for Pancho and bury him with honors. Then, as he would have wished, we will have a small *fiesta. Mañana* is soon enough to ride into danger."

Eli looked at Maria. She did not seem happy.

"Besides you have a beefsteak to eat, *señor.*" Maria smirked.

Eli nodded agreement. He picked up a fork and stuck it in the beefsteak. He walked out of the hut and over to the pig sty. He looked back at Maria and smiled as he threw it to the pigs.

CHAPTER SEVENTEEN

Stella was riddled with regret. She hated herself. She cursed herself for being so impulsive — so stupid. "How in God's name could I let that big dumb Irishman touch me?" she growled into her dressing mirror.

It was the morning after the day she had been so foolhardy. She had awakened with the worst headache of her life and the headache powders had not helped. She had poured two fingers of whiskey to ease the pain. She sipped the whiskey as she looked at herself in the mirror.

She was interrupted by a knock on the door.

"Go away!" she growled.

"Madam, it's Rosie. I have a letter …"

"… I'll read it later!"

"I believe it is from your mother and father. It has a New York posting."

Stella leaped from her stool and ran to the door. She pulled it open and reached for the letter.

She took the letter and shut the door in Rosie's face without comment. Her hands shook as she opened the letter and read:

My Dear Child,

As you know we are not able to write so Father Donegan is writing this for us. He read us your last letter and we have to say we were happy on the announcement of a grandchild. We do not understand all you told us about your new station in life, but we must admit to some satisfaction for you.

If you still wish, we would like to attend the baby's christening. The money you have sent is generous and we wish to thank you for it. But do not send anymore until we are able to talk.

We await your reply.

As always,

Sean and Mary

"Oh, thank you, God! Thank you!" Stella shouted as she ran from the room to Big Ben's bedside. She held the letter up and waved it around in the air as Big Ben looked at her with his laughing eyes.

Big Ben was going on three now and he loved to play. He thought his mother was playing and he laughed out loud. He jumped up and down on the bed like it was a trampoline. "Mommy! Mommy! Jump! Jump!" Big Ben wanted her to jump on the bed with him.

"Ben! Ben! They are coming. They are coming to see us! Oh, God! They have forgiven me! Oh, glorious day!"

Ben looked disappointed. Stella looked at him and thought it over. She took off her shoes and leapt up on the bed. She and Ben jumped and laughed until Rosie entered the room.

Rosie looked at them with a look of doubt, then shrugged. "Madam, I hate to bother you but there is a gentleman caller."

Stella stopped jumping and gave Ben a big hug. She walked over to Rosie and glared at her. She grabbed Rosie by the arm and dragged her into the hallway. She slammed the door shut before she addressed her.

"Don't ever! ... ever announce a gentleman caller in front of my son. You understand?" Stella snarled.

"I'm sorry, madam," Rosie looked scared. "I'll tell him to go away.

"No! Now that you've disturbed my fun, tell me who it is?"

Rosie looked even more scared. "I'm sorry, madam. It's Shannon. I told him to go away but he just won't. He brings flowers."

Stella's face turned beet red. "Oh? Well, you go tell him that I don't know any Shannon! You go tell him ... No, I'll do it!" Stella insisted as she stormed down the stairs.

Shannon waited at the bottom of the stairs holding roses in his hand. He smiled like a happy schoolboy until he saw the look of anger on Stella's face.

"I want you out of my house, now!"

"Stella? ... Stella, I ..."

"Don't you dare address me as Stella! Just go, now!"

Shannon looked intimidated for only a moment. "No! No, I won't. Not until you tell me what the hell is going on."

"There is nothing going on except your leaving this house. Now will you leave or do I have to summon the constables?"

"Yes, maybe you do. But first summon the loony boys. I think maybe someone *HAS* gone crazy here."

Stella looked at him with contempt. "You think what you like but I'll tell you this. That someone made a mistake and it was just that, a mistake. No one is to imply anything else. No one is to think that what happened meant anything to anyone. Most of all, no one is to say anything to anyone about it or they will be awfully sorry. Do you understand?"

Shannon could not believe his ears. He took the flowers he was holding and threw them on the floor.

"You *ARE* crazy." Shannon paused.

He looked her in the eye. "You are crazy but don't think that you can intimidate Shannon O'Bannion. I will do and say what I like and the likes of you don't scare me one damn bit!"

"You have no idea how much money I have and how much I'm willing to use it to destroy you if you so much as utter a peep about us."

Shannon knew that was no idle threat. He had never seen a woman as strong as Stella, and he had never hated and loved someone so much in his life.

"It's Big Ben, isn't it?"

"Don't you dare call my Benjamin, 'Big Ben'!".

Shannon shook his head in dismay. He thought it over. "Fine. Maybe this is a good thing. To do this early is best," he stopped and looked sad.

"I give you my silence if you give me your pledge that no action is to be taken against Rosie. I want no harm to come to her because of this matter between us. Understood?"

"I'll think about it."

"Well, you think a long time about it. Neither you nor your money scares me. But I know what scares you. I know you are scared to death of admitting what you really are." Shannon stared her down. "Just remember I know that."

"Don't threaten me, Shannon. Just go! Just go and do not come again. Understood?"

Shannon put on his hat, slowly.

"I don't threaten. I promise. Good day, Madam Winslow."

Stella did not reply but waited until he was outside the door, then she slammed it hard.

Stella picked up the flowers, reopened the door and threw them in the snow. She slammed the door hard once more then turned and stormed up the stairs. She entered Ben's bedroom and looked at Rosie, who stood in a corner looking very worried. Stella could not look Rosie in the eye.

"I think it is time you looked for other employment, Rosie. I will give you thirty days to look. I want you gone at the end of that time," Stella said coldly.

"No, ma'am! I cannot be held responsible for Shannon's actions. He has always caused the family trouble. I promise he will not ever come here again!"

"I can't take that chance. I will be fair. I will give you a generous severance bonus. I will not mention it in references."

"No, ma'am! I don't want to leave here. I love it here. I don't want to leave … Ben …"

"I'm sorry, Rosie. I have made my decision and it's final!"

"Rosie, jump! Rosie, jump!" Ben started jumping on the bed once more.

Rosie looked at him with tears in her eyes.

"No, Ben! Rosie isn't going to play anymore!" Stella moved to him and picked him up. "Rosie has to go back to her home. Mother will jump with you." Stella paused and looked hard at Rosie. "Will you leave us now?"

Rosie sighed hard. She smiled at Ben.

Ben smiled back and held his small hand out to her.

Stella pulled his hand back.

"Yes, madam. If that is your wish, I will go," she paused. "I do not require thirty days. I will be gone in the morning."

"Fine. See to it!"

Rosie took one last long look at Ben. He looked confused for only a moment before he pushed at Stella and reached his arms out for Rosie.

"Rosie, jump! Rosie …"

"See! See what you've done! You've turned my son against me."

"No, ma'am …"

"Don't give me that! You've been working on him day and night. God knows it'll take me months to purge you from his system! I want you to leave tonight!" Stella's eyes were drunk with rage.

Rosie had always been a little scared of her. Now she was afraid for her life. "Yes, ma'am! I will see to packing now." Rosie said, quickly, then turned and left the room.

"Rosie, jump, Mamma?" Ben looked disappointed.

Stella put Ben on the bed and took off her shoes once more. She got up on the bed and looked down at him.

"No! Mamma and Ben jump, see!" Stella started jumping.

Ben ignored her. He got down on the floor and started to move to the door.

Stella leaped off the bed, ran and closed the door before he reached it.

Ben looked at her with anger and sat down and began to cry.

Stella leaned back against the door and shivered with rage.

CHAPTER EIGHTEEN

Scotty looked at Eli and nodded agreement. "Sounds good to me. What about you boys?" he asked his men.

Shorty and the others nodded agreement.

"But you're tellin' me that Jules and Lyle knocked off a troop of soldiers and a bunch of *banditos?*"

"No, I expect they waited until they had mostly killed each other."

"Sounds like Jules, alright. When do you want to head out?"

"In the morning. Tonight you boys are invited over to Pepito's for a small *fiesta.*" Eli sipped on a glass of beer and looked melancholy.

"Well, that sounds mighty fine. What time we going?"

"An hour after sunset. You'll hear the firecrackers. Just follow the sound and the smell of fine *tortillas* cooking."

Scotty looked at Eli and knew something was wrong.

"Okay, spill it. What's goin' on? I get the feelin' you ain't in a party mood."

Eli shrugged. "I'm kind tired. It'll be a long day tomorrow. You boys go and have fun."

"I smell a woman. Hot damn! Eli's done got all tangled up with a woman. Maria? That's her name?"

"It ain't exactly like that."

"The hell it ain't! A man don't get moon-eyed like you over nothing else but a woman. Well, damn! I might change my mind about riding out with you. I don't want no lovesick dude watching my backside."

"I told you it ain't exactly like that!"

"Then what exactly is it like? You level with me, laddie, because we're talking about some serious business tomorrow."

"You're right, Scotty. I was out of line. I think I'd better go to the *fiesta* and decide what is what. If I don't, I don't expect you to ride out with me."

"That's the spirit, laddie. Let's go dance us a jig and drink us a lot of beer … because tomorrow? Tomorrow, well hell, let's worry about tomorrow when it gets here. Right, Mamacita?" Scotty smiled.

Mamacita looked at Scotty and agreed.

Her face broke into a mischievous smile. Scotty looked into her eyes and a pleasant memory passed between them. Eli picked it up.

"You? You and Mamacita, Scotty? Good, Lord! I leave you for a few hours and whoop de do! And you're on my back about getting tangled up with women."

"… it ain't … exactly like that, Eli." Scotty kidded.

Eli laughed. Mamacita and Scotty joined him.

"Your friend, *Señor* Scotty is a naughty boy," she paused. "But I think this is good."

"Yes. Well I suspect we'd better get going if we're to make it to this *fiesta,*" Scotty looked embarrassed.

"What about the boys?" Eli wondered.

"Mamacita found them some friendly company. They might join us later."

Eli nodded agreement. He left Mamacita a five-dollar tip and they moved outside the *cantina*. They walked down the street quietly for a long moment. Scotty sighed hard and looked worried.

"You worried that Mamacita is going to get serious?" Eli kidded.

"No. No, it's not that."

"Oh? I haven't seen you look so serious since your wedding day."

"There's something I have to tell you, Eli. You're my friend and I don't know how to tell you what I have to tell you."

Eli looked puzzled only a moment. "Just telling me would be one way?"

Scotty stopped and looked Eli in the eye. "Dr. Bulloch was in his cups and he said … he told me this and even though he was a little tipsy I put stock in it."

"What, Scotty? What is it?"

"Stella was with child when she left for Boston. I'm sorry. I thought you should know."

Eli looked stunned only a moment. It hurt him very badly to hear what Scotty had told him, but he was not going to let his friend see how much. For a moment his thoughts turned to Lydia and the unborn son that died with her.

Stella had killed all the love Eli had for her by sending Lyle to kill him. But for a child, a child of his, Eli might have to forgive her.

"Dr. Bulloch could be wrong. But those who saw her board the ship know this to be true," Scotty sighed. "I'm sorry, my friend."

"You have nothing to apologize for. Whatever is true, it will wait until this business is finished." Eli smiled. "As to Stella and Boston, well, I expect Captain Hopkins' good soul will look out for me on that." Eli seemed comforted with that thought.

Scotty nodded agreement.

Spanish guitars played a *flamenco* song as they approached Pepito's home. Eli paused and bought some flowers from a vendor. Scotty looked at him with concern.

"Pig food," Eli smiled.

Scotty shook his head as they walked up to the door and knocked. Pepito opened the door and greeted them. "Welcome. Welcome, *Señor* Eli and …"

"Scotty. Pepito, this is my friend, Scotty."

Scotty and Pepito nodded a greeting.

"Come in and meet all my relatives and those who will be riding with us, *mañana.*" Pepito moved aside and let them in.

Eli could not stop his eyes from searching for Maria but she was not to be seen.

"Maria is at the chapel. She lights candles for Pancho. But here we celebrate his life by drinking much *cerveza*. He would be happy for this."

Pepito read Eli's mind.

"Aye, a good old Irish wake!" Scotty agreed.

Pepito looked puzzled as he led them to the refreshment table.

Scotty almost cried as he saw a bottle of Scotch whisky. He picked it up and stroked it reverently. "My, God, laddie. Where on earth did you get this?"

Pepito looked sad then grinned. "It was Pancho's favorite. He was saving it for his wedding day. But he would be happy if a friend enjoyed it, I am sure. Please enjoy, *Señor* Scotty."

"I didn't know the man but I say God rest his soul!" Scotty opened the bottle and poured himself and Eli a small glass. He sipped it with a look of ecstasy. "… and his taste in whiskey was superb!" Scotty exclaimed.

Eli nodded agreement.

He and Scotty enjoyed several drinks as they met the friendly Mexicans who were going to ride to avenge Pancho in the morning. Eli grew increasingly melancholy as the guitar music seeped into his reverie.

Scotty was trying to teach a *señorita* a jig. She seemed to enjoy Scotty. Eli was happy for him, but feeling sorry for himself as he wandered off.

Children were playing in the courtyard, and their laughter made Eli feel tight in his chest. The thought that he might have a child in far off Boston made him feel both happy and sad. Stella had been a major disappointment in his life but if she had borne him a child — maybe a son, that would have to be dealt with.

Eli began walking out of Pepito's house, his mind foggy with these thoughts. He had gone some distance away, when he saw the small chapel.

Without realizing it, he wandered inside and saw Maria kneeling at a small wooden altar ablaze with burning candles.

She was wearing a black *mantilla* that outlined her chestnut Spanish eyes so that they outshone the candlelight. She was a breathtakingly beautiful woman and he found his legs were hard to move as he stood and watched her.

She looked up and saw him. She looked puzzled a moment.

Eli wanted to run but his feet would not move.

Maria made the sign of the cross and said a silent prayer. She got up and moved toward him.

"You wish to light a candle for Pancho?" she asked as she stood before him.

Eli would have rather fought another bear than be where he was. Maria intimidated him and he felt like a little boy in her presence. It was stupid but he couldn't get his tongue working right when she was near. "A candle?"

"Yes. Over there. You may leave whatever offering for the poor you wish."

"Oh? I see."

"Are you all right, *Señor* Eli?"

"Oh … yes. I'm fine. How are you?"

"I'm fine. I said the rosary nine times for Pancho. Are you Catholic?"

"Aaaahhmmm … no. No, I'm not … I'm sorry."

"You do not have to apologize to me. But this is a Catholic

church. Is that what you were looking for?"

"Ah! … well … you see …"

"The *fiesta*? It can't be over?"

"No! No, it's going fine. I …" Eli tried to think. Her intoxicating aura made that difficult.

"I came to thank Pancho for the Scotch whisky. Could I and Scotty donate to the poor in his name?"

Maria smiled. "Yes. The poor box is right there. Father Dominquez will appreciate whatever you want to give," she paused. "And so will Pancho."

"And you?"

Maria shrugged indifference.

Eli put three twenty-dollar gold pieces in the poor box. He looked at Maria, then put another two in. He was happy she seemed impressed.

She turned and began to walk out of the church.

Eli watched her go.

For some reason his hand reached out for the handle of his Colt. The feel of the walnut handle was, strangely, soothing. The gun was a good friend and renewed the strength Maria had so easily sapped.

"Aahhmmm … can I escort you back to the *fiesta*?" Eli moved up behind her.

Maria looked at him, doubtfully, then nodded quiet agreement. They walked along, quietly, for a long moment. The night was soft and warm and the *flamenco* music wafted down the street. A full moon nestled in a cradle of foothills in the distance.

The moonlight made Maria the most beautiful woman in the world.

Even the feel of the gun handle did not dispel the power her beauty had over him. It took more courage than Eli had ever used shooting a man, to reach out for Maria's hand.

Maria moved her hand away and Eli started to curse himself. "I'm sorry. I didn't mean anything by it."

Maria looked up at him with fiery eyes that turned mellow. Her face broke into a soft, inviting smile. "You know, you apologize too much!" she insisted as she put her long arms around his neck and pulled her lips to his.

Eli was caught off guard for only a moment. He eased his strong hands around her waist and lifted her to him.

She was wonderful to touch and hold.

There was a deep spiritual quality to this embrace he had never known. Some divine touch caressed them with a familiar innocence and their spirits blended.

They kissed subdued kisses like Lydia gave him. They kissed the hurried, formal kisses Stella had given him.

Then they kissed the intoxicating, fiery kisses of passion. Passion that had eluded Eli all his life, until this moment.

All his fears left him in an instant, and for the first time in his life, he believed he knew what real love was.

CHAPTER NINETEEN

Lyle looked at Jules suspiciously. Lyle knew he had struck a bargain with the devil. He only hoped that he could get out alive with his soul intact.

The more Lyle thought about it, the more he knew it had been a bad idea. Jules was no more a gun runner than he was. As he watched Jules try to maneuver himself into a bit of information that would lead to a legitimate gun runner he worried.

They had captured twelve cases of rifles and thirty cases of munitions, including grenades. It was a big haul and even covered with a tarp, Lyle felt it attracted too many curious eyes.

It was a bad time to be a *gringo* in Mexico and an even worse time to be involved in such a dangerous pursuit. Lyle prided himself on his nerves, but he looked at his hands and they were shaking. Lyle watched Jules move about the *cantina* which was said to be a gathering place for the Mexican underworld.

Lyle smelled a deadly tension in the air. His instincts told him to get out while he could. He turned to leave and bumped into one of the biggest men he had ever seen.

"You ... you are the American with the guns?" The big man with the German accent and the close-cropped hair addressed Lyle. Lyle did not reply as Jules stepped between them.

"Are you Gunnar Zimmermann?" Jules asked.

Gunnar nodded. "Yes."

"There is a back room. We can talk there. I am Jules and this is my partner, Lyle," Jules said then moved toward the back room.

Gunnar nodded recognition of Lyle then turned to three swarthy men and told them something with his eyes.

Lyle would have made it to the exit had not the three men stood in his way. Reluctantly, he followed Gunnar to the back room.

The back room was dimly lit, which was to Jules' liking.

Lyle moved into the background with his back to a wall and facing the door.

Gunnar moved to a small table and sat down. He pulled out a big cigar and lit it. Jules sat at the table with him.

They sized each other up quietly for a moment.

"So how is it you came by these guns?" Gunnar grinned.

"Is that important?"

"Not to me. But maybe to the government. They are very mad that someone has killed many soldiers."

"I don't know anything about any government. I just sell guns," Jules snapped.

"I see. You sell them many times before?"

"Of course. What is this anyway? I was told you were a serious gun dealer."

"And I am. But you? The question is, are you a serious gun dealer?"

"What the hell do you mean by that?"

Gunnar lay his huge hands on the table. He balled them into huge fists then unclenched them and smiled at Jules. His three men moved into the room and took strategic positions.

Lyle edged toward the door.

"I mean, *señor,* that you are not a gun dealer. You are a thief!" Gunnar posed.

"You're a damned liar!" Jules leaped from his chair and started to go for his gun. Gunnar's men already had theirs out.

Lyle held his hands up and tried to look friendly. He cursed himself for not leaving sooner.

Jules showed no fear as he growled at Gunnar. "Well, you think what you want, mister. I can sell those guns lots of places."

"I don't think so. Now sit down!" Gunnar barked like an Army drill instructor.

Jules was not easily intimidated, but Gunnar's tone and his men's guns were too much to deal with for now. Jules eased back down in his chair.

"Well, I can see I was told some bad information. Maybe we can just have a drink and forget it," Jules hoped.

"I don't think so," Gunnar said coldly.

"Look, mister. I don't know what you want but if we can't do business, I've got other things to do."

Gunnar gave Jules an icy stare that would have made some men mess their pants. Jules gave him an unblinking return stare. Gunnar seemed to like that.

"You are not afraid of me?"

"I'm not afraid of any man."

"Good! This is good. I have not met three men in my lifetime who could withstand my mojo. You are a thief but you are also a hard man like me."

"I told you I ain't …"

"Please, Jules. Don't begin our partnership with a lie."

"From what I've seen we ain't got no partnership."

Gunnar looked at Lyle. "Are you in this with him?"

Lyle hesitated a long moment. "He's the boss. I'm just along for the ride."

"You're the sharpshooter, aren't you?"

"I don't understand?"

"I'm told someone dropped five soldiers each with a single shot to the head. I do not think it was *Señor* Jules. I think maybe he is a backshooter."

Jules leaped to his feet again. "Look, mister! I don't have to take nothing from you!" Jules stopped as Gunnar's men cocked their guns. "You aim to steal my merchandise. Is that it?"

Gunnar looked hurt. "Jules? I am not the thief here. You hurt my feelings. I was going to make a most generous offer. Now I don't feel that is possible."

"That's okay by me because I don't aim to sell them to you anyways." Jules' anger was clouding his reason.

"I have something to say about that, Jules." Lyle stepped up and looked at Gunnar. "You have us at a disadvantage, Mr. Zimmermann," he grinned. "You know a lot more about us than we do about you."

Gunnar gave Lyle his stony stare. Lyle did not flinch. Gunnar grinned approval. "That was some shooting you did. A rifle?"

Lyle nodded agreement. "We rode into the situation. We did not start it."

"Of course. I know this or I would not be here. I have friends in the government, you understand?"

"I told you we ain't with no government," Jules snarled.

Gunnar got up from the table and turned his back on Jules as he addressed Lyle. "You understand, it would not be possible to deal with you if my friends in the government suspected who you were. It is good for you they think the *banditos* have the guns," he turned back to Jules. "I will deal with this man," he motioned to Lyle.

Jules started to object, then shrugged. "You got the upper hand, mister. It appears ... for now ... you can do what you like."

"So tell me. What are you asking for the lot?" Gunnar looked serious.

Lyle did not have a clue, so he looked at Jules. "He's the businessman, Mr. Zimmermann."

"I see. You heard the question," he turned to Jules. "How much?"

Jules was caught off guard. He had no real idea of the worth of the merchandise. He knew Gunnar was just waiting for him to name a silly amount.

"You know what they're worth. We don't need to haggle."

"Yes, I know. But do you? I think not."

"Well, you think what you want. Now you gonna make us an offer or not?"

Gunnar laughed. He looked back at Lyle. "I could use a good sharpshooter like you. How would you like to make a thousand a month?"

Lyle was impressed.

"We ain't here to talk about sharpshootin'. I want to know ..."

"Shut up, Jules! Just shut up!" Gunnar insisted. "We'll talk about guns when I say so. Now, Lyle, what about it?"

Lyle thought it over. "Maybe we should finish the business with the guns first?"

Gunnar looked displeased only a moment. "Five thousand American for the whole lot."

"The hell you say! Them munitions is worth a hundred times that!" Jules growled.

Lyle had to agree with Jules on that point. "I don't want to sound greedy, but that's mighty low, Mr. Zimmermann."

"Oh? Maybe so. Seven thousand five hundred, ... oh make it ten thousand."

"You know, mister," Jules looked at Gunnar then at his gunmen. "You think I'm a stupid hillbilly, but ain't nobody as stupid as you think. Now I think it's time you treated me with some respect or we'll just have it out right here and be done with it." Jules' hand moved toward his gun — without a hint of fear.

Gunnar studied their eyes. Lyle's look was steady. Jules eye was fierce. Gunnar had never seen the crazy look in a man's eyes he saw in Jules' one eye. Jules was a scary person to look upon, even for a strong man like Gunnar.

"Fifteen thousand and that's my last offer!"

"Them guns is worth at least fifty thousand!" Jules shot back.

Gunnar looked incredulous. "Then damnit, you find somebody who'll pay that! Everybody in the territory will be looking for those guns. They could get a man put up before a firing squad. You're lucky I'm even talking to you!"

"He's right, Jules." Lyle stepped up. "How about twenty thousand, Mr. Zimmermann. All things considered that seems a fair amount."

Gunnar thought it over. "Maybe so if I can get you to come work for me as a sharpshooter?"

Lyle thought it over and shook his head, "No, sir. I think I need to clean up a few matters and get on back home. Thank you, anyways."

"We ain't taking no pitiful twenty thousand!" Jules gritted his teeth.

"Shut up, Jules! I mean it!" Lyle growled.

Jules started to object but thought better of it. He was outnumbered for now. He would bide his time and kill Lyle some other time and place.

Gunnar smiled. "Twenty thousand it is. Deal! Now the drinks are on me. To the bar, gentlemen. Here they have the finest whiskey and the prettiest whores!"

Jules looked at Lyle and his anger did not dissipate even at the thought of such delights.

Lyle looked at Jules' evil eye and now knew for sure he had made a pact with Satan himself.

⊠ ⊠ ⊠

General Nogales was furious with his son, Carlos. Carlos was still a dreamer in a time when dreaming could get you killed.

He knew Carlos meant well but that did not make it right. He stared at the fear in his son's eyes and looked as stern as his heart would allow. "It is not enough that these men escape but I believe they have our guns. Do you know what this means?"

Carlos nodded agreement.

"Then what should I do to you for this? I would shoot any of my men for this. Am I to treat you different than my men?"

Carlos shook his head "No!"

"Aye, caramba! Your mother held you too close to her breast. It is my fault that I allowed this. For her sake, I will not shoot you.

But you will leave the barracks and return to the *pueblo* to live with the women."

"No, Father! Please don't! I'm sorry."

"Get him out of here!" General Nogales ordered two soldiers.

The two soldiers took Carlos by the arms and dragged him screaming and kicking from the room.

"*¡Padre! ¡Por favor!* Father, please!" Carlos begged.

General Nogales turned his back on his son and did not listen to his cries. He hurt inside when he thought of his son Carlos. He lived in fear every day that Carlos would turn out to be a sissy boy. He often wondered if he had been Carlos' real father.

To be ashamed of one's son was a terrible thing to admit, but General Nogales was ashamed of Carlos. In his mind, Carlos belonged with the women. He regretted ever trying to make him a soldier.

General Nogales fumed quietly, then called for Tomas, his orderly. Tomas, a cherubic man who always looked like he was laughing, ran to General Nogales' side.

"Yes, sir!" Tomas asked.

General Nogales did not answer immediately. He puffed on a cigar and sipped from a glass of red wine. "I want you to send some men to find that *alemán* Gunnar Zimmermann. If anyone knows where the guns are … and maybe the men we seek … it is Gunnar," he insisted.

Tomas thought it over. He looked puzzled. "But General, he works for the *Juaristas*, now?"

General Nogales looked displeased for a moment. It was hard to be mad at Tomas. "No, Tomas. Gunnar works for everyone."

CHAPTER TWENTY

Stella enjoyed the widow's walk that bordered the roof of her home. She could go there and look far out to sea. On a peaceful morning, even in a light snowfall, she found it a good place to go to think.

Stella needed to think this day. In a month her parents would be here. It would be a fulfillment of all her dreams to have them come to her elegant home. To have them see how well she had done. To have them look at her with love — with respect.

Stella ached to have her mother just say once, "... I love you, child. I forgive your past and respect your present. I hope for you a bright future."

The cool northeast wind blew, uncommonly warm snowflakes against her skin, as Stella turned her face toward the wind and dared hope her dreams would all come true in a few weeks.

She was mad at herself for firing Rosie. Rosie had been hard to replace.

Helga Von Strudel, the new German housekeeper, was efficient but cold and aloof. However, she did not know Stella's business and that was in her favor.

Stella had been a hefty contributor to Catholic charities headed by Father Brennan. Father Brennan was on her side and that too would please her parents. She and Father Brennan had an unspoken agreement that Shannon would not be discussed.

But deep down, Stella knew it was all a lie.

Everyone in the world outside knew she was of Irish descent, but she was wealthy enough to keep most of their mouths shut. Stella liked the way money could make believers out of the virulent Yankee Irish-baiter. It was true that the descendants of the Massachusetts colony despised the Irish, but they loved money more.

"Madam, a Reverend Talbot and a Mr. Winthrop Adams to see you?" Helga broke into her thoughts.

Stella started to tell Helga to dismiss them when she remembered she had sent for the Reverend. Reverend Talbot was the key to insuring everything was in order. Stella hated the man but he had the position and social persuasion that money could not buy.

Stella had heard the vicious gossip about her and Shannon. The talk of scandal was all about and her parents' visit was imminent. Stella lived in fear her parents would hear the rumors. She felt the solution was to find a respectable Yankee gentleman to parade as a suitor. If need be, she would marry him to be a proper father to Ben.

They would not wag their tongues so much if she took one of their own into her hearth and home.

She had agreed to invest in Reverend Talbot's scheme to buy the marsh land. Stella did not know much about real estate, but if he was right that was where Boston was going to expand. For her financial assistance, Reverend Talbot had agreed to act as a go-between and introduce her to a "proper Boston gentleman".

"Winthrop Adams?" Stella whispered under her breath as she went to her dressing mirror. It sounded "Yankee" enough. She wondered what he looked like. That he be handsome was not the most important thing. Stella had learned long ago how to imagine men were more handsome than they appeared.

What was most important was that she could control him. He must be just the right combination of "proper" and subject to feminine wiles.

But then she felt all men were subject to hers.

She dusted her nose with a last puff of talcum powder and touched the back of her ears with perfume.

She looked at the cleavage between her ample breasts and wondered if it was too much. She wanted to tantalize but not be risqué. It was a hard balance to strike. In some ways she missed the days when she was a sporting woman. It was easy to dress then. Her customers thought the more paint the better and were not scandalized by the sight of a woman's bare breasts.

In proper Boston, it was different. It was alright to hint at cleavage but not to show it. In Stella's mind, small-breasted women had made up that rule.

She thought to ask Helga for advice but knew Helga knew as much about fashion as a forty-niner. In the end, she decided to do the right thing and wore a high-collar dress.

She rummaged around in her jewelry box and looked for something to highlight the dress.

Her hand fell on Lydia's locket and she picked it up. She, quickly, put it down. For an instant, she thought of Eli. In the dark side of her mind she had to hope he was dead. It would be too complicated if he were not. The thought of him returning now and intruding on the life she was making for Ben was too painful to entertain for long.

She found a diamond necklace she liked to take her mind off such thoughts. She thought it looked too pretentious. Finally, she found a conservative brooch that would be accepted in any pew in town. She didn't like it but it seemed the right thing to wear.

She took one last look in the mirror and seemed satisfied. She thought to herself that she looked extra good this day. She was secure in her beauty and thought that whoever Winthrop Adams was, he didn't have a chance.

As it turned out, Winthrop Adams, the gentleman Reverend Talbot chose, was perfect.

He wasn't handsome in a striking way, but he had a nice face. He was a little taciturn and stiff but Stella could deal with that.

Stella felt no warmth in his company but he did have a name — a legitimate name. A name that as respected in Boston and beyond.

"Madam Winslow. Mr. Winthrop Adams," Reverend Talbot introduced.

Stella curtsied and extended her hand. Winthrop shook it weakly. Stella smiled and looked into his cool, blue eyes. She was pleased to see the look of stunned admiration in them.

She knew immediately she had him where she wanted him.

"It's a pleasure to meet you, Mr. Adams."

"You, also, ma'am."

"Yes. I see. Tea? Brandy?" Stella smiled.

"Oh, tea. Yes, by all means. It's much too early in the day for brandy," Winthrop insisted.

Reverend Talbot looked disappointed but agreed.

Stella called for Helga and ordered her to bring a tea service.

After Helga had gone, Stella looked hard at Reverend Talbot, then coyly at Winthrop. "So what has the Reverend been telling you about me?" she asked.

"Oh ... he's been most flattering. ... and I must say, he's been more than right in every respect … thus far …"

"… and do you think me rash, Mr. Adams?"

"Ma'am? I don't understand?"

Stella looked away and tried to look embarrassed. "That I would ask to be introduced?"

"No, ma'am! I respect that. By way of introduction is the only proper way for decent people to meet. I am here to honor that request. It is more than proper these times."

"It's just that I have to be so careful. A rich widow is a target of so many flimflam artists." Stella paused for effect. "I am the subject of so many scurrilous rumors. The good Reverend was kind enough to understand this and help me out."

"Yes, ma'am. But pay no attention to the fishwives. No one really does."

"It's not for me, but for my son, you understand."

"Yes, I do. I hear he is a fine boy."

"He is napping now or I would let you judge for yourself. Some other time, perhaps."

"Yes. Yes, I would like that."

"Winthrop is going to come in with us on the peninsula deal. I hope that meets with your approval?" Reverend Talbot wondered aloud.

Stella looked displeased only a moment. "I rarely mix business with pleasure, but in this case I'll make an exception." Stella watched Winthrop's eyes. He seemed a little embarrassed. She liked that. It would be easier to manipulate him than she had imagined.

"Mr. Adams has the front pew at the church. His family was one of the charter members." Reverend Talbot pursed his lips.

"I would be honored if you would attend services with me on Sunday," Winthrop said.

Stella did not like what he was suggesting. She felt cold for a moment.

She cursed herself for not remembering the religious factor. If she were to climb in Boston society she would have to turn her back on her church.

She would never do that.

She could see from the look on Reverend Talbot's face he liked the position Winthrop had put her in.

Stella knew Reverend Talbot still held some bitter feelings toward her and it was risky to trust him, but she had no choice. "I'm sorry, Mr. Adams. Didn't Reverend Fuller tell you I am a devotee of Margaret Fuller's writings, and I'm unsure at the moment where I stand on religion?"

Reverend Talbot looked confused for a moment. Winthrop looked sympathetic.

"... still a queen without guards a scepter or a throne?" Winthrop posed.

"You have read her?"

"I have engaged in her 'conversations' but I do not share all her views. However, I, like her, am a staunch abolitionist."

"You were invited to the conversations?" Stella was impressed. Only Boston's super elite were invited to the group intellectual discussions Margaret Fuller had held before she died in 1850.

Winthrop smiled "Yes."

"I understand. There are other lectures by prominent thinkers on Margaret Fuller's topics. Perhaps we could attend one of those together?"

"I would be delighted."

Reverend Talbot shifted in his seat. "I don't respect her notions of metaphysical realism. It goes against all that's holy ... Don't you agree with me, Winthrop?"

"Well, I haven't thought too much about that ..."

"I don't think it is a good idea to discuss religion. Particularly at a first meeting. Why don't you tell me where we're at on the peninsula investment?"

"Ah, yes. I have the papers of incorporation almost prepared. They will be ready for your signature by the first of next week."

"I see. You know I will have to have my San Francisco lawyer in-spect them before I can sign them." Stella did not trust Reverend Talbot at all.

"Oh, but Mrs. Winslow. We do not have time for that. Others know what we know and the property values will only increase as the word gets out. We must be in a position to buy within two weeks at the outset," he insisted.

Stella did not like it.

It had the smell of a fast shuffle. She had already put up a hun-dred thousand "good faith" money, but now she wanted out. "No, I do not move without Jason Rubin's approval."

"That will take months. We don't have that kind of time, Mrs. Winslow. I have to agree with the Reverend," Winthrop said.

"I wrote Jason six weeks ago. He should be here in three months, maybe two ..."

"I'm sorry, Mrs. Winslow, but that was not my understanding. I thought I impressed upon you the need for the utmost speed," Reverend Talbot insisted.

"Those are my terms, gentlemen." Stella said coolly. She paused and smiled. "You must understand I am very vulnerable in this arena. I have seen many widows flimflamed out of fortunes." Stella paused. "Jason Rubin is the only one I trust in such matters. Please try to see my side. I am risking everything here."

The Reverend Talbot did not like it. Winthrop nodded sympathy with Stella's position.

"Perhaps some compromise can be worked out that will satisfy everyone," Winthrop offered. "Why don't you let Mrs. Winslow discuss it. ... but not anymore today."

Reverend Talbot grunted reluctant agreement.

"I would be interested in hearing Mrs. Winslow's views on metaphysics, and, perhaps her views of Mr. Thoreau's essays on life in the woods?" Winthrop posed.

"Thoreau? God forbid! He advocates civil disobedience to right so-called social wrongs! Between him and Emerson I don't know who is the worst. I don't know where these radicals come from." Reverend Talbot shook his head in disgust.

"Tea is served," Helga interrupted them.

Stella was grateful for the interruption. "Thank you, Helga. Gentlemen, you may help yourself or Helga will serve it for you."

"Thank you, Mrs. Winslow but the hour is later than I thought," he stopped and looked at Winthrop.

"I have many errands to run. Perhaps another time," Reverend Talbot said as he prepared to leave. "Are you coming, Winthrop?"

Winthrop thought it over as he looked at the Reverend then at Stella.

"If it is alright with Mrs. Winslow, I'll stay a short while longer?" Stella nodded agreement.

"But you've only just met," Reverend Talbot was truly worried.

"It's okay, Reverend. You can trust him, can't you?" Stella kidded.

"Well, I ... I ..."

"It will be fine, Reverend Talbot. I will see you at Vespers this evening," Winthrop was, suddenly, forceful.

Reverend Talbot was not sure but he finally grimaced agreement. "Six o'clock sharp, Winthrop," he said.

"Of course, Reverend. Six o'clock sharp."

Reverend Talbot took his coat from Helga, looked at them critically, then turned and left.

Stella and Winthrop watched him go and both seemed relieved he was leaving.

Some time after he was gone, Winthrop turned and looked at Stella.

Stella was surprised to see the look on his face was now less strained. He had intelligent eyes and he seemed genuinely pleased that the Reverend was gone.

"Mrs. Winslow is that offer of brandy still open?"

Stella smiled. "Well, I suppose so. Yes. Yes, it is," she hesitated and looked at Helga. "That will be all, Helga. Thank you."

Helga shrugged indifference and left. After she was gone, Stella poured them a small glass of brandy.

Winthrop took his glass and raised it in a toast.

"To a new friendship and, I hope, a long one."

Stella looked at him over the edge of her glass. "I must say you surprise me, Mr. Adams."

"I understand. I too have to be cautious of appearances. So much in this town revolves around what one is perceived to be, not what one really is."

"Are you suggesting *I* put up a false front?"

"No! I did not mean that. I just meant you seemed as uncomfortable as I was. 'I am but a parcel of vain strivings tied by a chance bond together ...' "

Winthrop mused aloud.

Stella looked puzzled.

"Henry David Thoreau. Have you not read him?"

"No. ... no, I haven't."

"He is as radical in his own right as Margaret Fuller was in hers."

"Well, if Reverend Talbot doesn't like him, then I'll read him."

"I'll bring you a copy of his best essays on next meeting."

"Fine, I'll look forward to it."

"Well, there is a lecture at Faneuil Hall on Wednesday next."

"Faneuil Hall. Where the Know-Nothings meet?" Stella frowned.

Winthrop sipped at his glass of brandy as he nodded agreement.

"Yes. But the lecture I'm speaking of is a comparative analysis of the differences and similarities between Thoreau and Emerson."

"I see. Wednesday ... next."

"It would be my pleasure to escort you."

Stella sipped at her glass of brandy and thought it over. There was a certain cool, attractive charm about Winthrop. She had been prepared to dislike him but she was warming to him. He was taller and not as muscular as men she was usually attracted to. But that was not the important thing. She did not have to have any special yearnings for him, she just had to be able to tolerate his company. She thought to herself she might not only tolerate his company, but enjoy, it as well. "What time may I expect you?"

"The lecture starts at eight o'clock. May I call for you at seven?"

"That would be fine, Mr. Adams."

"Please call me, Winnie."

"Winnie?"

"It's not so pretentious. I had no control over my parents taste in monikers."

"Winnie it is."

"May I address you as Stella?"

"Please do."

"May I say, Stella, it has been a great pleasure meeting you."

"I must say it was a pleasant surprise meeting you ... Winnie."

Winthrop finished his glass of brandy and looked at Stella. "I would like to leave you with the confidence that whatever transpires between us will be treated with the utmost discretion."

"Oh? I see."

"I do appreciate your position. I just wanted you to know that."

"Oh, ... I see."

"I hope so, Stella. I really do. Until our next meeting then?"

Stella smiled as she thought it over.

"Good day, Winnie." Stella said as Winnie took his hat and left.

Moments after he was gone, she went to the widow's walk and watched him walk away in the soft afternoon snowfall.

Chapter Twenty-one

Maria was a heady intoxicant that awakened all of Eli's senses and numbed the smallest intrusion of reality. Eli had been denied the joys of childhood. When he should have been carefree and child-like he was made to labor as a man. He had never had a Christmas tree, notions of Santa Claus, or the simplest toy, and he had never enjoyed an easy laugh until he met Maria.

With her he was the little boy he had never been. With her he could leave the old, dank darkness of the coal mines and romp in sun-filled meadows chasing butterflies. With her, visions of sugarplums and long-forbidden dreams began to dance in his head. He drank her in as a man drinks from a well after days of thirsting in a bony desert. He gulped down her beauty and being and could not get enough. He did not want to leave her presence. He did not want her to ever go away.

Eli awoke to the rude reality of a cock crowing. The bright morning sun broke into the pleasant remains of the childish dream he was enjoying. He smiled as he reached over to put his arm around Maria.

She was not there.

He eased up in bed and wondered if last night had been a dream. His heart skipped a beat until he looked at the pillow beside him and saw the indentation. He sniffed the air and smelled traces of her perfume. He picked up a strand of her dark hair. He sighed hard. She had been here and it had not been a dream. Eli figured she was outside in Mamacita's courtyard washing herself. He was a happy man as he got up and dressed himself. He could smell the tantalizing smoke from the cooking of fresh *tortillas*. He knew that meant Mamacita was fixing breakfast — or maybe it was Maria?

Eli tried not to hurry outside, but his pace was measurably faster than normal. He entered the courtyard as the rooster that had awakened him scurried away. He was disappointed to see Mamacita was doing the cooking and not Maria.

"*¡Buenas dias! Señor* Eli. You slept late this morning. The sun she has been up two hours already."

Eli looked at the sun, climbing toward noon. He looked back at Mamacita and nodded agreement. "Could I have a dozen of those and some beans when they are ready?" Eli looked at the *tortillas* hungrily.

"*¡Sí!* You have the bad hungries? Did you work *mucho* hard last night?" She giggled.

Eli was too serious about Maria to laugh, at first. Finally, he grinned. "No. No, not at all."

"*Sí, sí.* I must tell you I have not seen such a smile from you since you come here." Mamacita paused and looked serious a moment. "But you are my friend so I say, *¡cuidado!* Be careful with thees one. She has broken many hearts."

Eli did not like to hear that. He did not think it deserved a reply. He shrugged and turned to a wash basin. He washed himself quietly.

"Have you seen anyone this morning?" Eli asked as he strapped on his gun belt and pretended to be talking about the weather.

"Anyone or someone?"

"Okay, have you seen Maria?"

Mamacita looked a little hurt. "I did not want to say anything to hurt you, my friend. You understand anything I say is because of our friendship?"

Eli gave her a half-smile.

"Maria left before the sun came up," she paused. "I will say no more, for if I do I think we will not be *amigos.*"

"Thanks," Eli said as he started to leave.

"But *Señor* Eli ... your *tortillas* ... and your beans?"

Eli was no longer hungry. He walked into the dusty street and took longer than normal strides as he made his way to her house.

He did not have to open the door. Pepito was coming out of it on his way to loading pack mules.

"*Señor* Eli. You are here and you are ready to go chasing the bad men today?"

Eli looked past Pepito to see if he could see Maria inside the house. Pepito shook his head knowingly.

"I am sorry. She is not here."

"Where is she? I need to talk to her."

Pepito hesitated.

"Where is she, Pepito?" Eli insisted.

"*Señor* Eli, we must ride this morning if we are to find a trail to follow. We have wasted too much time already."

"Where?"

Pepito pointed toward the chapel. He looked at Eli and looked sad. "She has been there all morning. I think she speaks with Father Dominquez."

Eli turned to go to the chapel. Pepito ran around in front of him and tried to stop him. Eli started to shove him aside.

"Please, *Señor* Eli! I do not think it is a good time to speak with her."

"What the devil is wrong with everybody! All of a sudden they want to poke around in my business!" He paused and looked at Pepito. "Get out of my way, Pepito!"

Pepito looked sad as he, reluctantly, moved aside. "*Señor*, you do not understand about Maria."

"I know all I need to know."

"No, *Señor* Eli. You do not!"

Eli saw the troubled look on Pepito's face and wondered if he did want to know what Pepito was determined to tell him.

"Spill it, Pepito. I'm in a hurry."

"Maria, she is ... she is sort of married to ... to a General in the Army — General Nogales. It is very bad for everyone if he knows your business," Pepito looked scared.

Eli felt a sharp pain in his chest. He did not want to believe Pepito but the look on his face was sincere.

"But she is a *Juarista?* How can this be?" Eli wondered aloud.

"She did not choose him, he chose her. It is the way of such powerful men. I am ashamed to say my house is a *casa chica!*"

"*Casa chica?*"

"The general, I am ashamed to say, he pays for all this. I am sorry."

Eli thought it over. "They aren't really married, like man and wife, right, Pepito?"

"No, it is not like that."

"Then, there is nothing between them?" Eli hoped.

Pepito shrugged. "*¡Sí!* But that does not matter to a man like General Nogales. It is said he had his first wife killed for disobeying him. It is not possible to leave him unless he allows it. I do not think he will allow it."

Eli knew enough about the dominance of the culture by powerful males to know Pepito spoke the truth. It made him angry to think of her with another man.

Even a man she might not love.

It gave him a very warm feeling to ponder the terrible risk Maria had taken just to be with him one night.

"I see," Eli thought it over and wondered what to do next. His first thoughts were not of himself but of how to protect her. As much as he loved her, he would get on his horse and ride away — forgetting all he had come for — if he thought that would be best for her.

Pepito read his thoughts. "No one in the village likes this man. If no one tells him anything then he will know nothing," Pepito sighed hard.

"Is she in danger, Pepito?"

"*¿Quién sabe?* Who can say?"

Eli thought it over a long moment. "Do you suppose, by now, General Nogales might have caught and hung the man I am seeking?"

"*¡Sí!* I believe this is possible."

"Then, maybe it's time to go home," Eli sighed. "Do you think she would come with me?"

Pepito's smile showed he liked the idea. "*¿Estados Unidos?* The United States? I could come also?"

Eli smiled "Yes."

"Then she *MUST* agree to come! I will see to it!"

"Did I hear the sweet sound of 'home'?" Scotty interrupted them, followed by Shorty, Chief, and Sam.

Eli looked doubtful. "Just a thought. How are you Scotty?"

"And I say it's a damn fine thought!" Scotty added. "But I thought we were riding to check on Jules?"

"It ain't exactly like that. Seems Jules is dead for sure this time ... and I'm tired, Scotty. Very tired." Eli tried to convince himself.

Scotty looked at Eli then at Pepito. "Well, if you're satisfied, then I'm satisfied. Hot damn! It will be good to get home to Mary!" Scotty was delighted.

Eli smiled thinly. He picked up Maria coming down the street out of the corner of his eye. "Yea. Let's head on back and get ready to ride. The sooner the better." Eli mounted his horse and turned his head away from the direction of Maria.

The feelings he had for her meant that he would be sure to do what would bring her the least harm. It would be hard to head home with so much unfinished business, but that seemed best for Maria.

He was determined to leave her in peace without saying goodbye. Pepito stopped him.

Pepito pulled on Eli's horse's rein. "*Señor* Eli. You must ask Maria if I can go with you? *¿Por favor?*"

Eli started to kick Pepito away and ride off.

He thought better of it.

"Go with him where?" Maria snapped as she approached them.

"Nowhere! We were just joking," Eli snapped back.

"*¡Estados Unidos!* We go to America!" Pepito almost danced.

Maria glared at Eli, then looked angrily at Pepito. "No, you are not!"

"Why not, if he wants to?" Eli glared back. "Get your stuff, Pepito. We leave in an hour."

"No! I said, no!" Maria yanked the reins out of Pepito's hands. Eli's horse reared up on its hind legs. It kicked its feet out toward her. A hoof struck her a glancing blow on the cheek and she tumbled to the ground.

Eli grabbed the loose reins and steadied the horse. He dismounted and moved to Maria's side.

Scotty took the reins and moved the horse aside.

The others gathered around.

"Doggonit, Maria! You shouldn't spook a horse like that! Are you alright?" Eli took his handkerchief and swapped, gently, at the small cut on her cheek.

Maria did not reply for a long moment. Eli's heart almost stopped until he saw her eyes open.

Their eyes met for a brief moment of tender understanding, before Maria shoved Eli away. She glared at him as she moved to Pepito's side. "Is it not enough that my brother Pancho is dead? You wish to kill this one as well?"

Pepito pulled away from her and moved beside Eli. "I told you, sister. I am a grown man. I can go where I please!"

"You will not go with this man!"

"I will!"

Eli stepped between them. "No, Pepito. She's right. You're the only family she has left."

"You take her side, *Señor* Eli? You are not my *amigo* because she is a woman ... a woman who you want ... you want to take her with you?" Pepito cried.

"Shut up, Pepito. That's uncalled for. Just button it up!" Eli insisted.

Maria seemed to agree with him. "Thank you, *señor.* *¡Vaya con Dios!*"

Eli tipped his hand to his hat. He turned to mount his horse. He took one more quick look, at Maria. Her face showed no emotion.

"Then we're leaving ... for sure, Eli?" Scotty asked dubiously.

Eli nodded "Yes."

Scotty motioned for his men to mount their horses. They were about to when a rider came down the street at full speed. He was a young Mexican and he looked very scared as he pulled his horse up in front of the house.

"*¡Señorita!* General Nogales. He is coming. He brings many men and he is coming this way!" he said before he slumped to his knees and fell over unconscious.

CHAPTER TWENTY-TWO

There was no honor among these thieves. As Gunnar and his men drank whiskey with Jules and Lyle, they did so with suspicious eyes — and their gun hands at the ready.

"So where are the guns?" Gunnar asked as he looked over his glass at Jules.

Jules was eyeing a small buxom brunette and did not reply for a moment. "Don't you worry none, Mr. Zimmermann. They's somewhere nice and safe."

Gunnar looked at Lyle for confirmation. Lyle nodded agreement with Jules.

"I see. Well, we still have five or six hours of sunlight. Will that be enough to ride to them?"

Jules thought it over. Lyle remained impassive.

"I ain't sayin' it is or I ain't sayin' it ain't. I'm just enjoying this good whiskey and lookin' at these fine women," Jules growled.

Gunnar followed Jules' eyes to the brunette.

"Maggie O'Riley? Hell, she's the ugliest whore in town. If you're hankering for a woman's pleasure, how about Suzy over there. Now she's a might more expensive but damn well worth it!" Gunnar said.

Jules looked across the room at Maggie then at Suzy. Suzy was a tall, voluptuous blonde and Jules could see Gunnar's point. But he would rather be hanged than admit it. "Well, you say what you want, but I choose what I want," Jules started to move toward Maggie.

Lyle grabbed his arm. "Maybe that's not a good idea. Like the man said, we have five hours of daylight. That should be just enough."

Jules shook his arm loose from Lyle. He glared at him angrily. "I'm tired of people tellin' me to do this and that! Just back off, Lyle!"

Lyle let his arm go but did not back away. He gave Jules a steady gaze. "I know where they are too, Jules."

Jules froze and looked at Lyle in disbelief. He looked at Gunnar who gave him a crocodile smile. He went back to the bar and picked up a glass of whiskey. He downed it in one gulp. "Well, if you're so damn all-fired in a hurry, let's be goin'. Now!"

Jules slammed the glass down and it broke, cutting his thumb.

The bright red blood spilled on the bar and mingled with the amber whiskey.

Jules wiped his thumb on his shirt, leaving a long, narrow trail of red from the top button to the bottom. He dripped blood as he moved toward Maggie. Maggie looked at him in disgust and started to back away.

"Ugh! You're bleeding," Maggie said.

Jules reached out and grabbed her with his bloody hand. "What's the matter. You think I'm ugly or something? You're just a whore! You ain't better than nobody! You hear?" Jules shook her until he felt the cold muzzle of a Colt against his head.

"Let her be, Jules," Lyle threatened as he cocked the hammer of the gun.

Jules started to reach for his gun but Lyle was joined by Gunnar and his men. He slowly released Maggie's arm.

Lyle gave Maggie his bandanna.

She wiped the blood off as she backed away, cursing Jules under her breath.

"Well, I guess these boys is ready to ride, Maggie. That's too bad for you," Jules grinned.

Maggie turned and ran upstairs.

Jules yelled after her. "Now you pretty yourself up and I'll be back later to come a'courtin'," Jules smiled, then turned and stormed out of the saloon.

Gunnar looked at Lyle for a long moment before he spoke. "You known this man a long time?"

"Hardly no time at all," Lyle paused and sighed. "And what time it is, I sincerely regret," Lyle concluded.

Gunnar nodded agreement. "You seem to be a man, that a man could trust."

"You trying to tell me something?"

"No. Just that I don't trust him and it might be best for everyone involved if he doesn't become a problem."

Lyle thought it over. He looked into Gunnar's eyes and tried to read his mind. "Does that mean I'm not a problem?"

"I told you, I can use a good sharpshooter. My friend General

Nogales would pay you a good salary for your talents."

"Nogales?"

"You know him?"

"No!" Lyle lied. "Is he a general like in a war? This *Juarista* thing?"

"Yes. Have you chosen sides?"

"Nope! I want no part of it."

"That is not possible."

"I don't understand?"

"You are in Mexico. Before you make it home, you will have to choose a side."

Lyle looked doubtful. The serious look in Gunnar's eyes told Lyle Gunnar spoke the truth.

"That may be so, but I'll wait a while if you don't mind?"

Gunnar shrugged. "You know where to find me when you're ready," he paused. "We'd better go before Jules gets any funny ideas." Gunnar motioned his men to follow him. Lyle waited a moment. He started to take one last drink of whiskey.

As he did a small hand touched his arm. He looked up to see Maggie smiling at him.

"I won't forget you, mister," She said as she gave him a fine silk handkerchief. "You come back sometime and get your bandanna. I'll be cleaning it up for you, okay?"

"Yes ... yes, that'll be fine. Thank you." Lyle gulped a whiskey before he hurried out of the saloon.

Jules and Gunnar were already mounted.

Gunnar's men piled into an empty freight wagon as Lyle mounted his horse.

Jules eyed the fancy handkerchief Lyle stuffed into his pocket and growled under his breath.

They rode, quietly, into the waning afternoon sun.

An unusually cold wind came out of the north and whipped dust into their faces. They covered their noses with their bandannas, except for Lyle.

Lyle refused to soil the lady's gift.

After three hours, they came to the secluded arroyo where Jules and Lyle had hidden the guns.

Jules had found such a good place to hide the guns that he had almost hidden them from himself.

All the foothills looked alike and for a moment he was lost.

Gunnar rode a horse a few yards behind and his men drove the freight wagon that would carry the guns. Gunnar could see from the look on Jules' face he was unsure of where he was. Gunnar had planned to dispatch this disgusting man at the first opportunity. He thought, for a moment, he might do it now and the hell with the guns. "Don't tell me you forgot where you hid them?" Gunnar shook his head in disbelief.

Jules looked at Lyle. Lyle was almost as lost. Lyle shrugged and moved his horse down a narrow canyon. The canyon led past a trickle of a creek that Lyle recognized. Lyle thought about pretending he did not know where he was. He knew he wanted to get out of this arrangement alive.

He also knew the minute Gunnar had the guns their lives were in serious jeopardy.

"Yeah! This is the canyon. I remember this one," Jules said as he kneed his horse into a gallop.

The others paused only a moment before they followed after him.

There was a huge rock that cast a shadow of a man.

The right arm of that shadow pointed toward the secluded corner where they had buried the guns. Jules pulled his horse up just before he reached that spot. He turned and looked at the others. "Now I suppose you don't trust me no more'n I trust you?"

Gunnar signaled his men to hold up. Lyle moved to a good position.

"Now what makes you say that, Jules?" Gunnar grinned.

"Well, let's just say I'm guessin'. But now that we's at the guns, why don't you show us the money?"

Gunnar and his men, instinctively, made their gun hands ready.

"Now, Jules. You think any man in his right mind would be carrying that kind of money around in these parts?"

Jules' eyes called Gunnar a lair.

"Well if that's the case, you done took a long ride for nuthin'," Jules spit.

Gunnar looked at Lyle. Lyle nodded agreement with Jules.

Gunnar shifted, nervously, in his saddle. He looked at his men. They looked ready.

"If you're thinking to outgun us and just take our goods, I can tell you there's a lot of dead men that thought like that!" Jules threatened.

"I see. Tell me, Jules. How were you planning on getting back home with half the army of Mexico looking for you?"

Jules looked puzzled.

"All I have to do is tell my friend, General Nogales, who took the guns and you won't make it twenty miles," Gunnar said as he eased off his horse.

Lyle saw what was coming and turned to face Gunnar's men.

"Well then, I suppose somebody has to shut you up!" Jules went for his gun.

Everyone else went for their guns at the same moment.

Gunnar turned and came up firing at Jules. Jules was faster and fired a bullet into Gunnar's stomach. Gunnar dropped to his knees in pain.

Gunnar's men aimed for Lyle.

Lyle, half-aiming, took one of them out with a rifle bullet through the throat. Bullets whizzed past his head as he threw the rifle aside and drew his pistol.

Gunnar, with his dying breath, fired a bullet at Jules that ricocheted off his horse's saddle. The horse bucked Jules to the ground.

The remaining two of Gunnar's men divided their fire between Jules and Lyle.

Lyle was better with a rifle than a revolver and his shots went wild. Jules spit dirt as he got to his knees. Debris from near misses spewed in his face.

He panicked when he could not find his gun.

One of Gunnar's men ran toward him. Jules spied Gunnar's revolver in his dead hand. He got up and ran for it. Gunnar's man fired two shots that whizzed by Jules' ear — then his gun clicked empty.

Jules reached Gunnar as the man was reloading. Jules tried to pry Gunnar's hand loose from the gun, but it wouldn't budge. Jules panicked as he saw the man almost finish reloading.

"Damn you, Gunnar!" Jules grimaced as he took out his knife and sliced Gunnar's gun hand off at the wrist.

Gunnar's man looked on in disbelief.

Jules took Gunnar's dead gun hand, and pulling the deadman's trigger finger, shot Gunnar's man to death.

Gunnar's other man made the fatal mistake of pausing to watch Jules. In that instant, Lyle put a bullet through his head.

When the smoke cleared, Lyle picked up and reloaded his rifle. He immediately trained it on Jules.

Jules looked at him and grinned as he tossed Gunnar's hand aside — still holding the gun.

Jules kept an eye on Lyle as he reached into Gunnar's bloody pants and withdrew his money belt. The money belt dripped blood as Jules opened it. He looked at the neat stacks of twenty dollar bills. He looked at Lyle and grinned.

"I expect there's more than twenty thousand here, Lyle," he chuckled. "Hell, we got the guns and the money!"

"No, we ain't!" Lyle moved up and leveled his rifle at Jules' head.

Lyle started to pull the trigger but thought of a better way to get rid of Jules. "You got the guns and all the trouble that comes with em'. Just count out my share of the money and I'll be riding on."

"Oh? I know about you."

"Just shut up and count the money."

"So you can go spend it on that whore? I seen that fancy hand-kerchief she done give you." Jules smirked.

"I should just blow your head off and be done with it!"

"Well then, I expect you'd better get to it."

Lyle leveled the rifle at Jules' head. "Get a shovel from the wagon, Jules."

Jules did not like it. He growled his displeasure. "I ain't digging up them rifles by myself."

"It ain't for digging up the rifles."

"What the hell you talking about?"

"First we got to bury these here dead men, then we'll see."

Jules picked up the knife and held it in his hand. Blood ran the length of the blade and made a steady drip to the ground.

"I mean it, Jules. Put down the knife and get a shovel."

"You mean to make me dig my own grave?"

Lyle answered with his eyes.

"That ain't Christian, Lyle. And it ain't anything I'm likely to do!" Jules paused and took on his "evil-eye" look. "You gonna have to shoot me while I'm lookin' in your eyes and I'll be lookin' up at you after I'm dead!"

Lyle did not know why he hesitated.

His finger danced on the trigger but he did not pull it. He eased his mind with the thought that he could leave Jules to General Nogales' men to deal with. In·that way he could kill two birds with one stone. He would get rid of Jules and maybe buy enough time to make it north of the border alive. Besides, with no money Jules would not last long in Mexico.

Slowly, Lyle eased down and picked up the money belt. Jules eye followed him all the way down and all the way up.

Lyle picked up the money belt and threw it over his saddle.

Lyle held his gun level as he eased up on his horse. He began to ease his horse back out of the canyon. "You know I can kill from long range with this gun, Jules. You keep the guns and do with these dead men what you want. I'll be riding out and I suggest you don't follow."

"Well, I think I'll be goin where that money is goin'." Jules snarled.

"If you do you won't hear the gunshot that kills you," Lyle turned his horses head and began to ride out of the canyon.

Jules ran after him and threw the knife.

The knife whistled through the air and lodged deep into Lyle's shoulder. The pain made him almost drop his rifle. He slumped over in his saddle as Jules found his revolver. Jules picked up the gun and began firing as Lyle whipped his horse into a gallop. The bullets were narrow misses that whacked into the canyon walls.

Lyle was out of gun range when Jules fired the last round and screamed curses that echoed down the canyon walls.

CHAPTER TWENTY-THREE

Stella had a hard time staying awake. The subject matter was interesting but the man presenting the lecture had a whiny voice that did not do it justice.

"Giving his motivation for his isolation at Walden Pond, Mr. Thoreau says, 'I went to the woods because I wished to live deliberately, to front only the essential facts of life, and see if I could not learn what it had to teach, and not when I came to die, discover that I had not lived,' " he said.

Stella enjoyed Thoreau's way with words but she did not share his philosophy. She did not understand how anyone could ever leave the fine things and conveniences of the city for a small cabin in the woods. But as something to ponder and discuss over brandy by a fire, it was interesting.

Mr. Thoreau's ideas were not popular with most people in attendance at the lecture, but his views made for titillating conversation and were fashionable.

As she sat in the third row of the hall and looked at Winthrop, she felt satisfied. They had been attending these lectures for seven weeks and her plan was working.

She could look all about and see Boston's finest people dressed in the latest fashions. There was some delicious irony, she thought, in all these fashionable people with their carriages and fine homes listening to and vigorously applauding Mr. Thoreau's simple philosophy.

" 'A man is rich in proportion to the number of things he can afford to let alone,' Mr. Thoreau says. He also says, 'Our life is frittered away by detail. Simplify! Simplify!' ... and to that I say, Hurrah!" The lecturer finished to applause and cheering.

Stella applauded politely and looked at Winthrop, who was cheering the loudest. Over the last few weeks she had come to enjoy Winthrop. He was tailor-made for her purposes. Wherever she went with Winthrop, she was treated with respect, although there was still a coldness, by some, toward her.

She knew there were still rumors about her, but no one dared wag their tongues in public.

Winthrop was too respectable.

She felt good about her parents' arrival in two weeks. They would be sure to like Winthrop and see that she was a respectable woman.

To further that end she wanted an engagement pledge and ring from Winthrop. She planned to make her move in that regard this very evening.

Stella had given the servants a night off, except for Helga who was instructed to sleep in Big Ben's room and keep the door locked. Stella had also purchased a magnum of the finest brandy available. She had also purchased an autographed copy of Mr. Thoreau's book *Walden* which she was sure would turn Winthrop's head.

She intended to go as far as she had to, to take him past his infatuation to a habitual dependency. She could tell by the way he looked at her that would not take much.

"I wonder if you share my delight in Mr. Thoreau's words?" Winthrop asked when the lecture was concluded and they made their way to the carriage.

"Why do you ask that? I applauded as long and loud as you," Stella replied.

"Stella? You were barely able to contain your yawns and I thought you might nod off anytime," Winthrop chided gently.

"I'm sorry. Ben kept me up most of the night he has a cough …"

"I'm sorry to hear that."

"That's okay. It's much better. In fact it's so much better that I think you should come to dinner tonight."

Winthrop's eyes lit up. "… but I can't get Reverend Talbot to chaperon on this short notice."

Stella smiled and brushed a speck of lint off his coat collar. "Is it alright if we have dinner alone?"

Winthrop almost fainted.

"I mean I don't want to scandalize Boston, but we're grown people. Doesn't Mr. Thoreau say that some people hear a different drummer?"

"Yes. He said 'if a man does not keep pace with his companions, perhaps it is because he hears a different drummer.'" Winthrop paused and smiled. "'Let him step to the music he hears, however measured or far away!'" Winthrop concluded with a flourish.

"I like that, Winthrop. A different drummer. How poetic."

Winthrop nodded agreement.

"By, God who cares what convention says. You and I will have dinner alone and proper Boston be damned!"

Stella nodded agreement as she got in her carriage and drove away.

Shannon O'Bannion didn't like it. It had stuck in his craw for months now. No matter what had passed between him and Stella, there was no call for Stella firing Rosie.

Rosie was a fine housekeeper, but because she had been fired was unable to find other work. To his undying shame, Rosie had been the main support of Shannon, his invalid mother, and their alcoholic father. The few jobs Shannon could find were short and paid little. His new job as a lamplighter was the most steady work he had ever had, but it paid little, also.

It was Rosie's steady employment that had been the shining economic light of their meager existence.

Stella had put that light out.

Shannon could not bear to look at Rosie's tears and watch her descend into poverty. Stella, to his mind, was an evil woman who deserved to be brought down and he had to find a way to do it. He believed that way was through politics.

The Democratic-Republican Party seemed to be the answer. Shannon was good at ward-healing. He was a master of saloon oratory and people liked what he said. He did not particularly care about the black man and was indifferent toward the slave trade, but if he found himself around Abolitionists he trumpeted their cause. If he found himself among radical women he espoused his love for women's suffrage — though he could never imagine giving women the vote. But it was the fight against the Know-Nothings of the Native American party that would be the basis of his success.

The xenophobia of the Native Americans was so pathological they wanted to put a twenty-five year resident qualification for citizenship into law.

This proposal united the Irish, at whom it was directed, like no other issue. Shannon would champion that cause. There was no compromise Shannon would not make to get where he wanted to go.

In that respect he and Stella were kindred spirits.

He knew what would hurt her most would be to be exposed as the Irish whore she was. Shannon had watched from a distance as Stella had sported herself around town in the escort of Winthrop Adams.

It made Shannon want to puke to see her fawn over the Yankee Brahmins he hated with all his heart.

"After I light the lamps I'm going down to the saloon, Rosie. I won't be too long and I'll bring back a sandwich or two, okay?" Shannon asked as he watched Rosie shivered, huddled in a corner wrapped in two shawls.

Rosie looked at him with red eyes that shone indifference.

"You do that, son … but don't be stayin' too late, now. You have to get in the employment lines early in the morning," Marian, his mother, coughed.

His father sat in an old chair at a rickety table and mumbled something unintelligible.

Shannon took a look around the small hovel in the North End of Boston where he lived. As he did every day, he made his vow to get out of this squalor no matter what.

If he could bring Stella down at the same time, it would be all that heaven allowed.

◈ ◈ ◈

"Come in, Winthrop." Stella opened the door.

"Thank, you, Stella." Winthrop looked puzzled. "Helga?"

"I told you we were dining alone. 'A different drummer,' remember? Let me take your coat."

Winthrop could not believe his good fortune, but he felt a little uncomfortable having Stella play the role of a servant. "Thank you very much," he said as he gave her his coat. He watched with interest as she walked away and put his coat in the closet.

"Go in by the fire while I put this away. Help yourself to the brandy. It's a new import I haven't tried yet."

Winthrop nodded agreement and walked, in a pleasant daze, into the parlor. He opened the fancy bottle of brandy and poured two glasses. "I assume you wanted one as well?" he asked as Stella entered the room.

"Of course. How is it?"

"I was just about to find out." Winthrop sipped from the glass. "Superb! My goodness, Stella, you have outdone yourself!"

Stella took a sip and looked at him in pleasant agreement. He looked back at her and she could see he was about to explode to say something.

"I must say, Stella. You are one fascinating lady. I have to tell you I have enjoyed the past weeks as I have enjoyed no others."

"… and I as well. I don't know how to thank you for introducing me to Mr. Thoreau. I think I like him best because so many people dislike him."

"Yes. Many think Thoreau to be but a pale imitation of Emerson. But I think someday he will be remembered as greater than Emerson."

Stella walked away and adjusted the shawl around her shoulders. She had worn a shawl because beneath it she had on her most revealing dress. The green silk dress she had bought the day Eli had left her was her favorite, and it showed off her cleavage, she thought, to its best advantage.

She thought she would unveil it at the most opportune moment. Perhaps after Winthrop had enjoyed one or two more glasses of brandy.

They sipped their brandy quietly for a moment and looked into the fire roaring in the fireplace. Winthrop poured another glass of brandy and sighed hard as he looked at her. "I hope it will not embarrass you for me to say what I must say."

Stella looked coy. She dropped the shawl slightly. "I thought we were kindred spirits. I hope we can talk freely to each other."

"Yes, I wish that to be true also." He thought it over as he took a long drink. "I am most fond of you, Stella. Please do not consider me forward but I cannot help it. I take it you can readily see my heart on my sleeve?"

Stella smiled as she looked at him with all the admiration she could muster. "Isn't mine?"

"Oh, Lord. I had no idea."

Winthrop shivered with the delight of fond discovery.

Stella turned her back on him. She walked over to a table and picked up a fancily wrapped gift. She brought it over and handed it to him.

"I was going to wait until after dinner to give you this. But now seems an appropriate time." She handed it to him.

He took it and looked at her with undying love and profound disbelief in his eyes. "But it isn't a holiday and my birthday is months away."

"A mere detail. ... our life is frittered away by detail ..."

"Oh, Lord, Stella you are something. You are really something!" Winthrop nervously tore open the package.

So great was his joy on seeing the book *Walden* that he almost dropped it. "Good God! How did you know? This is superb! I cannot begin to thank you."

"Open it."

Winthrop hesitated then opened it and saw the signature, Henry David Thoreau. He closed the book and clutched it to his chest. "Oh, good God! Good God, please excuse my blasphemy but this is too wonderful to believe. How... How ..."

"Don't worry about how. Just enjoy."

"I will, Stella. I will treasure it always. You are such a jewel. I can never .... ever repay a gift like this."

Stella smiled and turned her back on him as she walked over to the fireplace. She stared into the fire quietly as he moved up, slowly, behind her.

She smiled as she felt his hand fall gently on her shoulder. She smiled more as his warm breath fell on the back on her neck.

"Please turn and let me address you, Stella. I have something to say that must be said face to face."

Stella did not reply but held her position.

She waited until his hand became more firm on her shoulder. Finally she turned to him.

She did not look into his eyes. She waited until he put his hand on her chin and lifted her face to his.

"I am not good at this, but my heart compels me to speak. I love you, Stella. I know this is a most short courtship but what I feel for you makes me almost crazy sometimes. It must be spoken, so I speak it," he paused and sighed hard. "Please consider ... do not answer right away, but please take under consideration the ... the honor you would do me ... if you ... if you would consent to being Mrs. Winthrop Adams."

Stella tried to look surprised.

"Oh, my goodness, Winthrop!"

"I'm sorry. I'm so sorry to spring this on you like this, but it just spilled out."

"Then you don't mean it?"

"Oh, good lord, yes! Yes! I mean it with all my heart!"

Stella thought it over a long moment. She enjoyed having a man teetering on the brink of emotional death. She liked the powerful feeling it gave her to have him wait with his heart almost stopped to hear her answer.

She could almost hear the loud, frantic pounding of his lovesick heart.

She thought to really make him squirm as she dropped the shawl from around her shoulders. "You're saying this on an empty stomach. I prepared dinner tonight. Maybe you'll change your mind after you have had a chance to eat my cooking?"

"Never ... never, ever!" Winthrop's eyes glowed with lust as he looked at the cleavage between her ample bosoms. "I am not hungry!" He could not restrain himself as he lowered his face and kissed her on the neck.

Stella smiled the smile of victory as she stroked his neck and ran her fingers through his thick dark hair.

She smiled as he let his kisses descend onto the alabaster flesh that formed her breasts — mumbling unintelligible words of delight as he went.

CHAPTER TWENTY-FOUR

"You must go now!" Maria Christina insisted.

Eli did not like running from anything anytime. He particularly did not like running when he saw a friend or loved one in trouble. He saw the fear dancing in Maria's eyes upon hearing the name, General Nogales. He sensed Maria was in deep trouble and there was nothing that would make him leave now.

Eli dismounted his horse and addressed Pepito. "Does she have a horse?"

Pepito looked puzzled a moment before he shook his head "No."

"Then she will ride with me," Eli insisted as he looked at Maria.

Maria looked at him in disbelief. *"¡Es loco!* I do not go. You go!"

"Get on the horse, Maria!"

"Oh? And where would you take me?"

"We'll figure that out later."

"Oh? We just go for a ride anywhere we want? You *ARE* crazy, *Señor* Eli. If General Nogales is coming there is nowhere to go!"

"Well, as near as I can figure it, he's not coming in all directions," Eli paused. "You want to get on the horse or you want me to put you on it?"

Maria almost laughed. She looked at Pepito. Pepito told her with his eyes that he sided with Eli. "And what of my brother? You would leave him here?"

"He can ride with Shorty. Let's go!"

"No! You do not understand who this man is. You do not know what he can do."

"I don't care, Maria. You're wasting time!" Eli moved to grab her. She backed away. "Don't make me tie you up."

"You will have to kill me to make me go with you!"

"Maria, he is right. The town will talk and the General, he will know everything about you and *Señor* Eli!" Pepito made a throat cutting motion.

Maria was stunned by the truth of Pepito's remark. She knew

she had done wrong and Father Dominquez had already forgiven her.

She knew General Nogales would never forgive her.

She knew he would take it out on the village.

"What I have done is not your concern, but I do think it is best for you to go with him, brother. Please take him and leave *Señor* Eli. I beg you," Maria tried to sound pitiful.

Eli was unmoved. He took a rope from his saddle. He poised it at her. She backed away and Pepito blocked her path.

"You can ride free or you can ride strung up like a steer," Eli motioned for help from Scotty and the others.

They all dismounted and crowded around her, boxing her in.

Maria snarled at them but they did not back off. She tried to look coy but they didn't buy it. She kicked at the dust and sighed hard. "I will have to go pack a few things ..."

"We'll buy you new ones." Eli insisted.

Maria looked into his eyes and knew he was deadly serious. It was not in her nature to run either, but for now she would take the only obvious way out.

She gave them all one last look of anger. She pushed Eli aside and mounted his horse.

She slipped forward in the saddle and waited for him to mount behind her.

"... but who will feed the pigs, *Señor* Eli?"

Eli mounted the horse and snuggled in behind her. He put his strong arms around her waist and picked up the reins. "We'll send them flowers," Eli chuckled as he turned the horses' head and rode north out of the *pueblo*.

◈ ◈ ◈

General Nogales did not like it. The *pueblo* was too quiet. He did not expect a hero's welcome, but, at least, he thought he would see the usual camp followers.

Most of all, he expected Maria Christina to be standing in front of her house with a bouquet of flowers and a smile on her face. Instead, there was only Father Dominquez standing in the dusty street by the small chapel to greet him. General Nogales signaled his men to come to a stop. The dust from the horses swirled around Father Dominquez but he did not flinch.

General Nogales dismounted his horse and walked up to the

padre. "Where are all my people?"

"Your people, General?" Father Dominquez tried not to be contemptible.

"Don't play with me, *padre.* Where is Maria?"

Father Dominquez looked at the chapel then he looked back at General Nogales. "The last time I saw her she was at her prayers."

"She's in the chapel?" General Nogales pushed Father Dominquez aside and stormed into the chapel. He came back out a few minutes later very mad. "Why do you lie to me? You know I always get the truth. You know better than this, *padre,*" he paused and looked real mean. "So tell me where she is?"

"Did you contribute to the poor box?" Father Dominquez posed.

"You stupid old priest! You still do not know what is good for the people, do you?" He turned to one of his soldiers. "Go bring me the poor box, Pancho!"

The soldier dismounted and ran inside the chapel.

"No, General. What are you going to do?" Father Dominquez protested.

The soldier returned and handed General Nogales the poor box. General Nogales threw the box in the dust and shot the lock off. He was surprised to see five twenty-dollar gold pieces spill out.

He picked them up and held them, lovingly, in his hands. He looked at the padre with anger.

"Who has been here? Who has brought you this kind of money? Who?" he demanded.

"¿*Quién sabe?* Maybe it is the work of the Lord."

General Nogales leveled his gun at Father Dominquez. For a moment, he thought about shooting him. He hated the church.

More, he hated the influence priests like Father Dominquez held over the peasants. It was his hope to defeat Benito Juárez and drive the church from Mexico.

The late afternoon Mexican sun shone on the gold pieces in General Nogales' hand. The more he thought about them the more fearful he became.

Someone had come into a poor village who had money. Money enough to give it away. Whoever it was, was too rich and being too rich, was too powerful to let live.

General Nogales knew this and Father Dominquez knew this. This understanding passed between them as they looked into each other's eyes.

"*¿Quién?* Who?" General Nogales demanded.

"I will pray for you, General."

"Do you want to die old man?"

"Yes. Yes, I do. God forgive me, but I am more than ready."

General Nogales put the coins in his pocket and looked at Father Dominquez with disgust. "I am not an Indian scout but I can see the horses' hoofs in the dust. They are not three hours old. We will find this rich man and we will kill him," General Nogales stopped and looked hard at Father Dominquez.

Father Dominquez looked indifferent.

"You will not be so happy when we will come back and burn your chapel to the ground! *¿Comprende?*"

"You will not be so happy when the people are victorious!" Father Dominquez said with pride.

General Nogales would have shot Father Dominquez and enjoyed it, had not it been against policy to create martyrs.

"Maria Christina? She has gone with this man. He is a *gringo?*"

Father Dominquez looked beatific and did not reply.

"Only a *gringo* has this kind of money. A man who has this much money to give away is very dangerous. A *gringo muy peligroso!*"

"You are the only dangerous man in this vicinity. But I will pray for you," Father Dominquez replied.

"The guns? The guns at Batista? This man … he has them?" General Nogales wondered aloud. "That is why he has this money … that is why he has Maria. She goes with the man with the most money?"

"You know this to be true with certainty, General Nogales?"

"Yes. He takes the guns to Oaxaca to sell to the *Juaristas*. This is all plain to me, *padre*. I do not need you to help. I do not need you and this village does not need you." He stopped and looked sinister. "Pancho, Pedro, Tomas. Get the torches and burn this gathering place for the enemies of my people!" General Nogales ordered.

The soldiers hesitated as they looked at the look of defiance on Father Dominquez' face.

"General, you want we should burn … burn a church?" Tomas wondered.

"Do as I order or you will be shot!"

"No, General. Please. It is a modest chapel and the only one in many miles. The people have little else," Father Dominquez pleaded.

"Then confirm that they ride to Oaxaca."

Father Dominquez knew they were riding to Vera Cruz so he thought a little lie was not a great sin to tell such an evil man. "Yes … you are right. They ride to Oaxaca."

General Nogales sucked on his cigar and looked at Father Dominquez with contempt. "¿Padre? Padre, a lie from your lips is an ugly thing. Any fool can see the hoof prints lead toward Vera Cruz."

"Tell me, what has this *gringo* done for you that makes you do a sin of a lie to protect him?"

"If I lie it is not to protect a *gringo!*" Father Dominquez had a brainstorm. "I do not like Gunnar Zimmermann. I hope you do find him in Vera Cruz."

"Gunnar? This was Gunnar's work?"

"He thought to buy my blessing on his marriage to Maria with the money you took from the poor box," Father Dominquez prayed quietly for forgiveness.

General Nogales thought it over but did not buy it. "No, Gunnar is not stupid. He does not steal from me. You are lying again. I must meet this man that can make a *padre* lie so much. … Burn it!" General Nogales ordered once more as he moved to his horse and prepared to ride to Vera Cruz.

⊠ ⊠ ⊠

Eli enjoyed the feel of Maria's body pressed against his as they rode hard toward Vera Cruz. It was Eli's plan to get a ship out of Vera Cruz and take Maria out of Mexico.

He loved her.

He knew that she might not feel that way toward him, but he would work at it and maybe in time she would come to love him. He was prepared to wait as long as it took.

Eli did not completely accept the fact that Jules was dead.

But everything he had heard about this General Nogales made him tend to believe it was possible. Eli hoped Jules was afraid when the General's men put the rope around his neck. He hoped Jules' knees knocked and he messed his pants when the noose closed around his neck. He hoped the noose was not tied properly and Jules had to dance in the air and wretch and spit and choke — slowly and painfully.

Eli could see it all in his mind and it was somewhat satisfying.

Maybe he would not have to see the body. Maybe, if he could

accept that General Nogales had done it for him, it was time to get on with another life. A life with Maria.

Maria was worth putting the past to rest.

Eli would work to win her heart. Then he would get a bill of divorcement from Stella. He figured attempted murder was pretty good grounds. Once he was divorced he would give Maria the biggest diamond ring ever made. Then he would have the biggest wedding Sonora had ever seen.

Her hair smelled of spring flowers and he wanted to kiss it but wondered how she would react. He let his nose linger in it, as close to it as he dared. "You understand that what passed between us the other night was a mistake. I hope you do not think it has any meaning," she said over her shoulder.

The words hurt Eli but he showed no emotion. He did not have any respectable reply so he let her words go unanswered.

"Did you hear me, Eli?"

He still held his silence.

"You understand I do not do that kind of thing. It was dumb of me. Do you hear me?"

Eli shifted in the saddle and let his arms close around her a little more tightly.

"I am a respectable woman. You understand?"

Eli sighed hard.

"You think just being quiet has any meaning? Well, it doesn't impress me."

Eli said nothing as she shifted forward in the saddle and grimaced angrily. They rode quietly for a long time.

"Did you know your hair smells like spring flowers?" Eli offered as they passed a crude road sign that read, "Vera Cruz 50 miles."

"You didn't hear a word I said, did you?" she huffed.

"Yes, ma'am. I did."

"Well ... then ..."

"It ain't exactly like that."

"You're maddening. What exactly did you see it like?"

"I'm sorta married right now, but I can get out of that easy enough ..."

"What the hell are you talking about?"

"Well, I respect you as a proper lady and I want to do the right thing."

"Are you talking about what I think you're talking about?"

"I hope so."

"You are crazy!" Maria almost had to laugh. "You're talking about you and I ... getting ... married?"

"My intentions are honorable."

"Let me off this horse, right now!"

"That's not a good idea."

Maria tried to break free of his arms and jump. Eli held her tight. He sort of enjoyed the fight in her, but it took all his strength to hold her on the horse.

Scotty and the others rode ten lengths behind Eli and watched the action with amusement. They also watched the road behind them for any signs of being followed.

"Ain't true love grand?" Scotty looked over at Shorty.

"If that's what's goin' on up there then you can have it!" Shorty laughed.

"I just hope she doesn't claw his eyes out before he gets us safe on a ship out of Vera Cruz."

"From that sign back there it looks like most of two days' ride." Chief pulled up beside them.

"Well I'm betting on old Eli. In two days' time he'll have her bringing his meals and cooing love songs," Scotty said.

Chief looked doubtful. Shorty seemed to agree.

"It'll be good to get me feet on the deck of a good sailing ship, once more. Aye, I kind miss it, laddies." Scotty waxed melancholy.

"Not me. If it's all the same to you, I'll be parting company in Vera Cruz," Chief said.

"Me too," Shorty agreed.

"Did I hear you boys say something about a ship?" Sam pulled along side of them.

"Yep. A California clipper. With fine oak masts that go up to the sky," Scotty said.

"I'm with the boys. I don't hold much by being around too much water without having a side of whiskey," Sam said.

"Tell me, Scotty. What's going on up there with those two?" Sam motioned toward Eli and Maria.

"Why ain't you never seen true love before, Sam?" Scotty chided.

"Looks to me like she's got her claws out ready to scratch him up some," Sam added.

"Yep. Looks like she loves him a powerful lot, laddies!" Scotty said to the looks of disbelief on the face of the others.

General Nogales rode out of Puebla with the glow from the fire that burned Father Dominquez's chapel reflecting in his cold eyes.

Father Dominquez knelt in the dust of the street and let himself be enveloped by the smoke from the fire. He cursed General Nogales before he said prayers of repentance and forgiveness.

The burning of the church did not sit too easy with some of his men, but General Nogales did not care.

He knew the fire would teach the peasants the lessons of power he wanted to teach them. He pulled his men up in front of Maria's humble home. He did not have to give the order this time. His men knew his thoughts and put the torch to her home. After they lit the fire, General Nogales watched it burn and felt the bitterness of betrayal fill his mouth with bile. He was a womanizer of the first rank. In Mexico the old adage of "rank has its privileges" was more properly put, that "rank was all powerful." He took any woman he wanted and few dared say anything about it. He took them and used them then tossed them aside, but he could not bear the thought of any of his women in another man's arms.

Maria Christina was the only mistress he really cared for. Of the dozen or so women he had stashed in *casa chicas* throughout Mexico, she was the only one he might have considered marrying.

He wondered who this *gringo* was that could be so powerful as to make Father Dominquez lie and have Maria go with him.

It was not Gunnar. She despised him.

Whoever it was, he was a man to be approached with caution. But once he had him captured, he would take away his manhood and make Maria watch.

Then he would cut her throat.

CHAPTER TWENTY-FIVE

Shannon O'Bannion was in his cups in the smoke-filled dive that passed as a bar on the worst street in the North End of Boston. The worst street in the North End of Boston of the late 1850s was, perhaps, the worst street in any town in the world. The American definition of squalor was the Eighth Ward of the North End of Boston this winter's night of 1858.

Like many of his fellow Irishmen, Shannon found relief from the grinding poverty in the cheap whiskey and beer found in the dank bars filled with smoke and drunken sympathy from his Emerald Society Brotherhood.

The Emerald Society was one of the many "secret" societies the Irish formed to have the strength of numbers to try to survive. It was also a network of spies that dug up information on the enemy — the other secret societies formed by the Yankee Brahmins. Principal among the Yankee secret societies was the Know-Nothings.

The Know-Nothings were vehemently against "Popery" and "Papist" Irish. Shannon's Uncle Bernard had told him how he had watched in horror as they or their agents had set fire to the Ursuline Convent on Mt. Benedict in Charlestown. The burning had taken place in 1834 but the ruins still stood above the city to remind the "paddies" who was running things. Shannon refused to be cowed and he had founded the Emerald Society to help himself and his people fight back. He also saw it as a good way to build a political base from which to launch his dream of being mayor of Boston. There was to be a meeting of the Emerald Society this very night, but he was not feeling like conducting a meeting. He had read the announcement on the society pages of the Boston papers of the engagement of Stella to Winthrop Adams and it made him want to puke. Who did she think she was? She was as Irish as he, and when the Boston Brahmins of Mr. Adams' family found out they would bring her down and cast her out. He was going to make sure to have a ringside seat when that happened. He wanted to laugh at her myopia, but he cared for her too much and waves of melancholy made his eyes misty.

He knew he was a sentimental fool but he reveled in it. He pulled down a big draft of ale and called for another as his men began to fill the room.

"So Shannon, did you read the news?" Paddy O'Brien, one of three literate Irish in the group, asked as he sat at the table.

"They've made the Pope president and we're all appointed to high office? Is that what you be talking about, Paddy?" Shannon laughed. That thought made him feel a little warmer in the unheated confines of this dive.

"You know what I be talking about. That fancy lady you were sporting is marrying up with the high born," Paddy paused. "Didn't you say she was Irish?"

"No, she would not be admitting to that. You'd have to wash off the face powder and look at the freckles by her flaming red hair to tell that!"

"Sounds to me like she got to you a bit. You wouldn't be wanting any information that might put a crimp in her style now, would you?" Paddy looked mischievous.

"What are you talking about, Paddy?"

Shannon gave Paddy his undivided attention.

Paddy made him sweat a little before replying.

"Oh, nothing. Except you instructed us to keep a close watch on her comings and goings and find out whatever we could now. Did you not?"

"I'm sorry I wasted the Society's time on that. It was personal. I was out of line. I think it's time someone else took the rudder. I'm stepping down."

"The hell you say!"

"I'll be nominating you for president this very night, Paddy."

"Well, before you do that, you should let my son Jimmy show you what he has for your Christmas present." Paddy motioned for a young boy to approach the table.

Shannon looked at the big strapping boy and did not recognize him, at first. "Jimmy ... little Jimmy O'Brien? Is that you, lad?"

"He's all grown up since you seen him last. It's about all I can do to cuff him down these days!"

"Well, I don't think I'd want to be squaring off with him myself. He's about of age to join the society, isn't he, Paddy?"

"Oh, Mr. Shannon, there is nothing I want more. I would give anything to be a member. I'm more than ready, I really am!" Jimmy broke in.

Paddy nodded agreement.

"Well! I must say he doesn't lack for enthusiasm. We'll see, Jimmy. We'll, maybe, put it to a vote this very night," Shannon replied.

"Oh, for sure, Mr. Shannon? Do you really mean it?"

Shannon looked at Paddy. Paddy smiled, then looked serious. "Aren't you going to ask him what he brings to the table?"

Shannon shrugged.

"He's your son, Paddy. That's enough for me."

"The O'Briens don't come begging. Show him what you have, Jimmy."

Jimmy hesitated a moment. He looked around the room. He reached in an oilcloth bag and withdrew a thick letter. He laid it before Shannon.

Shannon looked at the return address:

"Jason Rubin, Attorney At Law

Fifth and Market, San Francisco, California."

He looked at Paddy and Jimmy in disbelief as he saw it was addressed to Stella. "How? Where did you get this, Jimmy?"

"I'm the fastest postal runner in town. They give me all the postings that are special delivery."

"I told him to intercept any important-looking mail going to her house and this looks damn important!" Paddy interrupted.

Shannon nodded agreement as he looked at the heavy wax seal on the envelope. He picked up a knife off the table and poised the point at the seal. "You realize if I break this seal Jimmy is going to lose his job. ... maybe even go to prison?"

"It's okay, Mr. O'Bannion. They treat me badly and I was going to quit anyways."

"Well, I don't know about that, Jimmy. Jobs is hard to come by and there might not be anything in here worth it anyways."

"Open the damn thing! I'm curious!" Paddy insisted.

Shannon nodded agreement and cut off the seal. He pulled out a letter on fine parchment.

He read:

> *My Dear Stella,*
> *This letter will serve to explain why I cannot come to Boston at any time in the near future. I send it post haste be-*

cause there have been legal complications here that might have potential adverse affects on your inheritance; your holdings here, as well as, your marital status. I did not anticipate any problems with obtaining the death certificate necessary to the purposes we discussed. However, there are those forces in Sonora extremely friendly to your husband and I have not, as yet, been successful in this endeavor.

It seems there are those here now who take seriously the fact of Statehood. They insist upon the use of legal channels I do not ordinarily rely upon. Therefore, I find it in your best interest to stay here and try to resolve these matters. I will keep you informed as I proceed.

As Always, Jason

Shannon was stunned into silence. He stared at the letter in disbelief.

He reread it again to himself as the others looked puzzled.

"Did he say her husband?" Paddy wondered aloud.

Shannon folded the letter almost reverently. He looked at Paddy and smiled; he got up and hugged Jimmy.

"Welcome to the Emerald Society, Jimmy. There will not have to be a vote. I declare you a member in good standing. Hot Damn! Hot Damn! I got her! I got her!" Shannon danced a jig and Paddy and Jimmy joined in.

Stella was worried. She had not heard from Jason in over six months and there was too much going on for her to feel comfortable. She had woven a complex web of deceit and she, at times, tired of trying to hold it together.

Winthrop was having trouble with his family because "they knew nothing about her background," but she could control him with sex-baiting glances and thinly veiled promises of love.

She felt she only had to keep it up a few more days. Her parents would be here any minute to stay for five days.

They would see how well she had done, then she wouldn't give a damn any more.

In her mind her parents would be overwhelmed with pride to see the high level of society she and Winthrop moved in. Big Ben was already benefiting as Winthrop was going to have a highly regarded English tutor begin reading lessons the day of his fifth birthday.

Stella did not pause to think of how Winthrop would take it when he found out her parents were very Irish. In her mind she had so much control over him that he would accept that — and make sure everyone else in town accepted it.

Stella was not one to bother with details.

She made plans that had fuzzy beginnings; very specific ends, and a lot of fancy footwork in between. She made her way to her goals through hook or crook, improvising rather than planning each step. Stella did not believe the old adage that "the devil is in the details." She believed hell was in not getting what you wanted anyway you could get it.

She had always made it through on beauty and guile, and she would once again.

It was all coming together nicely, but she still wrung her hands, nervously, as she waited for the carriage that would bring her parents to her doorstep.

She hoped her parents would not take umbrage at the fact she sent a closed carriage. There was no way they could know she had the driver bring them from the train station by the back streets. She intended they see and be seen by only a select group.

It was her plan to dazzle them with her social standing and get them back to New York without their finding out more than they needed to know. She watched from the widow's walk as the carriage stopped on the street below. She ran inside and powdered her nose once more. She smiled as she looked at the frumpy dress she was wearing with the old maid's brooch.

She did not know where Helga had found such an unfashionable dress but she thought it was perfect.

There would be no cleavage displayed this day, and her makeup was minimal. The brandy was in storage and replaced by a bottle of Irish whiskey. Stella anticipated offering her father a drink and her mother saying "No!"

Her father would be happy for the offer and pout for not being able to accept it. Her mother would let him stew awhile, but in the end, her mother would let him have "one glass to sip slow." He would eventually get her to take some also, and then things would flow smoothly after that.

She went to Big Ben's room and looked him over. He was dressed in a Little Lord Fauntleroy outfit and looked very uncomfortable.

"Mommy? Mommy! I can't breathe too good. This collar is too

tight!" he insisted as he pulled at the fancy lace collar.

"Well, you'll just have to bear it for a little while. Grandmother and Grandfather are here and I want you to look your best for them. Please, son?" Stella gave him an affectionate kiss on the forehead.

Big Ben still did not like it and his steel eyes blazed with displeasure.

At the age of five he looked to be ten and his feet hurt in any kind of shoes. Big Ben was most comfortable *au naturel* and Stella had a hard time keeping him dressed in anything.

She indulged his every whim except his love of running naked through the streets of Boston.

"Come now, son. It's time to meet your grandparents. Now tell me what you're going to say?"

"Ah ... Grandmother Mary and Grandfather Sean, I am so glad you came to see me. Welcome to ... to your house?"

"No, Ben. Welcome to our house. What else?"

"Mommy, what if I don't like them?"

Stella was angry with Big Ben. For the first time in his life she felt like slapping him. "Don't you ever say that and don't you ever think that! Understand?"

"Yes, Mommy."

"So what are you going to say?"

"I love you, Grandmother ... and Grandfather ..."

Stella hugged him. "Thank you, son. This means a lot to me," she paused. "It means a new train set to you. Maybe one that winds up?"

"Really, Mommy? Really?" Big Ben hugged her back. "I really do love Grandmother and Grandfather ... I really do!" Big Ben danced a childish jig.

Stella seemed pleased.

She pulled at her velvet gloves and stood nervously waiting for Helga to announce her and Big Ben.

Stella planned to make a grand entrance down the staircase after being announced. She had seen her mother's mistress do this in New York and thought it would signal her new status.

"Mrs. Daniel James Winslow and Master Benjamin David Winslow," Helga announced with her heavy German accent.

Stella took a deep breath and blew it out hard. She held Big Ben's hand tight.

They moved to the landing and looked down to see her parents looking up at her with a puzzled look on their faces.

Stella smiled, politely, as she and Big Ben descended the staircase and greeted them.

"Mother! Father! It's so good of you to come."

"Stella?" Mary seemed puzzled.

Stella seemed equally puzzled. "Yes. It's me. Father, how have you been?"

Her father looked as if he didn't recognize her.

"Stella? I'm fine. Fine. You look so pale, child. I heard so much about the California sun."

"I haven't been there for over five years."

"This is your house?" Mary looked around.

"Yes, Mother."

"This Winslow man? He left you all this?"

"Yes, Mother."

"He was a Protestant?"

"Yes, Mother," Stella said sadly, waiting for a hug or look of love that never came.

"And this is Benjamin?" Sean knelt down and looked at Irish eyes that reminded him of his own.

"I ... love .... you, Grandfather," Big Ben paused and looked at Stella. "Do I get the train now, Mama?" Big Ben said innocently.

"Benjamin, that's not nice. Not now."

Sean looked at his grandson and broke into laughter. Mary looked stern a moment until Big Ben pulled at her dress. "... and I love you too, Grandmother," he looked at Stella.

Stella waited until her mother almost smiled until she was able to relax.

"He's a bright lad who seems to know what's what and he's Irish alright. Just look at those eyes, Mary."

Sean took a shine to Big Ben.

Mary looked at Big Ben's sparkling eyes and had to agree. She nodded approval.

"Please let's go in the sitting room by the fire." Stella led the way.

"Does Madam wish me to serve the hors d'oeuvres now?" Helga asked.

"Later, Helga. I'll ring if I need you."

Helga turned and left without replying. Mary watched her go with a jaundiced eye.

"She's German?"

"Yes, Mother."

"You're telling me that in all of Boston you couldn't find an Irish maid?"

Stella looked to her father for support. He stood behind Mary and his eyes showed disapproval, as well.

"I had one ... but there were problems. Rosie ... was ... Rosie was a thief. I'm sorry, Mother."

"Rosie? Rosie is coming back to play, Mommy? I love Rosie, Mommy!" Ben's eyes lit up.

"No, Benjamin. We talked about this. Why don't you go help Helga in the kitchen. She'll let you lick the spoons!" Stella gritted her teeth.

"Oh, yes! I love the spoons!"

Big Ben turned and took off running down the hall toward the kitchen.

After he was gone, they moved into the sitting room. Mary and Sean sat in separate chairs, distant from each other, and Stella took the couch.

Sean's eyes immediately fell on the bottle of Irish whiskey.

"Would you like a glass of whiskey, Father?"

"No, he wouldn't!" Mary interjected.

"Just a wee glass." Sean licked his lips.

Mary looked disgusted and shook her head "No."

"I promise, only half a glass. That's all. I promise," Sean almost whimpered.

Stella anticipated her mother's reaction. She was not disappointed.

Mary looked angry then, slowly, nodded "Yes. Just one, Stella, and make it half a glass," Mary insisted.

Stella poured half a glass and remembering the stupid charade turned to Mary. "Mother, would you like some as well?"

"You know I don't drink it, Stella ... but I suppose this is a special occasion," she paused. "I'll take a small measure."

Stella poured her mother a glass of the Irish whiskey and wondered why she cared what this cold hypocritical woman thought about anything.

But she did care.

She cared desperately. She would have given up the house and most of what she possessed for one word of honest praise from her mother.

She would have given her life to hear her mother say, "I love you."

"I don't like that German, Stella. I want you to get rid of her. We hear the Irish are worse off in Boston than New York. Some of your distant relatives live here. ... I believe it's called the North End. I want you to hire a good Irish woman. A good Catholic with lots of children," Mary ordered.

Stella handed each of them their glass of Irish whiskey. "Yes, Mother. I'll see to it."

"It's a fine-looking house and you've a fine son, Stella. God's blessings on you!" Sean toasted before he took a long drink.

"Who is this Yankee man ... this Winthrop you are engaged to, Stella?" Mary asked as she nipped at her glass of whiskey.

"Winthrop Adams? He's from an old Boston family, Mother."

"A Protestant?"

"Yes ..."

"You're telling me there are no good Irish Catholic men in this town worthy of your attention?"

"I didn't say that." Stella was almost angry. "This isn't about me so much as it is about Benjamin."

"I understand that, Mary. A rich Yankee can ease the boy's way some," Sean said.

"Well, I don't like it. Does that mean Benjamin will be raised without benefit of Catholic teachings?"

"No, Mother. Winthrop has agreed to instruction in our church."

Mary looked doubtful.

"Benjamin will also have the best tutors in the world and he will go to Harvard."

"Harvard?" Sean almost dropped his glass.

For the first time in her life Stella saw a glint of approval in her mother's eyes. Stella wanted to shout for joy. Her mother's practical side had overcome her bias. Harvard was a dream no Irish person dared dream. That it might be a reality for flesh of her flesh, was even too much for the coldhearted Mary to let pass without being impressed.

"Well, when we see that we will believe that!" Mary tried to be cynical.

"Harvard? Hot damn! That would be something, child. Now you have to admit that would be something, Mary." Sean finished his glass and held it out to Stella. "I think it's something that we should celebrate."

Mary gave him an icy look of censure. Stella and Sean froze as they waited on her reply.

Mary thought it over as she looked around the room at the expensive appointments. It was hard for her to disguise her appreciation of such fine things. Finally she held her glass out. "One more glass and that's all. I mean it, Sean. I mean it!"

"Yes, dear," Sean agreed as he winked at Stella.

Stella smiled back, knowingly.

Shannon dressed in his finest suit. He had Miriam and Rosie dust it off and press it. He had stolen a carnation from a flower cart and put it in his lapel. He put the letter in his inside coat pocket. He threw an overcoat over his shoulders and moved out into the snowfall. It was Christmas week and he intended to play Santa Claus.

He was going to give Stella a gift she did not ask for, but one that he would enjoying giving more than any he had given in his life.

CHAPTER TWENTY-SIX

Lyle rode into Vera Cruz bleeding from his wound. He eased his horse around to the back of the saloon where Maggie worked. He hoped she had some nursing skills and would consider him a friend. If not, he had enough money to convince her to help.

The pain in his shoulder was intense and he cursed Jules Joshua under his breath. He was just at the top of the stairs, when he encountered the tall blonde lady.

"Customers come in downstairs, cowboy. You know that. Trying to sneak a freebie?" she said.

"Which one is Maggie's room?" Lyle grimaced.

"I just told you it don't work like that …"

"Damnit! Which one?"

She stepped back and looked impressed. She moved down the hall and tapped on the door. "Maggie? Maggie, you busy?" She paused. "Who shall I say is calling?"

Lyle thought it over a minute.

"Tell her it's a man who found one of her lost handkerchiefs."

The blonde looked puzzled. "Oh? Oh, you're that guy who butted in to stop that animal who attacked her. Why didn't you say so?" She smiled and tapped on the door once more. "It's that knight in shining armor …" She looked at the pain on Lyle's face. "Only he don't seem so shining …. you okay, mister?"

"Just open the door and see if she's there."

The blonde started to open the door but Maggie beat her to it.

"Oh, it's you?" She stopped and looked at the blonde. "It's okay. I know him."

The blonde shrugged and moved off, quickly. After she was gone, Maggie looked at Lyle suspiciously. "You okay?"

"I need a place to sit a spell."

Maggie hesitated then opened the door wide.

Lyle came in and stumbled to the bed. He fell face down on it as Maggie closed and locked the door.

She walked over and looked at his blood-stained shirt. She shook her head in dismay.

"I don't need any trouble, mister. I know you helped me, but this looks like real bad trouble."

"I just need to rest a while. I don't mean to cause you no trouble."

Maggie took a towel and wet it in a wash basin. She found a pair of scissors. "I'm going to cut this shirt some so I can get at that wound," she said as she cut at the shirt without objection from Lyle.

Once the wound was exposed, Maggie pressed the damp towel against it. She had seen many knife wounds. She could tell Lyle was lucky to be alive.

"Look's like you turned your back on the wrong man." She thought it over. "Was it that man you took on in the bar over me?"

"How bad is it?" Lyle mumbled.

"It's deep but I think it missed everything important. If I get this bleeding stopped I think it'll be alright."

"I'll be glad to pay you for your time."

"It was that man. Jules Joshua. If he did this, you don't owe me nothin'."

"I aim to pay you for your time, anyways."

"I'm not going to argue with you, mister. This is my room. It's the one place in all the world that I'm the boss. So we'll see what we'll just see. Meantime, you just rest." She thought it over. "I'm going to Doc's and get some medicines ..."

"No! No doctors. No one is to know I'm here. No one!" Lyle tried to get up. He was too weak.

"Okay. If you say so. But there is only so much doctorin' I know and I've about done it."

Lyle turned, slightly, in the bed. "You done fine. It feels better already. I thank you, Maggie ..."

"Rachel. Please call me, Rachel. Maggie is my stage name."

"Rachel?" Lyle mumbled weakly. "I just want to sleep awhile. Please remember ... if you leave lock the door and tell no one, I'm here. No one! Please ..."

Rachel dabbed at the blood on his strong muscular back. Rachel was as cynical as the next "sporting lady" but there was something about him she liked. "Lyle? They call you Lyle?"

Lyle did not reply for a long moment.

"Lyle are you alright?"

"Yes. Thanks. I feel better ..."

"Lyle, I have to ask you just one more thing," Rachel insisted. Lyle mumbled agreement.

"Those men. All those men that left here with you. They were not your friends? Am I right?"

"I really need to rest, Rachel"

Rachel, suddenly, did not like it. "And I need to know if they'll be riding this way. If Gunnar is mad at you I can't help you!"

Lyle was drifting in and out of consciousness but he was alert enough to appreciate her position. "I swear to you, you don't have to worry about Gunnar. I swear ..." he slipped into a deep sleep.

Rachel felt he sounded sincere but she could not afford to take a chance. She decided she would let him sleep a few hours, then if Gunnar showed, she would tell Gunnar where he could be found.

◈ ◈ ◈

Jules was in a quandary. He knew instinctively that the guns were now big trouble. Yet it was against his nature to leave so much money buried in the ground. Jules had looked at the place he and Lyle had buried them and decided it was too much work to dig them up now. He had, finally, decided that he would come back for them after all his other business was finished. He figured if he could catch Lyle and kill him he would have the guns and money once again. As he rode into the outskirts of Vera Cruz, he thought he knew right where Lyle would go to hide out. He was extremely pleased with himself to see Lyle's horse tied behind the saloon. He backed his tired horse into the shadows and looked at the upstairs rear window. He fingered his Colt and pondered the best way to approach it.

It was almost sundown and he figured it would be best to wait until the salon filled with the usual drunks and whoremongers. He knew Gunnar had friends and he had to move cautiously around them. When he had left Gunnar's body the vultures were already circling. He expected by now someone had found them.

◈ ◈ ◈

General Nogales was furious. He was mad at Gunnar and he was mad at whoever had killed him. Gunnar was General Nogales' best gun runner and paid informant. Whoever had killed him was a man to be approached with caution. Gunnar had survived some very nasty situations and escaped with his life. General Nogales wondered how he had come to allow someone to kill him and cut off his gun hand.

General Nogales watched as his men dug graves for Gunnar and the others. He had no way of knowing the graves were only a few yards from where Lyle and Jules had buried the guns.

"*¡Andale!* Hurry up, *amigos!*" General Nogales encouraged them.

His men responded by digging faster until they had the graves prepared. General Nogales motioned for them to lower the bodies in the graves and cover them over. Once that was done, he made the sign of the cross and mumbled a quick prayer.

"Now we go!" he ordered as he mounted his horse.

His soldiers looked to him for instructions on which way to ride. General Nogales looked at the fresh tracks leading west. Whoever had killed Gunnar had left an easy to follow trail.

He said nothing as he turned his horse's head toward the setting sun and rode hard toward Vera Cruz.

Eli and the others stopped at a watering hole within three hours ride of Vera Cruz. It was almost night and the weak sunlight made it hard to see.

"We gonna set down here or ride on in tonight, Eli?" Scotty wondered aloud.

Eli was about to reply, when Maria pushed him aside and jumped down from his horse. She broke into a run and disappeared into the bushes by the water hole. He started to go after her but figured there was nowhere for her to run in the wilderness.

"She's a feisty one. Reminds me a little of Stella," Scotty mused aloud.

Eli scowled and showed he did not like that thought.

"I didn't mean anything by it, Eli."

"I know. I'm bone tired. What do you say we bed down here and ride in early in the morning? There's no sign that General is following us."

Scotty thought it over as he looked at his men.

"Well, that might be alright if we put a scout out to give an early warning."

Eli nodded agreement.

"Chief, you want to do some scouting?"

Chief looked doubtful, then shrugged. "I expect so, but I hope I don't nod off in the saddle."

"I tell you what. You ride out first and one of us will ride out and relieve you in a few hours. Okay?"

Chief tipped his hat and moved to refresh himself and his horse before riding out.

"I'll relieve him, Scotty," Shorty offered. "Just give me a lot of black coffee and a few nods."

"Thanks, Shorty. That'll work out just fine. Okay by you, Eli?"

"Yea. I think about four hours is all the rest we should take, and that with one eye open," Eli sighed.

"Right!" Scotty nodded agreement. Sam nodded agreement, as well.

Eli looked in the direction that Maria had disappeared. "I expect ... it would be a good idea ... I reckon ... I should make sure the little spitfire hasn't tried to run away," he half-laughed.

Scotty looked disgusted as Eli moved into the bushes to find her. "It's a mite nippy, Sam. You mind building us a fire?"

"You think that's such a good idea?" Sam wondered as he looked down the road behind them.

"I see what you mean. Maybe a small one to brew up a pot of coffee?"

Sam agreed and dismounted his horse. He took one look at Eli disappearing into the bushes and chuckled under his breath.

❖ ❖ ❖

Lyle was resting uneasy. Rachel had stopped the bleeding and had managed to rig up a passable bandage. His shoulder hurt but he felt himself regaining a little of his strength. He was rational enough to know that staying in this place much longer was dangerous.

He had just finished taking a bowl of hot soup from Rachel and he felt it was time to move on.

"I want to thank you for all you done, Rachel. I'm just about feelin' well enough to be gettin' out of your hair."

"I didn't say you were in my hair."

"Well, that's awful kind of you, but you know and I know there might be some trouble comin'. There ain't no need for it comin' your way."

Rachel was impressed by his honesty. She liked Lyle, but knew what he was telling her was true.

"Is it Gunnar?"

"No! Gunnar won't be troublin' you no more."

"He's dead, ain't he?"

Lyle nodded "Yes."

Rachel turned pale as she thought it over. "That's mighty bad. Mighty bad …"

"It couldn't be helped."

"But you don't understand. This is his town. All these people … even me. He's the one we all made our livin' off of. He's got friends here. Friends that make that Jules man look like a pussy cat!" Rachel seemed scared.

"I didn't say I killed him," Lyle said.

"If was you or your friend it don't make no never mind," she backed toward the door. "I have to ask you, kindly, to please leave."

Lyle nodded understanding. He eased up, painfully, and tried to stand up. He was too woozy to stand.

"I'll go get the bartender to help you out. I'm sorry, but I hope you understand."

"You ain't asking anything that I wouldn't be asking in your place. Just do me one more thing and I'll ride out. I promise."

"I don't know …"

"I need a fast horse. Could you have someone go to the livery and buy it. I'll pay top dollar." Lyle reached into his money belt and withdrew a substantial amount of money.

Rachel almost fainted as she saw it was Gunnar's money belt.

"No, sir! I don't want your money and I can't help no more. You've got to be going, mister! I mean it!"

Lyle sighed hard. He made another effort to stand. This time it was easier and he was able to walk stiffly. "Just help me down the stairs and I'll be leaving," he paused as he spied a bottle of whiskey on a table. He reached over and picked it up.

He took three long pulls from the bottle. The fiery fluid made him cough but somehow seemed to make him feel better. He put the money on the table.

Rachel started to pick it up and give it back.

"No! You deserve this and more. Thanks,"

Lyle paused and looked at her with admiration. "Maybe some other time we can have a drink together. Bye!"

Rachel did not reply as she ran to open the door. She reached the door, paused and turned. She looked at Lyle with pity and concern. "Look. You're in no condition to ride. Tell you what. I know a ship's captain who has a bark anchored nearby. For the right price he'll take you aboard and keep his mouth shut."

Lyle thought it over only a moment. "Thanks, but I ain't no sailor boy."

"And right now you ain't much of a horseman!"

Lyle winced in pain and looked at Rachel. He sighed hard and agreed with his eyes.

Ericka, the big blonde, heard a strange noise as she dismissed her timid banker friend with a kiss that made him blush. "Until next week, darling!" She tickled him in the ribs. He blushed and hurried off grinning from ear to ear. Ericka shrugged and started to go back into her room. Then she heard the noise again.

She thought it over and started to ignore it. Finally her curiosity overcame her good sense and she moved in the direction of the strange sound.

The sound came from the back staircase and she wondered if it was Jack, her impoverished lover, whom she often treated to a freebie. Jack sometimes came around this time of day but he had always made a date in advance. She smiled as she thought how he just couldn't keep away from her. "Jack? Jack, is that you?" Ericka reached the head of the back staircase and peered into the darkness.

There was no answer.

"Jack, I'm not ready for you today. This is a bad day. We can set up something for tomorrow …" she stopped as she saw a shadow of a man. "Jack, don't play scary games." Ericka moved onto the staircase to get a better look.

The man moved back into the shadows and seemed to disappear.

"Well, I don't have time for this. I've got work to do!" Ericka turned and started to walk back up the stairs. Moments later, she felt a firm hand on her shoulder. She turned to see the ugly face of Jules sneaking up the back stairs.

"You? You aren't supposed to be here. Rachel!" Ericka started to warn Rachel when Jules pushed his fist into her face and knocked her down the stairs.

Rachel had just opened her door when she and Lyle heard Ericka's cry then the sound of someone tumbling down the stairs.

Lyle sized up the situation and closed the door. "Damn! I don't have a gun. Damn!"

"It's him, isn't it?"

Lyle nodded. "Yes."

Rachel ran to her bed and reached under the mattress. She withdrew a Colt and handed it to Lyle. "Yes, you do!"

Lyle looked at the gun then at Rachel and smiled. "Thanks."

"Just kill him!"

"I certainly aim to, ma'am," Lyle saw a door on a far wall. "Where does that lead?"

"It goes into Ericka's room. You can get to the back hall that way." Rachel liked the idea. "Yes. You can get behind him through there. Hurry!"

"Lock your door and sit tight!" Lyle insisted as he moved through the door and out of the room.

After he was gone, Rachel turned her lock quietly and moved to a dark corner to wait.

Jules waited until he saw no movement from Ericka, then he eased, cautiously, up the stairs. Once at the top of the stairs he looked at the five doors on each side of the hall. He did not know which room was Maggie's, but he knew whichever one it was — Lyle was in it.

He hefted Gunnar's Colt in his hand and rattled the doorknob on the first door. It was the room three doors from where Rachel waited in the darkness but she heard it rattle. Jules pushed the door open and moved in ready to fire.

The room was empty.

Lyle was out into the hallway around the corner from Jules. He was slowly moving up behind Jules. He heard Jules rattle another doorknob and, slowly, cocked the hammer of the Colt.

Lyle was still weak but gathered strength at the idea of blowing Jules away.

Jules broke into a sweat as he closed the door to the second room which was also empty.

Jules wondered if he was checking out the wrong side of the hall. He thought it over and moved across the hall to a room door. He put his ear against the door and thought he heard noises. He grinned as he felt he had found what he was looking for.

Lyle readied himself to jump into the hallway where Jules was and fire before Jules had a chance to shoot back. Lyle figured, in his physical condition, he would have one chance. He was determined to make the most of it.

Jules turned the doorknob, slowly, and eased the door open. He grinned as he saw a hat like Lyle's on a bed post. He saw a gun belt and a pair of pants. He saw the back of a man in the bed with a woman. He leveled his gun to fire.

Lyle came around the corner and saw Jules aiming his gun into the room. Lyle aimed at Jules and fired.

Jules heard the bark of the Colt and turned to see Lyle shooting at him. The bullet missed and crashed into a window at the far end of the hall.

Lyle cursed his incompetence with a pistol. He wished to God he had his rifle.

Jules turned and fired at Lyle. A bullet tore Lyle's left ear off and he backed around the corner.

Jules was about to move down the hall when he felt a gun barrel against his head.

He turned to see a half-naked man with a mean look on his face, holding the Colt.

"What the hell is going on here, mister?"

"Aaahhmmm ... I'm the sheriff. I'm here to arrest that man," Jules tried.

The man cocked the hammer of the gun as he looked at Jules with disgust. The lady he had been with ran by him and disappeared down the hall. "That's funny. Last time I checked you were a fat Mexican with a big mustache. I guess you shaved the mustache."

Jules swallowed hard and wondered at his next move.

Lyle held his hand to his ear and felt the hot blood ooze between his fingers. He decided he was no match for Jules with a pistol. He had to get to his horse and get his rifle.

To get to the front staircase and down to his horse, he had to move across the hall.

Carefully, he eased around the corner. He raised the Colt and fired as fast as he could in the direction of Jules as he ran for the stairs.

The bullets distracted the man holding the gun on Jules. In that instant, Jules rammed his Colt into the man's gut and dropped him with one slug.

Then he turned to pursue Lyle.

Lyle was breathing hard as he reached his horse. He was covered with blood and weak but the sight of his rifle made him feel much better. With strength of purpose, he pulled the rifle from its holder. He lay it across his saddle and aimed at the doorway.

He waited for Jules to appear.

Jules moved past Ericka who lay at the foot of the stairs. She stirred, slightly, and he ignored her groans of pain. Jules knew Lyle would be waiting to waylay him outside.

He paused at the door and wondered if he shouldn't go around the other way and sneak up behind him.

Then he had a cunning idea. He removed his hat and eased it out of the door. He hoped to draw fire. Instead he drew laughter.

"That's about as dumb an idea as a man can have. Come on out, Jules. You been hiding behind the womenfolk too long," Lyle sneered.

"It ain't me that come here to hide behind a woman's skirt, Lyle!"

"Just come on out, Jules."

"Now, Lyle. I expect you got that rifle pointed right at this door. That ain't no fair chance for me."

"It's about as fair as you deserve."

"I don't think so, Lyle. I think I'll be goin' to the saloon and havin' a drink. You come join me and we'll straighten this whole mess out," Jules said as he eased to the door and prepared to jump out firing.

Lyle held his rifle steady and waited. He saw Jules' shadow and knew he would be out in a moment.

Jules saw a big fence post a few feet away. He figured if he made it there fast enough he could find cover and have a better angle to shoot at Lyle. He respected Lyle's aim but had pride in his speed.

Lyle opened his aiming eye wide and peered the length of the gun barrel. He eased his finger on the trigger and waited.

Jules was about to make his move when Ericka dug her claws into his shoulders. "You bastard!" Ericka snarled as she jumped on Jules' back.

Lyle heard a commotion and thought Jules was trying something else funny. He decided to fire at the first movement out of the door.

Jules was staggered by Ericka's attack.

Jules stumbled backwards out of the door with Ericka hanging from his neck.

Lyle smiled as he pulled the trigger.

The rifle barked and Lyle was about to shout for joy when

Ericka came between the bullet and Jules.

The bullet dropped Ericka to the ground and Jules came up firing. One round bounced off Lyle's forehead and he staggered backwards before he fell to the ground.

Jules ran to Lyle's side and put his Colt to Lyle's head. He pulled the trigger but his gun was empty.

Jules looked at Lyle's blood-covered face and figured him for dead. He spit in Lyle's face as he reached down and removed Gunnar's money belt.

Jules checked the money quickly. He took out his knife and started to cut Lyle's throat, but he heard the sound of a lot of people coming his way.

He put this knife away, mounted his horse and rode into the cover of night.

CHAPTER TWENTY-SEVEN

Eli watched Maria as she took off her sandals and waded out into the small pond. There was a full moon that lit up the night much too much for Eli's comfort. But the way it outlined her beauty with a circle of diamonds on the still water eased his concern.

He felt a little bad about interrupting her privacy. He looked around to see that she was safe and turned to go back to the camp.

"Can I not have one moment without you interfering in my life?" Maria yelled at him.

Eli started to keep going and not reply. He thought better of it. He paused and turned to look back at her. "I'm sorry, There are wild coyotes and rattlesnakes out here. And *banditos* ..."

"... and wolves!"

"Look! Look, I was just concerned for your well-being. You ... you take too much of what I do the wrong way!"

"Well, that's mighty easy to do since I haven't seen you do too much right."

"What's that supposed to mean?"

Maria looked disgusted as she moved out of the water and sat down on the sand. "I think you know the answer to that."

"No. No, ma'am! Why don't you just spit it out! We can settle all this now!" Eli said as he walked back to within a few feet of her.

Maria looked up at him and watched the moonlight reflect in his sparkling eyes. He stood tall and he was a handsome man. In another time and circumstance she would have considered him a marital prospect. "As I remember I had a good life ... a peaceable life, before you came along. Now what do I have? I cannot even bathe in privacy!"

Eli had to agree with her but he refused to accept all the blame. "The way I hear it, that General decided whether it was a good life or not. I don't expect he always made it so peaceable."

Maria looked hurt. "That's none of your business! You just stay out of my private life!"

"Well I guess you'd of been happier if I left you back there?"

"Perhaps?"

"Well Pepito don't think so. And I .. I don't think so."

"I think you think too much," Maria paused and looked at the moonlight. "But it really doesn't matter. He will come for me and in the end I will be back in his *casa chica* or I will be dead."

Eli did not like that thought but Maria always made good sense. He delighted in her common sense as much as he delighted in her beauty. "There are ships in Vera Cruz. I know ships. I can help you leave him if you have a mind to."

"Oh? I see. Just leave Mexico for the wonderful *Estados Unidos!* The United States where I will be treated with respect and honor?" Maria snarled, cynically.

"I will pledge myself to see that you are."

Maria looked deep into Eli's eyes and knew that he meant it. She also knew what prejudices she would face in the United States.

For all the pain General Nogales had caused her, he was at least a *compadre*. General Nogales was a bad man but she knew he would never look at her as if she were second class and call her a "dirty Mexican!"

She suspected Eli would never call her that either — except someday in a heated argument when reason had failed.

"That is noble of you but it is not enough." Maria replied.

"Then what is?" Eli insisted.

Maria looked confused. "I don't understand. What is what?"

"What is enough for me to say to make you come with me?"

Maria had never seen Eli look so strong and resolute. He was, suddenly, not the timid "schoolboy" who had confronted her in the chapel. He was, now, a man who knew exactly what he wanted.

"I understand you have a wife."

"I told you that is something on paper that I can make short work of. I have no feeling inside for Stella except feelings that are better left unsaid."

"You really don't like her, do you?"

"I can't say that I do."

"So why did you marry her?"

Eli was taken aback by the question. He had to think it over a moment. "I was lonely."

"Oh? I see. And are you lonely now?"

"It ain't exactly like that …"

"What is it like, Eli?"

Eli grimaced. He sighed hard and knelt down. He moved close beside her and looked her straight in the eyes. "It's like I ain't been able to put you from my mind since … since we … since the other night …" Eli paused and gathered strength. "I never had this feelin' and I don't know quite what to do with it. It ain't like Stella or Lydia or nobody."

"Lydia?"

Eli flinched. "Lydia was my first wife."

"How many have you had?"

"It ain't exactly like that."

"Oh? You are something, Eli! You just love them and then leave them? Well you can go loving in some other place, *señor!*"

"Lydia … she was killed!" Eli sighed hard. "She was killed along with my unborn son."

"A son?"

"That's what I figured it to be," Eli stopped and looked genuinely sad. "It was a long time ago. It don't have much to do with you and me."

Maria had never seen him so determined. She had never seen so much pain in his face.

"I'm sorry, Eli. The man you hunt in Mexico. He killed them?"

Eli nodded. "Yes."

Maria stood up and walked away. She had to think. She had to separate sympathy from feelings of love. She had fought hard to keep this *gringo* out of her heart and had been successful until this moment. She had regretted succumbing to passion and sadness when she made love to him on the night of Pancho's wake.

Her self-loathing for that act was finished and she could now see the real reason she had yielded to Eli. Eli was very lovable. Eli had all the good qualities she wanted in a man and she felt he loved her deeply. It would be easy to give herself to him again.

Eli moved up behind her and she could feel his warm breath on her neck. He put his hands gently on her shoulders. "I didn't mean to hold anything back from you. It shames me to know I don't think of Lydia much anymore."

"It's okay, Eli. We all have put some kind of hurt behind us."

"It ain't exactly like that …"

"You don't have to explain ..."

"I don't want all that past stuff gettin' in the way of what's goin' on now. I can't help none of that. I'm sorry, that's just what was."

Maria turned and looked up at him and smiled. "You know you apologize too much!"

Before Eli could reply she kissed him tenderly on the lips.

Twenty miles into the hills Shorty brought his horse to a stop. He looked disturbed by what he saw.

The moon was behind a wall of dark clouds and the night was suddenly pitch black. He looked down into a distant arroyo and saw a hundred campfires.

He grimaced as he turned his weary horse and rode hard back to camp to alert the others.

CHAPTER TWENTY-EIGHT

Stella knew a storm was coming, though the sky was devoid of clouds and there was no wind. Stella had heard of old-timers who could predict the arrival of a nor'easter days in advance. Stella was no Boston old-timer but she could predict this one.

As she stood on the widow's walk she could see dark clouds on the horizon that boded no good.

Stella could not hear the doorbell and Helga, cleaning the back bedroom, did not hear it in time to respond before Mary opened the door.

"Top of the morning, madam. I'm sorry I haven't had the pleasure." Shannon looked puzzled.

"You're an Irishman?"

"Yes, ma'am. I'm that alright. With no apologies."

"And why should you apologize?"

Shannon picked up Mary's Irish brogue and knew he had found a soulmate. "You're Irish?" Shannon looked at her and thought it over. "I'll bet you're Stella's mother."

"Aye! And who might you be?"

"He's Shannon O'Bannion and he's not welcome here," Helga tried to shut the door.

"Oh? Well let me be the judge of that. Come on in, Shannon," Mary said as she moved in front of Helga.

Helga mumbled something under her breath and moved back upstairs to her chores.

Shannon came inside and his eyes searched for any sign of Stella. It seemed Stella's mother liked him and he was inside the house without a fight. He patted the letter in his pocket and thanked whatever gods that be for his good fortune.

"I'm Mary. Come into the parlor and meet my husband, Sean. We're from County Down. And you?"

"Wexford. Stella didn't say anything about relatives here in Boston."

"Well, she should have spoke of us and she should have told you we were in New York. I sometimes wonder if she's ashamed of her heritage."

Shannon thought to himself, if Mary only knew how right she was she would give Stella the back of her hand. He found that idea appealing.

"Sean," Mary addressed her husband who sat back on the couch as they entered the room. "Get up and meet a fine Irish lad that Stella has been keeping form us."

Sean got up and shook Shannon's hand. "Well, that calls for a celebration. We just happen to have some good Irish whiskey on hand."

"Sean! It's too early in the day for that!" Mary stopped him from reaching the bottle.

Sean and Shannon's eyes met in common disappointment.

"What are you doing here, Shannon?" Stella interrupted them.

Shannon smiled thinly as he replied. "Mary was kind enough to invite me in. Why didn't you tell me you had such a fine Irish parents?"

Stella could barely contain her anger, but she saw the way her mother looked at Shannon. "Well to be honest, Mother. I thought after our last lover's quarrel I would never see him again."

Shannon smiled in admiration of Stella's quick thinking. "Ah, but I could not stay away. I cannot stay mad at her for very long."

"You know it's too late, Shannon. I'm sorry but I am betrothed." Stella said with a tone to invoke sympathy.

"I came here today to ask that ... that maybe you reconsider," he made his Irish eyes mist.

"Well, if you want my opinion, I say undo it. Adams is a damn Yankee Protestant!" Mary insisted.

Stella gritted her teeth. She glared at Shannon, then looked agreeable. "I don't believe that's possible, Mother. But I should give Shannon the courtesy of listening to what he has to say. Do you mind if we talk it over in private?"

Mary's eyes lit up at the prospect of an Irish man for her Stella. "Yes. By all means, yes. Come on, Sean. Let's go in the kitchen."

"Can I take the bottle?" Sean reached for it.

Mary started to object, then shrugged. "Why not. There might be something to celebrate today after all," she smiled at Shannon and gave Stella a hard look before they left the room.

Sean whispered prayers of thanksgiving as he picked up the bottle and followed after her.

Once they were gone, Stella glared at Shannon with an intensity that made him feel awkward.

"You opportunistic bastard! How dare you come into my home and try to slip your way into my parents' good graces. If we were in San Francisco I would have your sneaky throat cut and no one would ever hear from you again! Do you understand me?"

"You have no call to talk to me like that, Stella. They invited me in."

"They don't know you. I do."

"No, you don't! You know that I'm not a rich Yankee, that I'm just a poor Irishman on his way up. You think I'm nobody and that might be true now. But someday I'll be somebody and then maybe I won't give *YOU* the time of day!"

"I thought I told you not to come here anymore."

"Oh, you did and I fully intended to honor your wishes. I certainly do not want to be anywhere I'm not wanted ..."

"... then why are you here?"

Shannon gave her a leprechaun smile and walked over to the table holding the decanter of brandy.

He poured himself a big glass.

"No one offered you a drink, Shannon. You have some nerve!"

"Will you not allow me to toast your betrothal?"

"I want you out of here, now!"

"But what will Mary and Sean say? Aren't we supposed to be discussing our reconciliation?"

"I'll take care of them. I don't want to have to tell you again!"

"Here's to Stella and Winthrop C. Adams."

Shannon paused and lifted his glass. "May they have a happy and prosperous marriage. May it last as long as ... as ... well as all of Stella's marriages. Or at least as long as her present marriage."

Stella did not like the mischievous look in Shannon's eye. He knew something and she was afraid to know what. "Have your drink and your little game then go! Do you understand me?"

"No! Do you understand me?"

"If you have something to say to me, spit it out. I don't have time to dilly dally with you, Shannon!"

Shannon poured another glass of brandy.

He gave Stella a cold stare. "You know I could have cared for you a lot. We would have been good together. But you wanted to be a Boston Brahmin. You spit on me because I wasn't socially acceptable."

"I'm not going to listen to this!"

"Oh yes, you are!" He looked resolute.

Stella stepped back as his eyes danced with affection and hatred.

"I don't care so much about me. Yes, I'm mad about it, but that's alright. But you hurt Rosie to her bone. She would have died for you. Rosie has a good heart, Stella. You and I can have our differences and survive, but Rosie is not a survivor."

"I liked Rosie. But you know there was a problem."

"Yes! You wanted to be a social climber and we were both in your way," he paused and grinned. "Well, you didn't make it after all, Stella."

"What the hell are you talking about?"

"I'm talking about a woman who turned her back on her people to try to be somebody she wasn't. A woman who had a past she thought was buried and is making wedding plans but forgot one important detail."

Shannon stopped and looked into Stella's eyes. He waited for her response.

Stella sensed he knew something but she did not want to give him the satisfaction of showing any emotion. She moved to the table and poured a glass of brandy. She smiled at Shannon as she sipped it. "And what might that be, Shannon?"

"Well, it's my understanding, polygamy is illegal in Massachusetts."

Stella almost dropped her glass before she regained her composure. "I don't know what you're talking about."

"Well, Jason Rubin knows what I'm talking about."

"You bastard! How do you know Jason?"

"Oh? Now I have her attention."

"Just spit it out!"

"Okay, I will," he thought it over. "I have a friend who brought me information ... reliable information ... that you are not a widow or even a divorcee. You have a husband in California, Stella. Winthrop, and his family, would find that a little difficult to take, don't you suppose?"

"What friend? You don't have such friends. Besides he's a lair!"

"Come on, Stella. You built a house of cards. Didn't you stop to think it would come tumbling down someday?"

"Who do you think you are to come into my house with these vicious accusations. I can have you fixed permanently for this!"

"This isn't California, Stella. And besides you didn't fix it too good there." Shannon handed her the letter.

Stella took it and her hand shook as she read it.

"I have friends who watch out for me, Stella. I did not do this myself."

Stella drank her brandy in one gulp. She looked at Shannon with hatred, then with her seductive gaze. "Do you still care for me, Shannon?"

Shannon wanted to say "No!" but his eyes revealed his answer was "Yes."

"I'm sorry if I hurt you, Shannon. It wasn't personal. You have to understand it was all for Benjamin. All of this was for him, for his future. If you care for me, for him, you'll forget about this letter. And if you do, you will have my undying affection. Please, I beg you?"

Shannon shook his head in dismay. "You are something, Stella. You never quit. God, I love that about you. But you have such a blind spot. What kind of future could Benjamin have built on a lie?"

Stella gave Shannon a steady gaze. "He will have all that you and I never knew or ever dared to hope for."

Shannon sympathized with Stella's motive but did not have any sympathy for her methods. "Benjamin will do fine on his own. Boston is changing even now. We will have political power soon, then everything will fall into place. I tell you, Stella, in our lifetime, Benjamin will be proud to walk the streets and declare he's an Irishman."

"Pipe dreams. Stupid pipe dreams!"

"No! I will be the mayor of this town, someday. I an Irish immigrant, a shoe-shine boy and lamplighter. I see it coming, Stella. You could have come with me."

Stella sighed hard. She walked over to the window and watched the storm clouds increase in size and intensity. "What do you intend to do next, Shannon?"

Shannon picked the letter up off the floor. He put in back in his pocket. He put down his glass and moved to the door. "I want nothing for myself."

"Oh, really? How about twenty thousand dollars up front? How about a monthly stipend of ... oh, let's say, two thousand dollars?"

Shannon looked disgusted and shook his head sadly.

"I want you to be a friend to your people, Stella."

"That is not possible."

"Not possible, Stella?"

"I won't go back, ever, Shannon!"

"Go back? You have never left! You have been so busy trying to be what you are not that you can't see you are not one of them and they won't ever let you be," Shannon stopped and patted the letter. "I won't let you be."

"What are you saying?"

"I'm saying proceed at your own risk."

"You have no idea what you're dealing with! I don't like threats."

"No threat. A promise. You'll thank me someday."

"Never! If you do any damage to me, Shannon, I will see that your political career is the shortest one in history. Do you understand?"

"I understand, Stella, but you don't. It's sad but you just don't see it."

"I see an opportunist who had better be careful who he makes mad. Winthrop Adams has powerful friends."

"Yes, and they will destroy you much better than I ever could." Shannon picked up his hat to leave.

Stella wondered what to do. She did not have a plan yet, but she did not want him to go away mad.

"Have one more glass of brandy before you go. After all, it's almost Christmas."

Shannon looked suspicious. He put down his hat and took a glass that Stella poured. "Plying me with an Irishman's weakness, Stella?"

Stella gave him her best sincere smile. "I have wronged you, Shannon. You pulled me from the ice and I have treated you shabbily. I'm sorry."

"I wish I could believe that, Stella."

"I promise, from now on I will make a conscious effort to earn your trust."

Shannon knew Stella to be an accomplished liar but she was now telling lies he wanted to believe. He loved her and he had now had his revenge for her scorn.

Emotionally, he could now afford to give her the benefit of the doubt. Now, if he had an opportunity, no matter how slight, to win her love he would gamble on dealing with her lies.

"I would like that, Stella. You don't mind if I remain cynical for some time?"

"I would expect it."

"... I see ..."

"No, Shannon I don't think you do. I am a stubborn woman but a very practical one. I do what is necessary. I think it is necessary for us to try to be friends and, if you wish me to be ... a friend to my people."

"Holy Mother of God! I would give anything to believe that!"

"Will you accept deeds instead of words?"

"Of course? But what ..."

"You will have to go along with me until I have it all worked out. I cannot disengage all at once, but I will give you something to hold on to today."

"I told you I don't want your money!"

Stella looked at him with affection. "Would you accept my hand in marriage?"

Shannon dropped his glass. It shattered and splashed brandy all over Stella's dress.

Moments later, Mary and Sean came rushing into the room.

"Stella? Stella, are you alright? We heard ..." Mary stopped and looked at the broken glass. "My goodness!"

"It's okay, Mother."

"Are you sure?" Sean joined Mary.

"Oh, yes. Shannon has convinced me to call off my wedding to Winthrop. Looks like he and I will get back together."

Shannon, Mary, and Sean looked dumfounded before they all broke into rejoicing.

Chapter Twenty-nine

Shorty rode hard into camp and pulled his horse up quick. Scotty saw him first and ran to find out what was going on.

"It's the General and his army. There's a whole passel of them camped about twenty miles out." Shorty stopped to catch his breath. "I don't think we'd better be campin' here tonight."

"Damn! How can you make that good of time with an army? Where's Eli?"

"He went off thataway. He was looking for … Maria …." Sam looked cynical.

Scotty nodded agreement. "Well, go get him. We've got to ride out tonight. We got to be in Vera Cruz by morning."

"I'm here, Scotty. What's goin' on?" Eli entered the camp with Maria trailing just behind him.

"You heard Shorty?" Scotty wondered.

"Sort of."

"General Nogales … seems he's camped out not too far from here. I think we'd better ride."

"How many, Shorty?"

"There's a bunch, Eli. I never saw so many campfires."

Eli grimaced and agreed. "Let's saddle up. Thanks, Shorty."

They all went about preparing to leave quietly and efficiently. When they were ready to leave, Maria moved to Eli's side and mounted his horse without objection. The others noticed her change in attitude and shook their heads, knowingly.

Scotty was Eli's friend but he, now, wondered at the wisdom of keeping Maria. It occurred to him that maybe the General would not follow if they cut her loose.

Eli saw the look in Scotty's eyes. "If you boys want to split up, now's the time to say so."

Shorty started to say something but looked at the others and remained silent.

"It's not that, Eli. You know these are good boys. It's just the odds don't seem to be in our favor." Scotty spoke up.

Maria saw what was going on and looked sad. "Scotty is right, Eli. It's time I went home."

"No! They can leave, but you ain't going back!" Eli looked at Scotty. "I understand, Scotty. You go on ahead. Maria and I will take our chances. Thanks for coming this far."

Scotty looked at the others. They all seemed doubtful.

"I always wanted to see the ocean," Chief spoke up.

"Me too," Sam added.

"You boys is crazy but you ain't goin' anywhere without me," Shorty insisted.

Scotty sighed hard. "I must be crazy too. Let's go. The smell of the ocean seems right appealing to me also."

Eli smiled at his friend as they turned and headed toward Vera Cruz.

◈　◈　◈

Jules knew he had to get out of town. He had the money to buy his way out and he looked around for the safest way possible. He figured if the General was going to come looking for him, the last place he would look would be on board a ship. Jules did not like water. He, particularly, did not like water that moved.

But he had casually met unscrupulous sea captains in Vera Cruz and sailing back to California seemed like the best way to go.

"Them boats of your'n. They seem mighty rickety to me," Jules said as he looked at Captain Rogers across a table and a glass of whiskey.

"The Eureka has made the voyage thirty-seven times without incident. From Panama to San Francisco there is no more reliable ship!" he insisted.

"Like I told you, I need special passage."

"We are experts in "special" passages. Discretion is my middle name."

"That may be so, but you understand I don't just take a man's word for nothin'. I got to see things afore I make up my mind."

"Well, in this case, that's not possible. You either sail with us or you don't."

Jules had heard about the shanghaiing of able-bodied men and he did not like the look the Captain gave him. "I've been shot up and ain't able to do no hard labor. You understand?"

Captain Rogers laughed. "My crew is made up of people whose gold fever has played out. I pay them well. I do not need to gang-press anyone … specially men who've been hurt."

Jules still did not like it but knew the Captain sailed in the morning. He wanted to be out of town by then.

"Fifteen hundred dollars seems like a powerful lot of money just to ride on a boat."

The Captain looked very irritated with Jules. He got up to leave. "I picked up a full compliment of passengers in Panama. There is barely room for you. If you want to come, the pick-up boat will be in the south cove at daylight."

"I didn't say I didn't want to come. I just said what I had to say." Jules counted out seven hundred and fifty dollars. "I'll pay the rest when I'm on board."

Captain Rogers took the money and put it in his pocket. He nodded agreement and walked out of the dark *cantina* without further comment.

Jules growled under his breath. Jules prided himself on reading a man's intentions in his eyes. Jules knew there would be no boat waiting in the cove come tomorrow morning.

❖ ❖ ❖

Eli could tell Maria was very tired as they reached the outskirts of Vera Cruz. Eli was tired also. He could tell that the others could use a rest so he looked for a safe place to set down for a spell.

Eli knew their best chance of survival was to hide out on the seedy side of Vera Cruz. There they would find the most *Juaristas* and most friendly sea captains.

There they would find the most people who had reason to hate General Nogales.

But Eli had no illusions. Many *Juaristas* would turn their back on their ideals for the right price. Eli was low on funds and knew he did not have the right price to buy much of anything in Vera Cruz. He prayed he had enough to buy his and Maria's passage to California.

Eli signaled the others to pull their horses around to the back of the saloon. They dismounted and walked their horses to the hitching rail.

"*Señor* Eli! Look! Look!" Pepito exclaimed as he pointed to the horse with the rifle in the saddle holster.

Eli saw the gold plated butt of the rifle with the initials L.J. and looked at Scotty and the others.

"Lyle Jameson. Looks like he's here. You fellas go have a drink. I'll look around some." Eli grimaced as he scanned the area quickly.

"He rides with the man you seek?" Pepito wondered aloud.

Eli looked at the single horse and thought it over. "Maybe … maybe not."

"Shorty, you, Sam, and the Chief take Maria and go have a drink. Eli and I will meet you there in a while," Scotty insisted.

"That's not necessary, Scotty."

"Don't start that, Eli. You need someone to watch your back."

Eli looked doubtful, then nodded agreement.

Maria did not like it, but she knew better than to waste words trying to stop Eli. "There is a red lantern in the upstairs window. Perhaps he is there."

"Go along with the boys, please, Maria. I'll be along directly," Eli replied.

"No! I know some people here. I will go find out about the ships," Maria said firmly.

Eli looked deep into her eyes to read what she was thinking. "A ship to California, right, Maria?"

Maria leaped into the saddle of Eli's horse. She half-nodded agreement then rode off.

"Should I follow her, Eli?" Shorty asked.

Eli thought it over.

"No! No, she would most probably shoot you. She'll … be back …" Eli wondered aloud.

Scotty looked doubtful and could see that Shorty, Sam, and the Chief agreed with him. Eli ignored their cynical looks as they moved into the saloon and left him and Scotty alone.

"I'll ease up the stairs first, Scotty." He stopped and checked his gun. "I would appreciate it if you would watch my backside."

Scotty withdrew his gun and checked it.

The steps creaked as Eli eased up them toward the room where they had seen the red lantern. He stopped in his tracks as he saw a trail of dried blood that led to the door of the room.

Quietly, he pointed the blood stains out to Scotty. Scotty looked worried as he moved more and more cautiously behind Eli.

Once at the door, Eli paused and put his ear to the door to listen. He heard the voices of several people. He held up three fingers to Scotty.

"That many?" Scotty whispered.

Eli shrugged as he put his hand on the doorknob. "You take anybody I don't see first." Eli said softly.

Scotty nodded agreement.

Eli took a deep breath and blew it out hard. With one quick motion, he turned the doorknob and shoved the door open. He and Scotty burst into the room ready to fire. They both were unprepared for what they saw.

Rachel and an old sawbones were attending to what looked like a semiconscious Lyle lying in a pool of blood.

"Who the hell are you?" Rachel snarled.

Eli figured Lyle to be mortally wounded, so he slowly put his gun away. "Who shot him, miss?"

Lyle's eyes opened slightly at the sound of Eli's voice.

"You men have no business here. Can't you see I'm tending to a severely wounded man?" Doc tried to shoo them out.

"Was it Jules?" Eli pressed.

"You know him? Are you friends of his?" Rachel's voice trembled with rage.

Eli shook his head. "No!"

Lyle raised up, slightly, and motioned for Eli to approach. Scotty still held his gun on Lyle as Eli moved up to the bed.

Lyle's eyes were weak but burned with hatred.

"Kill! Kill! ... kill him for me, Eli!" Lyle coughed up blood.

Eli said "Yes!" with his eyes.

Lyle lay back down and sighed hard.

"Please gentlemen. he doesn't have the strength for this," Doc insisted.

"I'm sorry but there are some things we need to know," Eli replied.

"Well, can't you see he's in no condition to be carrying on no conversations!"

"It's okay, Doc. I know all he knows. I'll talk to these gentlemen," Rachel said as she motioned Eli and Scotty aside. "If Lyle wants you to kill this man then I trust you. What do you need to know?"

"Where is Jules?" Eli asked.

"He rode out after he shot Lyle."

"Which way?"

"I believe he rode toward the water."

"The water? … a ship? Damn!" Eli thought it over. "Where would such a man find a ship?"

"Miramar, the sailor's *cantina?* Juan Mirabella!" Pepito appeared and spoke up proudly.

"Where? Who? Pepito?" Eli looked shocked and pleased.

"Yes, *Señor* Eli. The *cantina* where the sailor men go. *Mi tio* Juan he knows everything." Pepito smiled.

"Pepito? What are you doing here? You are supposed to be resting at camp."

"I followed to help. I can take you to the Miramar."

"You are well?"

"Sí, señor Eli. I can go on the ship also?"

Eli shrugged.

Pepito looked disappointed but broke into a smile.

"This uncle of yours? He can help?" Eli hurried.

"He is not a real uncle but he was like a brother with Pancho."

"God! Maria? That's where she would have gone! Yes. Pepito! Where is it?"

"It is on the waterfront, of course." Pepito stopped and shared Eli's concern.

Eli did not reply but turned and hurried downstairs. Scotty and Pepito followed behind.

"You come with me. Get on Chief's horse," Eli motioned to Pepito.

Pepito nodded "Yes," and leaped up, obediently.

"Tell Chief I'm borrowing his horse. Meet me at the sailor's *cantina* as soon as you can!" Eli said.

Scotty nodded agreement.

Eli mounted Chief's horse and sat behind Pepito. He turned the horses' head and they rode hard off toward the waterfront.

Scotty watched him disappear then moved into the saloon to get his men.

◼ ◼ ◼

Jules sat in a corner in the dark and watched the pretty *señorita* enter the *cantina.* He thought she looked out of place in this seedy bar.

She was too young and beautiful to be a common whore. He figured her to be some powerful Mexican's kept lady.

Jules had terrible judgement, but once in awhile his instincts were right.

Jules did not like the hard edges of most of the whores who plied their trade in this place. Sailors were not much for being picky after so many months at sea. Jules figured he deserved the best and this *señorita* was the very best. He spit on his hands and patted down his hair before he got up to intercept her.

Maria saw him coming and found him instantly repulsive. She searched the *cantina* for any sign of her friend Juan Mirabella, the owner.

"Pardon me, missy. But I have a table in the corner over there. I can get a fresh bottle if you'll join me." Jules grinned.

"Get out of my way!" Maria tried to push past him.

"Hold on, little lady! I don't mean no harm, I made you a right friendly offer. Now you just have no call being so uppity ..."

"Leave me alone or I'll have Juan throw you out!"

"Maybe you didn't understand. I offered to share my table with you."

"And I told you to get out of my way!" Maria glared as she backed away.

Jules gritted his teeth and balled his fist to punch her. "I ain't lettin' no whore talk to me like that!" Jules reared back and a huge hand closed on his arm. He turned to look up in Juan Mirabella's eyes.

Juan was as big around as he was tall, and he was over six feet tall. His arms were bigger than Jules' legs and he had a fierce look in his eyes. "You want to apologize to Maria?"

"What for? I ain't ... ow!" Jules stopped as Juan twisted his arm hard. "Okay, missy, I'm sorry ... okay?"

Maria shrugged. Juan let Jules go.

Jules glared at him as he backed away. "You ain't heard the last of this, mister. You ain't, you hear?"

Juan did not reply, but watched as Jules disappeared into the shadows.

"Maria, what are you doing here? You know this is no place for any decent person."

"I'm in trouble with the General, Juan."

"Nogales?"

"Yes."

"Jesus! That's big trouble." He looked worried. "That's trouble

I can't help you with."

"You know lots of ship captains."

"Yes?"

"You know captains who sail to America and do not care who rides with them?"

"… you want to sail to America?"

"No! It is not for me, it is for my four *compañeros.*"

Juan looked behind her and saw no one. He looked puzzled.

"They are still at the saloon on the other side of town. They will be here in a little while. … if they do not get killed."

"What have you done, Maria?"

Maria hung her head in shame. "That is not important. These men have done nothing for which to die. They are not *Juaristas.* Can you help them?"

Juan looked doubtful.

"Maria, I support the cause of Benito Juárez, but I have to do it in a quiet way. It would not be good to make General Nogales mad," Juan paused and looked very worried. "The General, he is coming? … here?"

"Yes. But do not worry Juan. I will take care of him if you will take care of my friends."

Juan thought it over. "I do not know, Maria. Where is Pancho? He could help you with this …"

"… Pancho is dead." Maria let her eyes mist. "General Nogales hung him and dragged his body through the street for hours before dumping him on my doorstep."

"*¡Aye caramba!* None of this is good for business,"

Juan scratched his head. He did not like it, but Pancho and he had been childhood playmates and Juan had loved Maria from afar all his life. "I know this one captain. I believe he can be trusted."

"Good! Can you have him meet my friends here later?"

"Perhaps. … and where will you be?"

Maria looked sad then regained her composure. "I ride to met the General."

Juan sighed and nodded understanding. Then he looked fearful.

"No! I will not let you do this. You must sail for America also. There is a ship leaving this very morning."

"No, Juan! I must delay the General. If I do not stop him he will kill everyone."

"Maria? Maria, you always see things so simply."

"I don't understand?"

"If he is very mad then he will kill everyone anyway." Juan thought it over. "This killing of Pancho, you saw this?"

Maria looked very sad and nodded a quiet "Yes."

"I am sorry for this so I will help you. We will go get the Captain now."

Maria put up her hand and stopped Juan. She had a determined look in her eyes. "Please, just help my friends. My friend Señor Eli is a big man and he rides with three others, one *blanco*, one *es Indio*, one *muy pocito.*"

"Your friend, *Señor* Eli? He is the reason the General is mad?"

"I'm sorry, Juan. Now you see I must ride to meet the General."

"No, Maria. For such a thing his blood will be *muy caliente!* No! I will hide you and your friends until Captain Rogers sails. Maybe with enough *tequila* and women I can make the General believe a lie."

Maria started to object but thought better of it. She was still determined to ride to intercept the General. But she would wait until Juan helped her friends — until she knew Eli was safe.

"Come with me. I will have Diego take you to Simeon's house. It is close by the cove where the ship waits. I will meet your friends and bring them along."

Juan held out his hand.

Maria, reluctantly, took his hand and followed him to the back of the *cantina* where Diego waited.

Jules did not take his eyes off of Maria for a second. He took his gun from his belt and lay it on the table in front of him. He pondered where he would place the shots that he would use to kill Juan. He shivered with pleasure as he thought of how he would take Maria.

Jules waited until Maria and Diego disappeared out of the back of the *cantina* and Juan moved into the shadows. He spit twice on the floor, picked up his gun and followed after them.

General Nogales was tired and mad. He was a dangerous man when he was mad, but even more dangerous when he was tired and angry. In such a mood, he had once shot one of his men for

giving him a crazy look. It did not matter that the man was naturally cross-eyed. As he led his men into Vera Cruz he was ready to
end the chase. Whoever had made him ride this far was going to
pay. Someone would die today to satisfy his anger and allow him
to rest easy this night but he knew he had to be cautious. Parts of
Vera Cruz were thick with *Juaristas*. General Nogales was, in his
own way, a brave man. He did not fear much, except being shot
in the back by a turncoat.

He knew even in his ranks there were those who might shoot
him in the back given the right opportunity. His fatigue came
from always having to look over his shoulder and his anger from
the thought that anyone would dare betray him.

He thought this day it would be Juan Mirabella's day to die.
Juan had been useful until now. He had let Juan get away with
many things because Juan had supplied he and his men with many
pleasures.

He also knew Juan trafficked in contraband and helped smuggle
people out of Mexico and that was, where Maria would be.

And she, for her betrayal, would die also.

Shorty saw them first.

Shorty, Scotty, Chief, and Sam had just started to ride to meet
Eli, when the dust cloud in the distance told Shorty the General
was coming.

Scotty followed Shorty's eyes and grimaced. "Let's ride hard,
laddies!"

"Amen!" Sam added as he saw the dust cloud and checked his
revolver.

Chief swallowed hard as he leaped up on Shorty's horse. "Good
thing that you are not too heavy, short stuff!" he kidded Shorty.

"I told you not to call me ... Oh, the hell with it!" Shorty snapped
as they rode hard toward the waterfront.

Eli was uneasy. He did not see his horse tied up in front of the
cantina. He looked at the name, Miramar, written in faded red
paint on the front of the *cantina*.

This was the right place, but where was his horse and where
was Maria? He relaxed when he figured she had tied it out back.

Eli paused to see if Scotty and the others were coming. The street seemed empty in every direction. An erratic wind blew dust into tiny tornadoes that caused temporary blindness.

Eli covered his face with his bandanna as he motioned for Pepito to follow. Sailors were packed elbow to elbow in the smoked-filled *cantina*. Eli searched through the smoke to see her, but there was no sign of her.

"This Juan, do you see him, Pepito?"

Pepito searched the room. "No, *Señor* Eli, I do not see him. But he is always here. He is easy to see, He is *muy gordo!* Very fat upside and downside."

Pepito laughed. Eli did not.

The old familiar feeling of dread began to overcome Eli. He smelled the presence of Jules.

Eli's gut told him Jules was either here or had been here. "Well, we've got to find him. We've got to find Maria. Let's look in the back …"

"Over there. There is Juan!" Pepito ran over to Juan as the smoke cleared enough for Juan to be seen. Eli followed behind and watched as they greeted each other like long lost brothers. They chatted a long moment before Eli joined them.

"*Señor* Eli, this is my 'Uncle' Juan Mirabella."

"Juan …"

"*Señor* Eli."

"Good news! Juan has sent Maria to Simeon's house. They are getting us a ship."

"Where?"

"A ship in the cove …"

"No! Where is this house?"

"Oh? It is not too far. You want to go there now?"

Eli felt a chill that went to the bone. His nostrils flared with the smell of danger. He felt an evil coldness in the air. He knew he had to get to Simeon's in a hurry.

He knew he had to get there before Jules did.

Jules hung back in the shadows and watched two riders heading to the remote little hut just above the cove where Captain Rogers' ship was anchored. Jules did not like it. Jules expected the worst of people so he figured the riders were heading to set him up.

Jules would have shot them in the back by now if he had not wanted to know what they were up to.

He almost fell off his horse when he saw Captain Rogers walk out of the front door of the house and light his pipe.

Jules watched as Captain Rogers took a lantern and signaled his ship.

Moments later, a lantern on the ship sent a return signal.

The fiery top of a crimson sun broke through a black woolen sky bringing the first light of morning as Jules watched men on the ship lower a boat into the water.

"Damn them to hell!" Jules cursed. "They gonna leave without me!" He paused and thought it over. "Well, they got another think coming!" He eased his horse into the shadows behind the house.

He dismounted and crept up to the window. He sneaked a look inside.

Maria was seated at a table talking to Diego and another man Jules had never seen. Jules decided that if he killed them all, that would impress Captain Rogers. He hoped it would impress him so much that Jules would have no further problems. He, slowly, withdrew his pistol from his belt and made sure it was fully loaded. He eased toward the back of the house. He was about to kick the door in when he heard hoof beats.

He turned in the direction of the sound and could not believe his eyes. It was still early morning light but it was bright enough for Jules to see what he thought he would never see again.

Coming at him out of the morning mist was Eli followed by a young boy.

Jules grinned from ear to ear as he raised his Colt and fired.

Eli knew he would never doubt his instincts again. They told him Jules was near and the man firing at him was sure enough, Jules, the devil incarnate.

The muzzle flashes from Jules' gun did not cause Eli to slow his horse one bit. Instead he kicked it into a full gallop and headed straight toward the gunfire. Bullets whizzed by his head in near misses as Eli drew his Colt and returned fire.

Jules cursed himself for missing as he emptied his gun. The sight of Eli bearing down on him was unnerving as he drew his other gun. Near misses from Eli's gun blasted adobe into Jules' eyes — then it occurred to him.

This woman inside? This Maria who rejected him.

Could it be his good fortune that this woman was someone Eli cared about?

Jules decided she was.

He fired two shots at Eli then kicked the door open. Simeon confronted him with an ancient shotgun that fired more smoke than lead.

Jules dropped Simeon with one shot.

Diego grabbed a table knife and took a defensive pose. Maria backed into a corner.

Jules fired a shot through Diego's chest. He dropped to the floor.

Jules kicked him to make sure he was dead, then advanced on Maria. "You know Eli Llynne?" Jules growled.

"Who are you?"

"Yeah, you know him alright. Well, you ain't gonna be knowin' him much longer!" Jules grabbed her by the hair and pulled her in front of him.

He backed into a corner and waited for Eli to come through the door.

Eli dismounted on the run and headed straight for the door of the hut. He did not know what lay behind the door but he knew he was not going to hesitate this time.

The door was partially open and he could see two bodies on the floor. He was relieved to see neither of them was Maria.

"I'm coming in shooting, Jules. God help me, I'm gonna kill you real dead this time for sure!"

"You do that, Eli! I got plenty of bullets for you … and one for this pretty lady!"

Jules fired two rounds at the door.

The bullets ripped through the thin wood of the door, splintering it into pieces.

Eli saw Maria and Jules' arm around her neck through the smoke. He did not have a clear shot.

Jules grinned, knowingly. "I thought you was comin' in shootin'!"

"You gotta hide behind a woman's skirts, Jules?"

"I ain't hidin'. I'm right here."

Eli moved to the right of the door frame toward a small window. The window was cloudy with grease except for a small clear patch.

He could see Jules but wasn't sure if Jules could see him.

"Look's like you're doin' the hidin', Eli."

Eli raised his gun barrel to the small clear patch of glass. He cocked the hammer of the gun.

There was just enough clearance between Maria's head and Jules that Eli thought he could put a bullet.

He was about to fire when Captain Rogers opened the front door and peeked in.

Jules was distracted by the Captain and Maria broke free. Eli fired two shots and both smacked into the wall inches from Jules' head.

Jules moved toward the Captain and cracked him over the head with his gun. The Captain dropped to the floor.

Maria ran toward Eli. Eli came through the back door as Jules was just about out of the front door.

Eli did not have a good shot because Maria was coming toward him. He saw Jules raise his gun and grin just before he fired at Maria's back.

Maria grimaced in pain as she stumbled forward and fell into Eli's arms.

Eli emptied his gun at the door but Jules had already disappeared.

"Maria! Maria? Good God almighty! Maria!" Eli cried.

Eli heard gunshots form outside, then the sound of a horse galloping off. He knew Jules was getting away but he could not leave Maria.

Moments later, Juan staggered into the room and fell against a table. He was bleeding from a wound in his arm. "I am sorry, *señor*. I am not so good with a peestol." Juan stopped and looked at Maria. "*¡Madre Dios!* Is she ..."

Eli nestled her in his lap. He caressed her hair. She was breathing but her eyes did not open.

He felt the back of her blouse and it was blood-soaked.

Pepito ran into the room breathless.

"*Señor* Eli, that man he took the horses and rode away ..." he stopped. "Maria? Maria she is ..."

"No, Pepito. No ..."

Captain Rogers stirred and got to his feet. He rubbed his head and mumbled curses. He picked up his pipe and, calmly, relit it. He looked at Eli then Maria. "If you like I'll have a look. I tend to my men often." Captain Rogers moved to Eli's side and looked at Maria. He carefully examined her back. He looked serious then smiled. "Good fortune has smiled upon you. The bullet appears to have made a glancing blow to her scapula. I believe she is in shock but not seriously injured."

"Are you sure, mister?"

"Captain Rogers is the name. And I'm sure the bullet did not penetrate. Let's elevate her feet and see if we can find a blanket."

"Then I can count on you to tend to her?" Eli eased himself up and found a blanket on an old bed.

"I can't tend her long. I have to be sailing before the tide goes out."

"Do you sail for California?"

"Yes."

"I'll pay you whatever you ask for your assistance. I have something to attend to. Will you take her aboard?"

"Yes. Passage is ... fifteen hundred ..."

"That's fine," Eli took most of the money from his money belt. He counted out five thousand dollars. He looked at Pepito. "You go with Maria. You take her to Sonora and tell her to wait for me there. You understand, Pepito? Sonora."

"So ... no .. ra. *Sí,*" Pepito repeated. "But you, *Señor* Eli?"

"I have to catch the man who did this, then I will come to Sonora and join you ..." Eli stopped as he heard the distant sound of a lot of gunfire. "Go now, Captain!"

Eli moved to the door to see Scotty and the others heading toward them at a full gallop.

Scotty pulled his horse up and looked at Eli. "The General is about five miles back and headed this way."

"Jules? Did you see Jules?"

Scotty shook his head "No! Did you hear me, Eli? There's a whole army headed this way."

"I heard you. Come in, Scotty, I need your help."

"Eli, we have to ride, now!"

Eli looked hard at Scotty and moved inside. Scotty looked at Shorty and the others and dismounted. He walked inside to see Eli put a blanket over Maria.

"Jesus, Eli! I'm sorry."

"You have to go with her to Sonora, Scotty."

"I don't understand?"

"This is Captain Rogers. He's sailing for California this morning. You take the passage money for you and the boys out of my account. Take care of her for me, Scotty."

"And where the hell are you're going?"

Eli sighed hard and checked his guns. He mounted Scotty's horse. "Wherever he's going. Bye, Scotty."

"Eli! You can't. That's insane. General Nogales will take care of him for you."

Eli did not reply as he rode away.

"Eli, there's an army out there! Eli!" Scotty yelled after Eli in vain.

CHAPTER THIRTY

The storm Stella had expected had come. It came out of the northeast across the ancient stones of the Salisbury plains, down the Thames aside the treacherous halls of Parliament, by way of the desperate reaches of the hallowed coldness of the Irish Sea.

It blew in mean and merciless and sought to blow Stella's house of cards to the ends of the earth.

She had always known that she was building a house that would not withstand such a storm. She had only wanted to keep it together long enough to gain her parents' love and respect, and for Benjamin to grow up under the right conditions.

But they were all coming at her now. All trying to break her castle doors down. All trying to send her back to the retching darkness of a new coffin ship. All wagging their tongues and mocking her.

It would be easy to correct things if she were in San Francisco.

In San Francisco everyone lived in a house of cards.

In San Francisco she would have been able to call everyone's bluff and come up with the winning hand.

In Boston it would be difficult, if not impossible, to withstand this evil wind.

For the first time, in a long time, she considered returning home.

But before she did she had to put some things right.

Stella was not a religious person, but she believed in the biblical admonition that there was a season to all things. Now it was a season for her enemies to take advantage of her mistakes.

They had the upper hand for now.

She would have to endure some setbacks — but some day soon it would be her turn again.

Now was the season of their triumphs. In due time it would be her season for return payment. Her season of setting things straight. Her season to prevail.

Her season of reckoning.

DON'T MISS

A Season of Reckoning

THE EXCITING CONCLUSION
OF THE
JOSHUA TRAIL TRILOGY

ORDER FORM

Don't miss any of the action…
Order your autographed copies today!

THE JOSHUA TRAIL TRILOGY

Volume One: *Six Notch Road*

Volume Two: *The Joshua Trail*

Volume Three: *A Season of Reckoning*

Name _____

Street _____

City _____

State & Zip _____

	Price (U.S. dollars)	Number Ordered	Total Amount
Six Notch Road	$16	_____	_____
The Joshua Trail	$16	_____	_____
A Season of Reckoning	$16	_____	_____
Shipping & handling included			
		TOTAL	_____

Fill out this form and send with your check to:

OZ
Osteen-Zalar Publishing
P.O. Box 1349
Sacramento, CA 95812-1349

Printed in the United States
4739

9 780971 643710